Never Trust A Stranger

NEVER TRUST A STRANGER

Prince Kwatchey

FIRST EDITION

ISBN:
Paperback: 978-1-80227-581-0
eBook: 978-1-80227-582-7

This novel is dedicated with gratitude for love and encouragement to my late mother, Eudora Kwatchey-Johnson, Emmanuel Kwatchey, my son, and my wife, Mrs Lydia Kwatchey, the daughter of the late Mr Emmanuel Anum, also known as Try Again...

Chapter One

Two weeks after I had returned from a three-month course sponsored by the company, the new Managing Director from our sister company sent for me. He had arrived in my absence, during which time, a lot of water had passed under the bridge.

Some junior and senior officers were sacked, and others were sent on compulsory leave in order not to interfere with the investigation of various claims. Mismanagement and embezzlement of funds, corruption and maladministration were the order of the day.

The nonchalant attitude of some of the workers had disappeared. The new Managing Director's approach to the various problems facing the company had minimized this.

Anyone caught indulging in illicit deals was given an outright dismissal, and, if the amount involved was huge, those involved would be handed over to the police. People came to work early; the usual gossiping and character assassinations were greatly reduced.

Some of the staff were redeployed or transferred to other branches of the company in the region.

On Monday, at almost ten o'clock in the morning, Mr Freestyle, the personnel manager, dressed in a two-piece suit with a woollen vest over his shirt, strode down from the company's car park to the accounts section on the ground floor. He had someone on his mind.

It had rained last night. This had made the morning very chilly. He nodded to everyone who greeted him or waved till he pushed the sliding glass door to one side to allow him entry.

He came straight to where the three of us sat, putting our heads together over a problem.

"Good morning, gentlemen," he said, smiling.

"Good morning, Sir," we said in unison.

He heard the sound of the typewriter, turned his head and smiled, then moved towards the typist.

The lady wore a shining white collarless silk blouse with a rose printed on the left side of the pocket, over a pink silk skirt with a white leather belt. A white and pink handbag hung on her chair. On her feet were a pair

2

of high-heeled shoes and she wore shiny red lipstick with pale makeup.

Before Mr Freestyle got there, she was eating a toasted cheese sandwich. By the time Mr Freestyle reached her desk, she had finished eating and was cleaning her mouth with a white tissue from her bag. It was cleaned so carefully that the lipstick was not disturbed. He returned to our table after going to two other desks.

"Pardon me for breaking up your conference," he said, smiling. "The Managing Director would like to see Jerry."

The expression on my face changed as we were aware of what was going on. My heart jumped. He extended his hand, and I did the same, and we shook hands. It was a surprise. Nobody in the hall understood, watching with open mouths and mixed feelings. They glanced around at each other as we went out of the sliding door.

Before we got to his office, he had asked me a lot of questions which I had answered accordingly. He was impressed. In his office, he offered me a chair and we talked over some hot tea.

"I know you speak French," he said. "It is in your file."

"Yes, I do."

"But I want to know if you can communicate fluently."

"I can, Sir. Please may I ask why all the questions? I took it at school and, what's more, some of my relatives are French."

"There is nothing to worry about," he said, "but how come some of your relatives are French?"

"My great-grandfather, I was told, worked in Lomé and married there. Since the marriage was fruitful, there had to be children. I have travelled extensively in that country."

"That makes you the right man for the job," he said, fetching his matchbook from the breast pocket of his jacket. "About driving… any hope?"

"Yes, I am good at it. Even though I don't own a car, I got my driver's licence two years back."

"Think you can drive from here to Togo and then tour places of interest like the beach, parks, zoo and museums and go to some decent clubs?"

"It is no problem," I said. "If there is any difficulty at all, I can go to the Togolese Embassy for information."

"I do not think there is anybody in the company more suitable for the job than you. You are taking a very important person to Togo."

"Me, Sir?" I asked, puzzled. "But we have drivers."

"Yes, we do," he replied, "but the fellow wants you and he is none other than the new Managing Director."

"Me? Drive the Managing Director?" I gasped, startled.

"You will leave Accra in two days' time. He is going sightseeing and having a rest. I don't know how long you'll be away."

"But he is still doing the house cleaning and, moreover, he has not been here for a year."

"You ask too many questions."

"I am sorry, Sir."

"Don't go and ask questions like this if you value yourself. His annual leave was due when the board of directors asked him to come down."

"He has brought a lot of changes into this organisation," I said.

"For the few months that he has been here, we have seen a lot of action. He talks little but…"

"He must be some sort of guy."

"You'll be equipped with everything that will make the journey go smoothly. From my office, you'll have to go home and make all the necessary arrangements. Go to the Information Centre of the Togolese Embassy."

He handed over some sheets of paper to me.

"This is the routine you'll follow. If you don't have any knowledge of where anything is situated, they'll help you at the embassy. Good luck."

I got up, ready to go.

"Thank you very much," I said, shaking hands. "I will do my best."

"Before you go, let this guide you and it will do you some good," he said, like a father giving a child advice. "Try to be always neat. Faultless and blemish-free. Tidy at all times. Let this be your watchword."

For a moment, I stood silently, biting my lower lip.

"Sounds like there is something good for me, but I don't really know the man. His lifestyle, what he likes and hates."

"I know you are a brilliant guy, so have no fear. I will take you to his office tomorrow."

The Managing Director's office was on the top floor of the new five-storey building.

At nine am the following day, we joined three others already in the elevator going up. He was not in, but his Confidential Secretary was at hand to receive us.

The reception was clean and well-arranged, decorated with flowers and pictures of the founder, the past Board of Directors and the present one. She ushered us onto a sofa and went to continue with her work. The secretary went through some papers as if there were fake ones amongst them. She never raised her head or turned her eyes until she had finished with the papers.

"He will be in any moment," she said, after returning from the M.D.'s office. "Would you care for some tea or coffee?"

"Coffee for me," Mr Freestyle said.

"Tea, thanks," I said, with my fingers interwoven on my lap.

She went into a small room. I heard her talking to somebody. The telephone rang and she raced back to receive the call. It was the Managing Director from the accounts section, she later told us.

"Mr Freestyle, the M.D. says you can go and leave Jerry behind; he will be here in a moment."

We shook hands and he left. I saw him off at the door.

"Do you have any idea of what to do?" she asked.

"Not quite."

She brought out a paper and handed it over to me.

"Go through it. It might be changed tomorrow before you go. If not, then you can rely on this."

I read it to myself while sipping the tea. It was written like an order.

'At exactly nine am, you'll drive from the Managing Director's house to Lomé; you have to drive fast and carefully. He might stop on the way to see something that fascinates him. Most important of all, you have to be at the Hotel de la Paix before noon or, if you are running late, it must be during lunchtime. He is staying at the hotel for four nights. You will make a brief stop at the Hotel Sarakawa before going to the hotel to spend the night there. From here, you will drive to the

National Theatre for five days. Then, on to the National Stadium. After that, you drive to Victoria Island over the Third Mainland Bridge. This is where you'll stay for the rest of the day till you return home. Separate rooms have been booked for you both.'

"Are you through with it?" she asked when she noticed I was not looking at the paper.

I nodded and rested my head on the back of the sofa.

"The M.D. will advise you on places of interest and for entertainment. You can also suggest places you think he'd like." The phone rang. "Okay, Sir. I understand; it's alright."

She turned to me and said,

"He is a bit busy. It will not be possible to meet him this morning. You can come in the afternoon or around six."

"Okay, thank you very much."

"There is one more thing; his official car is in the garage near the gate. The driver will be on hand to tell you some dos and don'ts when you are driving him."

"Bye. See you in the afternoon."

Before going out of the hall, I turned back and smiled at her. She had all that charm you just can't shy away from.

Jones, the senior driver/mechanic, was the official driver of the M.D. He was short, about 35, a bit fat, with a round face and big eyes. As soon as I left the secretary's office, I went straight to him. I found him snoring. It was after I sneezed that he woke up. He had locked the M.D.'s white automatic Mercedes 200 in the garage and was asleep at the back of the garage. I had to shout his name and go round the building before I found him still asleep. Having roused him, I intended to greet him. Before I opened my mouth to tell him why I had come to see him, Jones told me not to worry since he knew everything. He unlocked the door of the garage. I went round the car, opened the door and looked inside the boot and the bonnet. Everywhere was clean. Here, I remembered what the personnel manager had told me. He stood at the door staring at me.

"You are taking the M.D.?" he asked, teasingly.

"Why?"

"Nothing. You'll enjoy the trip if only you do what I tell you about this car and yourself."

"Man, be serious," I said. "I am not here to joke."

"I know; who is here to joke? I have a family but I don't finish early at night. He'll work throughout the day, but when night begins, that is when he'll have his own fun."

"That's why you get a good pay," I said, sneering.

"Look at the rims," he said, pointing at them. "How do they look? As if they've come right from the factory. He likes them polished and spotless. Any time he goes out in the car, you clean every part that is visible to him. Sometimes he'll even ask you to open the bonnet in the middle of the street."

"But this is absolute madness."

"Don't let him hear you say that," he said, straightening his tie. "Your tie must always be straight. Another thing too is the ashtray; don't say I didn't warn you."

He opened the door; the car was spotlessly clean. The seats had white cotton covers, bleached and well-ironed even though he had used the car that morning. He gave me the keys to try my hand at it. The engine sounded perfect. Everything was alright.

"Man, this baby is good," I said.

"Any stupid thing you do or mistake you make, do not think he will forget about it, because it has been stored in his big head. Don't say I didn't tell you so. Just refuse to take my advice and on your return, you'll live to regret it," he said.

I touched the glass of the driver's door.

"You have not gone on the trip yet and now this," he said, pointing to my fingerprint on the glass. "Don't say I did not warn you."

He brought out a spotless duster and cleaned it as if his life depended on it. In fact, I was amazed.

"Just make sure you do everything I told you and don't do what I told you not to."

"I will remember. Thank you very much."

"When you return from the trip, it is then that you will realise that it is advisable to listen to an elder. But don't worry, when you get to know and understand him, you'll love him and his car."

"Are you sure?"

"Yeah, I am sure. You won't believe me now. When I was first posted to him, after the first two weeks, I threatened that I would quit but as time went on, I got to know him."

I had a close look at the car once more.

"But you could have gone with him and then he would have a guide."

"Me? Go with him? Leave my wife and follow him? No, this trip is not mine; moreover, I need some rest. Since I came to this country, I have not had time to pay attention to my woman's problems. She has even threatened many times to leave me. I can't afford to let her go. I would rather resign than let my woman go. She is good and sweet. It is very difficult to come by a woman like her in this modern world. There is no problem if you heed the advice I am offering you. There will come a day of peace and happiness for you."

What I heard of the M.D. convinced me that if I took chances, it would be a sad trip for me. I wouldn't like it, so I had to be very careful.

"You'll see things for yourself. Actions speak louder than words, so watch out."

"He must be a very difficult man to work with. His servants are in for a rough time."

"He seldom stays at home," he said. "They understand him, so they all live in peace. It is just a matter of time."

He came close to me.

"The M.D. told me there have been many attempts on his life, but every attempt has failed. They say he is hard to deal with and difficult."

"It is not the right time," I said. "If you want to eliminate him, it has to be a smart person. I just don't understand why up until now, no one has been able to do the job."

"He drinks a lot and when he is drunk, he can raise hell. He knows they can poison him so he takes precautions. But you could make it look like an accident."

"Do you mean me?" I said, the words rattling in my mouth. "I can't do it. Why haven't you done it? You who goes out with him day and night. Let's forget about that topic. I have heard rumours that I would be promoted when we return."

He laughed loudly.

"Why are you laughing, you fool? I said, angrily.

"Is that why you want to go with him?" he asked me. "For him to recommend you? He'd rather recommend you for demotion."

"To be a man is not an easy task. It needs courage and a lot of dedication," I smiled. "When I was at the secondary school, I lived under a strict housemaster and a great disciplinarian. If he does not give me peace, I will not make his leisure trip a difficult one for him."

"You compare your housemaster with the Managing Director?" he asked with a cold face. "You must be sick. It's not a joke, man. I am on it. I know what he is made of. You have the guts and brains enough to travel with him but listen to me. I am older than you, even though you are better educated than me. Look on me as your father and take my advice. I am much more experienced than you in this business so do what I say."

I glanced at my wristwatch. He was becoming monotonous and I was fed up with him.

"Very soon, you will know why I told you to forget the idea of being promoted when you return. Tomorrow morning, you have to report early to his residence for further instructions from his steward."

From here, I went to meet the secretary who, in turn, announced my arrival to the Managing Director. He asked his secretary to show me through. He was impressed by my appearance and behaviour. As I expected, the chit-chat had not lasted even thirty minutes when the arrival of the company's legal adviser was announced. I bowed out.

who stood in his way and she broke her back. He might even want to drive, but never give him the key to the car - never. He will yell and curse but do not submit to his order. A driver once gave him the keys to his car when he was drunk. He ended up colliding with a pole when he drove across the railing dividing the road. Now, let's go in and look at his clothes and other things."

Before going into the building, he put the stool back in the right place. In the guest room, he had laid out the luggage. He opened each case for me and gave me all the instructions I would need. After explaining, he gave me the keys to the car and helped me to carry the luggage.

I was still in the garage when Jones arrived. We exchanged greetings. The steward left.

"Man, I am going to be with my woman till you return, just the two of us," he said, jokingly. "It's just a joke," he said, seriously. "I am meeting two guys in town this morning; we've got some stones and gold. We will take them there. Since you know the place very well, you must have some connections. You can give me the address of the hotel where I can find you; it's a business deal. We don't have passports, so we'll come through the bush path. Man, hurry, I am already late. I should have given you this information yesterday, but first I had to study you."

"Do you have the guts to do it?" I asked.

"I am just taking a risk; it's all because of my woman. I don't want her to walk out of my life, no, no."

"If you are arrested, you would be shot as an enemy of the state."

"I don't mind dying for her," he admitted. "Don't worry, we have people at the border."

As soon as he got the address of the first hotel, we shook hands and he hurriedly left. I checked on the engine, water and oil and cleaned everywhere that was visible to him, in and out of the car.

At a quarter to nine, I put on the air conditioner, combed my hair and straightened my tie. I did not see the steward till it was nine o'clock on the dot when he came to signal that the M.D. was ready.

I drove to the entrance of the hall and got out quickly, looking smart. I greeted him and opened the door. He climbed in, and then I closed the door and hurried to my seat. I released the brake and set the car in motion.

"Fast but carefully and not too fast," the baritone voice murmured behind me.

In less than a hundred miles, he was asleep. Inside the car, it was quiet and cool. He did not wake up till we got into a road full of potholes.

"Pull over," he ordered.

I did as I was told.

"Now, open the bonnet."

He drew a big, white handkerchief from his pocket, opened the water and oil reservoirs then closed them again. He looked at my face. He turned away from me and closed the bonnet, and before he had stretched his hand out to open the door, I had done it already. He stared at me once more then climbed in. I closed the door, saluted him and quickened my steps. He had not fully settled down when I changed gear and then set the car in motion.

Jones and the two other boys alighted from a green 120Y Datsun at the Aflao bus station. Since they had no passports, they were on the footpath which ran by the new model market. They hired a guide from among a group of young boys who spoke French and their native dialect. After the market, they came to a much wider path. There was another, smaller path, but the guide chose the much wider one on the left.

About a hundred metres away, they entered a family compound and then their farm consisting of cassava and coconut trees. After this farm, there was water with tall, dense green weeds spread all over the surface. One had to remove one's footwear and, if wearing trousers, these had to be rolled to the knees. Jones and company did that and waded into the water clinging to their shoes and canvas bags because of what they kept inside.

They stepped onto a footpath; if you had not been there before, you would hardly notice it was a path. Thick bush with tall, mature trees grew on both sides. Jones had told me he had wanted to return and call it quits but his other two friends persuaded him to continue by saying that, after all, they had made it half of the way.

For over thirty minutes, they trekked without coming across anyone. It was difficult to even see the clouds above.

A beautiful, layered cassava plantation was what they passed through next. Jones said they went to a cottage after the cassava plantation to ask for water, which they were given. The cottage had a fence made of palm tree leaves with two gates, one going into the cassava plantation and the other to the river. He said when they went in to ask for water, it was around lunchtime. The head of the family was eating a local dish of corn dough (ugali) and okra soup (okro). He was in the company of a friend. I wish you were there to witness the amount of stuff they ate. It was really hot with the steam coming out of it.

The guide went forward to tell the man why they were there. He had a canoe that carries passengers from his side to the other end. He was enjoying the food but did not want to lose the money. Two boys were also eating from the same plate as three other boys. The rest of the boys had to wait till the others returned. Without washing their hands, they ran out and took their places in the canoe. When the man collected the fare, we had to pay extra.

The canoe was an old woman; she had holes in her. We sat on some wood laid across it. The slim boy, being the elder, stood at the head of it with a long, strong bamboo pole; he controlled the movement of the boat whilst the younger one sat on the floor of the old canoe baling out the water so that it wouldn't sink.

The two boys were between the ages of ten and twelve. The wind blew against us which made it difficult for the boys to steer the canoe. Instead of us going straight to the other end where about five people were waiting, halfway across, the wind increased. The boat moved right, we all pushed to the left so that when the boy put the pole in the water, it would not move right. We finally got to the end of the water but far from where we were supposed to land. It took about twenty-five minutes to trek back to the point. This part of the land was hilly but you'd not notice it till you got far into the cassava farm. On top of the hill, one would see the Lomé township and the villages surrounding it. It was not a stone's throw from there. This was the most dangerous part of the journey because we had outwitted the border guards.

A guard on patrol might have seen us and announced our presence to the others around. As we descended from the hill, we heard someone shout.

"Hey, you," a voice called from the bush. "Stop there or I'll shoot!"

Jones and the two others froze at the point when they heard the voice. The guide disobeyed the orders and ran into the bush.

"Stop! Stop!" He still refused and indiscriminate shooting followed. He slumped forward and died. Then, they knew the whole place had been surrounded. They later learned that the path was used by notorious smugglers.

The stern-looking border guards rushed out wearing camouflage khaki uniforms which had made it difficult to differentiate them from the bush. Some had green leaves on their uniforms and caps and were equipped with guns, knives and walkie-talkies.

They were led by a sergeant; his structure made Jones tremble, his eyes wide open and looking like those of a drunkard, hair dirty and unkempt with some leaves in it.

"What are you doing here?" he asked, moving forward.

"Going to the next village," Jones said.

"Which of the villages and from which one did you come? You can see for yourself there are a lot of small villages."

"Do you have a cigarette?" a private asked.

No reply.

"What do you have in your bags?" the sergeant asked.

"Clothes," they replied in unison.

"Search them," he ordered.

Three of the guards came forward, snatched our bags and threw them down. The sergeant went for them and began his search of them whilst the three worked on us. A passport was found in one of the bags along with two letters addressed to some people in Lomé.

"Going to the next village with a passport?" the sergeant asked, showing the passport and the two letters.

"I know they have it. Search them, Jacob," the leader mentioned.

He stepped forward. There was a volley of kicks, slaps, and the butt of the gun into his stomach; he was booted and fell on his face. They stamped on him, then the butt made several trips to his head. The teeth fell out of his mouth and the butt of the gun made some more hits to his back. He was kicked straight in the face. They were asked to bring everything out voluntarily. No one did. Jones told me it was a terrible and sorrowful experience. Everything they had on them was removed and they stood naked.

"The sergeant came right in front of me," he said. "With his huge palm, he whacked at my jaw and the pieces of stones fell out. Then, a kick to my belly. Oh my God, I cried!"

There was a groan in the bush; it was the guide. They tore open the soles of the sandals and shoes and removed the gold stuffed inside them.

One of the guards kicked Jacob; there was no movement, so he held his wrist - he was dead. The same man went into the bush and brought a shovel and pickaxe.

"We dug a pit; it took us over an hour to dig it because of the rocks. With guns pointed at us, we were ordered to put the dead body into it. This we did with great pain all over our bodies. It was difficult for us. A few hours back, we were alive and now one of us was being buried."

Jones told me that if he had the power of a juju man, it would have been bad for the guards.

Slowly and reluctantly, they carried the body into the pit. He even jumped into it to receive his body and placed him on the bare, hard, stony ground. They filled in the pit and placed branches over it.

They were taken deep into the bush where they had their tent. Soon, night came and they had nothing to cover their bodies except the blood-soaked cloth. They looked dirty, hungry and thirsty. The guards ate and drank some food and water provided by some girls from a nearby village. The sergeant brought out two bottles of gin which they kept amongst themselves. One after another, they drank from the bottle. They slept in turn.

Jones told me he decided to run and seek refuge in a village. Since he did not know the area, this would be a difficult task for him. Moreover, if his escaping was detected, the guards could alert the others beyond. The fire they had set to keep out the cold lit up the whole place. In the middle of the night, the two border guards, who were supposed to keep vigil, fell asleep. Stealthily, he crawled to where the leader was asleep on a bench. He was sound asleep like his companions.

The passport was on his chest with the gun lying on it. Jones took the risk, raised the gun with one hand and took the passport. With patience, he put the gun back. The gin had put the leader into a deep sleep. He stretched his arms and touched the gun; Jones nearly dropped dead. He woke his friend and they disappeared into thin air. However, it was not all that easy; his friend nearly gave them away.

By the time the gin would have cleared, they would have been long gone if they didn't meet any checkpoints. The guards would not waste their time and energy going after them since they had the stones and gold. What might prompt them to give chase would have been the passport.

Early in the morning, they were at the hotel with clothes someone had given them in one of the villages.

Chapter Three

From the spot, he checked the engine. He said nothing to me until we reached a checkpoint. I did not understand - as soon as he got into the seat, he would sleep. Although he was with me in the car, I felt lonely. I sometimes forgot that he was in the car until the odour of his perfume reached my nose.

For the next three weeks or so, what would it be like? People are unique and have different ways, but this man? Only God knew. I couldn't imagine being this type of man.

It was lunchtime when we arrived at the hotel New Season on the island. I dashed to open the door for him, then closed it and went to park in the car park. I called some porters to help me with carrying the luggage. When we brought his things to the reception, he was not there. I went to the receptionist and mentioned his name. The fair-complexioned female receptionist gave me two keys, one for a double room and one for a single. We carried the luggage up and as soon as I got to the room, I put on the air conditioning. I arranged his luggage and took mine to my room before tipping the porters.

I found him in the bar and gave him his room key.

"You can have lunch, rest, clean the car, get dressed and meet me at the reception by six pm sharp."

I went up and arranged for lunch to be brought to my room. After lunch, I showered and instead of resting, decided to go into the town.

During the days I spent in Lomé, I had a girlfriend called Antonia. It had been a long time since I had seen her and didn't even know if she was still around. There were rumours that she had married and moved out of her former house.

I hailed a taxi, told the driver the address, and, in fifteen minutes, we were right in front of the house. The place had changed. I offered the driver a thousand francs but he had no change, so I bought a packet of Silk Cut and asked the seller to give me one hundred and fifty to pay for the taxi. I returned for my change and asked the seller if I could sit for a while as I was waiting for somebody.

Some children were playing by the seller. One kicked the ball and it landed on the items for sale. The seller seized the ball. The children pleaded with him but it fell on deaf ears. I joined in with the children and he finally gave it to them. I called one of the boys closer.

"Do you know Antonia?"

"No, no, I don't," he said, about to go.

I took his wrist and put some coins into his palm. He opened his hand and smiled.

"Be a good boy," I said, smiling.

"I am going," he said, running into the house. He came back with her address and telephone number.

As soon as I got the number, I left for the hotel and went straight to my room. I picked up the phone and asked the operator to put me through to her number.

"You are through," the telephonist said.

"Thank you."

"Hello, hello. This is Jerry. How are you?"

"I am fine," she said. "Oh, I have missed you! I can't wait to be in your arms."

"I will come over tonight. By the way, is it true what I heard?"

"About what?"

"That you are married?"

"Who told you that? They must be mad, it is ridiculous."

"Okay, let's forget about that."

"See you tonight, bye."

I dropped the receiver and jumped in celebration. After resting for a couple of hours, I left my room to wash and clean the car inside and out. Sweat poured out of my body whilst I washed the car.

I hurried to the elevator which took me to my floor. When you came out of the elevator, my room was the second on the left. On entering the room, I went straight to the bathroom to have a cold shower. I dressed and went to the balcony overlooking the Atlantic Ocean.

At five minutes to six, I was in the reception to report to him, but he was not around. I went to the bar but he was not there either. I rushed to go out but as I went back into the reception, he was entering. He had changed from a beige suit to a cream suit.

We met halfway and I greeted him. He asked me to follow him to the bar and went to sit at the far end of the room. The Managing Director asked me to sit on the sofa opposite him. The atmosphere in the bar was splendid, with people of different races, ladies and gentlemen. It was not a surprise to see different people in a country with various tourist attractions. Young chicks with their bellies protruding, sugar daddies, couples and customers in groups.

He ordered three shots of whiskey on the rocks, and I requested a Star lager. The waiter left.

"There is not much to do tonight," I said, whilst he brought out a cigar from the inside pocket of his jacket.

"I would like to sit here for a while then have my supper, watch some movies and sleep."

The waiter returned.

"Tomorrow, we start visiting places of interest. The museum first in the morning and in the afternoon, we'll go to the seaside to watch the fishermen. Then to the National Theatre - after breakfast, we will visit the National Stadium and Victoria Island. We will come back to the hotel, have some lunch, rest and go out for the afternoon. Can you guess where?"

"I don't want to get it wrong."

"Third mainland bridge after lunch and then drive to the market before it closes for the day. You can go now," he said, "but report in time. I want to learn about the people, how they live, their customs and heritage…" He paused, staring at me. "My nightlife depends on you. Make all the arrangements. I want real fun, that kind of leg show, strip tease. Sentimental music."

"Oh, I understand."

"Clubs, cafés. I want action, women, lovely ones, sophisticated ones."

"Do you mean call… call…"

"Yes, call girls," he said. "What do you think I came here for? I came for fun."

I couldn't believe it.

"Why has your face changed?"

"Nothing, Sir. It's a stomach upset, Sir. There are a lot of places we can go for a real show. It's the private places in the call house that cost a lot. They make you feel at home, but they cost a lot."

"Money is not a problem," he said, bringing out his fat wallet.

"There is a private club; it is very private. The dancers are nude, I mean, maiden ones with plump, round breasts and pointed nipples."

He stretched his legs.

"That's it," he said, shaking my hand. "You are the right guy."

"The dancer will dance right on your table, hug you and kiss you. You can arrange it on the spot. As soon as she finishes dancing, you follow her to her dressing room. She'll be yours for the rest of the night, but it will cost. Since she has to cut short her show, the manager has to be tipped. But if you can't stand it, you'll have to wait till she finishes her shows.

"She can come on stage in pants, work on your body to show her appreciation and you'll put some notes there, you understand? It's a trick they use to cheat customers. This is done when the house is full."

"It does not matter provided that she is to my satisfaction."

I jeered and noticed his face change, so I stopped.

"Why this?" he asked, indicating my face.

"Some of the places that have these ladies are dangerous and some are peaceful. As a gentleman, you would like the peaceful one."

"How are they dangerous?" he enquired.

"Pimps, pickpockets and drug dealers. The women themselves are sometimes dangerous. You'll be drugged then they will flee with your cash. There are a lot of nightclubs so it would be difficult to find her. Even if you do, she'll deny it. Don't think of making trouble because they have bribed the police. She might even tell the pimps that you duped her some time ago and if you're unlucky, it can cost you your life."

"Shit, that's nothing. I have seen real action before. I would prefer the dangerous spot."

"Okay, Sir," I said, rising.

"See you tomorrow at nine."

He called the waiter as I left. Before I got to the door, I turned and looked at him. I saw him move his head to the sentimental French music. I wondered if he understood the music. Perhaps it was the music and not the lyrics.

Since I had a date that night, I did not order my dinner but showered and changed into something more casual. A pair of black, wool trousers, a blue checked cotton short-sleeved shirt, and a pair of black shoes. I had a cool ride in the elevator to the ground floor and hurried to the car park. I waved down a taxi which arrived as soon as I had raised my hand. You had to be smart or else someone would take it first. In some cases, accidents occurred, serious ones.

The driver beckoned me to enter when I showed him the address. It was a ten-minute drive and even though it was short, I enjoyed it. Cool music and cool, fresh air from the Atlantic Ocean.

The street lights lit the street and the entrances of the houses lining it. A stone's throw from the house, he pointed to the number clearly marked on the white wall with black paint. There she stood, already dressed and poised for action. I asked the driver to wait and take us back to the hotel. She jumped and ran to me as I approached, kissing and hugging me.

"Jerry, this is a dream come true," she said, putting her arms around my neck.

"My workload stopped me from coming here, then I had to travel for a course. I wrote two letters to you but got no reply. So, when this little chap I met at your former place told me you had left, it wasn't a surprise. Let's go over to my place."

"Won't you come in?" she asked.

"No, the taxi is waiting."

"I am sorry, excuse me." She ran into the compound. In less than five minutes, she was back. "The windows and doors have to be shut in case it rains or an intruder comes around."

We returned in the same taxi, but this time, the journey was longer since the driver had to take another route. The road we took originally was one-way. It was a nice relaxing ride. We sat close to each other, holding one another and doing all the things you might imagine. The taxi driver played some cool old French tunes, reminding us of the good old days.

Arm in arm, we went straight to my hotel room. It was just the two of us. As soon as we entered and closed the door, we kissed. Just imagine it; we had not seen each other for a long time and now we were together behind closed doors.

I phoned to order some wine and a sumptuous meal for two from the restaurant then ordered some beer and soft drinks for two from the bar. While we waited for the drinks, we were in each other's arms relaxing with a musical playing on the television.

A few minutes later, there was a knock on the door when I had gone into the toilet to relieve myself.

"Jerry, there's somebody at the door."

"Hold on, I am coming." I hurried to do up my zip.

"Who is it?" I asked.

"Waiter," the voice replied.

He came in with the drinks. I paid him after he gave me the bill. There were some things I had to foot myself.

"Give the receipt to the cashier and keep the change."

He turned to go.

"Sir, Sir." It was the waiter with the food and wine.

That night will always remain in my mind. How would you behave when you see your baby who you've not seen for a long time?

Her kisses were more passionate and caressed me with some tenderness. She was more beautiful now, and her hips and bust would have made me grab her if I had seen her nude.

It was just the two of us and only the four walls could say anything. We did it over and over again, making up for everything we had missed.

Since I did not want to report late to the Managing Director in the morning, at dawn, we had sex again, relaxed for about thirty minutes and went to bathe. She dressed and I saw her off in the taxi with a nice kiss and a promise to call her. Since I would be busy, she could also call me.

Breakfast was cornflakes, French toast with a boiled egg and grilled bacon washed down with a cup of tea. Whistling, I went to the balcony to enjoy some fresh air and watch the fishermen. Before having my breakfast, I washed and cleaned the car and checked the water and engine oil. I topped up the water and did not forget the ashtray or the rims. I made sure I cleaned every part visible to him. It took me about an hour and a half to polish the damn thing. Whether I liked it or not, though, I had to do it since I was looking forward to getting a better deal at home. After cleaning, I went up to wash my body then I went down to the restaurant. Before I went up to the balcony, I had about thirty minutes to rest and smoke some cigarettes.

Chapter Four

At ten minutes to nine, I was in the reception going through some daily papers. It was a bit busy with guests checking in and out, and some taking part in early morning sports. I moved to the desk in the reception area to talk to the female receptionist, who I later got to know as Connie, a citizen in that country. Since it was a busy morning, I didn't get to talk to her much. I got the chance to tell her who I was and my mission there and she promised me a nice time if she got the chance.

At two seconds to nine, he entered the reception and I hurried to meet him. His green safari suit with cream pockets and cream shoes made him look young and smart.

"Bring the car. I will be out in a minute. I think you know the routine, spend an hour and move on. Before we return, we'll stop at a florist; I need some flowers."

"Okay, Sir."

A bird pooped on the windscreen in the process of removing the tarpaulin. With the tissue paper I brought out of the car, I was able to get rid of it and then cleaned the whole surface with a dry duster. As soon as I had finished and drove to the entrance, he was already there with a cigar in one hand and his other hand in his pocket. As soon as I stopped, he opened the door and got in.

"Sit down and move," he said, as I opened my door to get out.

In all the places we went, he asked me a lot of questions. I was the guide, mind you. For almost all of the photographs, carvings and paintings we saw, he wanted to know where, when and by whom they had been made. He jotted down notes in a small pocket book he carried. Even the attendants frowned at some of the questions that he asked me. The Managing Director was so generous that when he noticed your face change, he would grease your palm.

He praised the staff at the museum after we left and thanked me for accompanying him. I saw him smile through the rear-view mirror. I began to wonder if Jones and the steward had tried to frighten me. By and by, I would understand him.

He put on a serious face and looked at the postcards, mini crafts and drawings he had bought at the museum. After looking at everything, he took out the small notebook.

The car came to a halt and he got out, then I drove to the car park, washed and cleaned the car, collected his purchases, and covered the car with the tarpaulin.

From what I heard from Jones and the steward, then what I heard yesterday of clubs he wanted to visit, I became confused about what sort of man he was. There was something strange about him that I didn't understand. He was not in the reception, bar or restaurant but I found him on the phone in his room. After delivering his things, I left and went downstairs to the restaurant for lunch. Still pondering over what sort of man he was, I fell asleep. I woke up when I heard some knocks on my door. I glanced at my wristwatch; it read six pm. When I opened the door, it was a waiter.

"Mr Hunter would like to meet you at ten in the reception," the waiter said.

"Thank you very much." I closed the door, yawning. Laid on my back staring at the ceiling, I jumped to my feet and called Antonia.

"Hello, Antonia, my dear. I received your message but I was too tired to call you."

"Won't I see you tonight?" she asked.

"I am very sorry, I don't think I can make it," I said. I heard her grumbling at her end. "We are going out tonight and I don't think we will be back early. If you don't mind spending about two hours or so with me now, you can come because we are leaving at nine."

"Why not? I am coming straight away."

"See you."

Twenty minutes later, she was in my room, dressed in a white V-neck dress with a blue bag and a pair of blue and white shoes.

Nothing serious happened after we had dinner; rather, she complained about me not paying attention to her and accused me of not caring. At nine o'clock, she refused to go and I had to protest at her not being grateful for staying beyond the two hours. Finally, at nine-thirty, she agreed to leave. I then escorted her to the taxi rank and saw her off.

There was enough time for me so I went to the bookshop. I bought a French magazine, an English magazine and a novel.

As I closed the glass door of the reception area, I glanced at my wristwatch. It was ten o'clock. When I raised my head to look for him, he was walking toward me. He had raised his hand, waving at a white couple.

"Good evening, Sir," I greeted him.

"Nice evening," he replied. "Where are we going tonight?"

"Le Réve," I replied as we moved to the door.

"That's it. I like that name," he said, patting me on the shoulder.

His eyes were restless, and their colour had changed. The M.D. had been warned and attempts on his life had been foiled several times, but that did not stop him from drinking. His legs were not steady and he was tottering as if he had been sitting for a long time. If I am not jumping to conclusions, I would say that the ashtray on the round glass table was full of ash from the kind of cigar he smokes and two almost finished ones. He sank into the sofa like someone who had just been saved from drowning.

He removed his white handkerchief from his pocket and wiped the beads of sweat from his forehead. He found it difficult to speak but controlled himself.

"Bring the car to the entrance," he said. "I will be with you soon."

Now that he was drunk, what would I do when he became uncontrollable as I had been warned before coming here? I sat looking at him.

"What are you sitting for?" he shouted. "Are you crazy?" Little bits of saliva flew from his mouth. "Would you leave me alone?"

I had been warned about him and since he was getting out of hand, I did not want to leave him.

Some waiters and three guests came over to our table and said he could do as he wished with the promise that they would keep an eye on him. A confused man, I left for the car park. Was it the beginning of the worst to happen? Were we still going out tonight?

The car park was fully occupied with cars parked in a haphazard manner. One had blocked me in and I had to copy down the car number and make and give it to the manager of the hotel for it to be announced on the public address system before the owners moved out of my way. Even at the entrance, there was a notice with 'NO PARKING' inscribed on it. Luckily for me, the driver of the car, a Citroen, was behind the wheel. He was asked to drive away from that place by the hotel manager.

A few minutes before eleven, he came out; he was not himself. Because of the stairs, I hurried to assist him by holding him at the elbow. The M.D. shook my hand away and pushed me like a massive two-hundred-kilogram weightlifter would push a fifty-kilogram fellow.

Behaving like a man of eighty years and dragging one leg behind, he came down the steps, got into the car, pulled the door from my fingers without realising, and slammed it.

I hurried to my seat.

He cleared his throat. Although he looked tired, I knew he would go.

"To the club," he rattled, with his head resting on the door.

Before I drove fifty metres, I noticed that he was asleep. Driving at sixty and with great care not to jolt him on the broad street lined with tall coconut trees, after a ninety-minute drive from the hotel's car park, I stopped at a junction which was controlled by a traffic light. I drove into a quiet and deserted street flanked by beautiful and well-designed houses. The next street I entered led to the dual carriageway a hundred and fifty metres from the shores of the Atlantic Ocean. I drove sixty metres and turned right, then into a sharp left. The street was lined on both sides by cars of different makes. The four-storey, black and white building housing the club was surrounded by palm trees and seemed to be styled on medieval times.

As soon as one turned into the street at night, the signpost with the club's name inscribed on it, surrounded by various colours of fluorescent light, shone brightly. I brought the car to a standstill and started gazing at him, thinking that now the car was stationary, he might wake. But no, I was fooling myself and had to get out and open his door. The driver of a car waiting to drop their master made a lot of noise with the horn and some went to the extent of shouting abuse at me. A lady kicked the car with her boot when I refused to answer her. That made him wake up.

"Sir, we are there,' I said.

"Why didn't you call me?" he asked, stepping out of the car. "Have you seen all the confusion you've caused?"

He was as fit as a fiddle. I did not say a word.

"Do not go far; I will be back soon. If there is no parking space, leave it somewhere and hang around the gate."

As I had told him, the body-sellers, their traders and buyers were around. Driving slowly, looking for a space to park, I saw a car reverse from between the seventh and eighth cars from where I was. I increased my speed. After the car had driven away, I parked between a green TS Renault and a blue Volvo 244DL.

Since the entrance to the club was lit, as soon as he stepped out of the door, I would pick him out of the rowdy night-crawlers.

The speakers on the radio cassette recorder in the car gave me a clear sound of the cassette I put into it. I shook my head and lit a cigarette. I sat there waiting for him, but it would turn out to be into the early hours of the morning before he emerged. Sitting on the white, dry duster I had placed on the boot of the car, I spotted him out of the crowd. I threw away the cigarette I had just lit, quickly entered the car, put on my shoes and reversed since, at that time, the street was quiet. I stopped before I got out of the car, as he had already got in. If he had stayed and waited for me to open the door, a bottle from the crowd would have hit his fat head. It missed him by inches and hit the top of the door near the side of the back windscreen.

"Where did you park?" he asked, bending over the front seat.

"About seven cars from here."

"Drive to that same place and park."

Still in that position, I glanced at my wristwatch; it read three-thirty.

I did as he asked. Ten minutes later, he called out, "Brenda!" I opened the rear side door, she got in and I closed it. She was fairer in complexion, in her late twenties, heavily perfumed and with a round face, broad nose and small lips with partly-smudged lipstick. He might have kissed her. She stared at me as I got into the car.

"Anything... anything wrong?" he asked her.

A while ago, they were strangers, but she had offered to give herself in return for some notes. Two strangers who were not just strangers - both had something to offer.

"Jerry, right, left," he said. "You'll see the signboard in front of the car park."

The man beside her, does she know who he is? And this lady, does he know if she is a criminal?

As I kicked the car into motion, they became strangers once more. I was glad; I didn't want to hear anything that would cause them embarrassment purely because I had heard it.

I drove using the directions given to me. She smoked till we arrived at the car park of the hotel where she had a permanent room.

"Room number 723," she said, pointing through the back windscreen. "On the fourth floor, third room from the end, the one without light. Come up the stairs at the back of the building; it will save you from going through the reception. When the red light comes on, you come up too."

I liked her bosom; it suited her figure. She kissed him and got out. As she stepped out of the car, he spanked her lightly on the buttocks. She turned and looked at him, then closed the door.

"Wait here and keep an eye on that window. I got her through somebody. As we left the club, she left to talk to some rough guy. I did not like him. If anything happens to me, you will be held responsible."

"Did I tell you to go further?" I asked.

"I think they are up to something. Her face changed when I brought out my wallet to pay for the drinks."

The light went on in the room of sin.

"Sir, the light is on."

"Okay, I must go. Take care and watch out in case I am in danger."

He got out and I closed the door. Resting on the car, I watched him move unsteadily. I reached for my packet of Silk Cut from the glove compartment. As I was about to light one, a Honda Accord drove past as if it was running in a grand prix. A few seconds later, I heard the siren of a police car.

I climbed into the car to get some rest since I was tired, and my eyes needed some sleep. What if that troublemaker calls? The whole place was quiet. Even the security guards who were supposed to be watching had fallen asleep. I took one of the magazines I had bought and went to rest on the boot. I had not even read through two pages when I put it back.

Some people have a way of doing things; look at all the beautiful and decent ladies at home. He had refused to date one, but rather, chose to pick a whore. I wondered why. I just didn't understand him.

The light went on while I was still pondering over him. He was in the window waving at me. What if the guards woke up to see a man waving from the window? I remembered the lady telling him that men are not allowed after midnight.

The lift attendant questioned me for being in the hotel since I was not a guest.

"I carried a lady in room 723. She was so drunk that her fake pearl necklace fell off. You know, she came to our party." I dipped my hand into my pocket, and he smiled as he received the necklace.

He allowed me to enter the elevator. On the fourth floor, I went straight to the end of the corridor where I saw '723' boldly written on the black door in white paint.

I knocked twice but nothing happened. Same with the third knock. As I was about to knock for the fourth time, there was a response.

"Who?" he said

"Jerry, Sir."

"Open."

I went in, and I was greeted with an unusual smell.

"What kept you so long in coming?" he asked with his back to me.

"The lift attendant refused to allow me in till I gave him a tip."

"That's what you should have done in the first place rather than stand and argue." He still didn't look at me.

The lights had gone out when I got into the room, but it was lit from outside. The moment I saw him with his back turned to me, I knew something had gone wrong. He locked the door and put the key in his pocket.

"Would you mind doing something for me?"

"I will do anything you ask me to, except murder." His face changed and he turned away from me.

"Okay, put on the light and go into the bedroom." It was in a higgledy-piggledy state. It made me step back. He was right behind me.

"What's holding you back?"

I went in as he passed and picked up the table lamp from the floor. The door to the bathroom was partially closed. I went in; the sink was painted with blood.

"Where is she?" I asked, trembling. On the carpet, there were pieces of cigarettes and cigars. The smell in the room was too much for my liking. He moved the scattered clothes on the bed to one side.

"Oh God," I said, closing my eyes. "May her soul rest in peace."

Her abdomen had been ripped open and beside her was the kitchen knife used for the brutal job. She lay there, once gorgeous, now naked and covered in bruises. The bed sheet and some of the clothes were soaked with blood. The carpet, which was once cream, had ash spots all over it. I wondered how a lady like that could engage in this kind of job. He pointed at her.

"Come closer," he beckoned. "You would not like something like this to happen to you."

"No, no, Sir. But why?" I asked.

"Come closer."

I turned my head away.

"Never mind, she'll not bother."

As I moved closer, beads of sweat began to form on my forehead. My mouth was filled with saliva. I had seen the brain of a woman hit by a long truck, but it wasn't like this. A bus had run over a sheep and the intestines had spilt out, but this was too much for me. I had never seen a murder in my life before. It was horrifying.

I left for the bathroom as I could no longer stand the scene. He went to the cupboard and poured himself a brandy and gave me some. The sight of the awful act had made me sick. I reached for the bottle of whiskey and drank it straight from the bottle. I sat on the dressing table with my head turned away from the corpse, trying to pull myself together. With my face buried in my hands, I waited for him to say something, but no words came forth. He stood by my side with the knife he had used to murder the lady. He had covered up the body.

We looked at each other - trouble was brewing. Staring at him, I noticed his unsteady eyes and realised that he could harm me. He had removed the key, but I could knock him out with the bottle. Any mistake I made would end with a knife in my flesh. He asked me to pour myself some whiskey.

"No, I have had enough, Sir."

"If you do not want it, I will order you to drink it," he said, closing in on me. "If you attempt to do anything silly, you will be as dead as her."

I stretched my trembling hand for the bottle of whiskey. I stared at him and, accidentally, the bottle fell. He frowned and threatened to knife me if I refused to co-operate.

"Look, we don't have enough time. If you co-operate with me, there will be no trouble."

"Okay."

He wiped the beads of sweat with his white handkerchief.

"I had her twice and fell asleep. Stretching my hands to touch her, I realised that she wasn't on the bed. It had occurred to me that she would do something like that. When I turned, I saw her stiffen, my wallet in her hand. She ran to the cupboard for the kitchen knife. She charged toward me like a wounded lioness. With my jacket, I was able to disarm her. She then went for the chair as I reached for the knife. She jumped at me. I picked up the knife and it went straight into her.

"Look at my neck; her long fingernails found their way into my flesh. I grabbed the knife and pierced her."

"But Sir," I stammered.

"But Sir what?"

"You could have over-powered her. Even though she was a harlot, you have committed a crime."

"Yes, you have made a point. It is not that I am crazy, but it has been part and parcel of me all my life and I had always got away with it. All the staff of the company - if I had my own way, I would have shot them outright."

"But Sir, you cannot take the law into your own hands! You can never get away with this," I protested. "You have startled me."

There was no word from him.

"I now know what sort of human being you are. From the moment I set the car in motion at your house, I never understood your life. I had a strong feeling that there was something sinister going on."

He moved back and rested on the window.

"I will make a deal with you. Let's work together as a team. You don't understand me; I feel relaxed."

I searched my pocket for the last cigarette. It was wet.

"Do not stay and argue here, because I can cut you into pieces."

"Did I commit this unholy crime?"

"Hold it; you don't understand. The lift attendant saw you coming up, but no one saw me. Do you see the point I am making?"

"Yes, I was seen coming up. This brutal killing has nothing to do with me."

"Stay here and argue with me if you want. Very soon, the attendant will alert security that an intruder was upstairs, and they'll come after you. I am your boss, and they won't believe I did it. Let's help ourselves. Don't try to be difficult. Let's settle this before we get out of here. I will assist you to flee Lagos. Everyone is going there; you can make a better living there. Are you satisfied with your salary? As an accounting officer, you can make it. I am the Managing Director, and you are just an accounting officer, so who is more important?"

No word from me. There was absolute silence.

"You."

"Then let's make a deal," he said, putting the cigar between his lips.

I inhaled some smoke. It choked me. With my left hand covering my mouth, I coughed.

"You will have enough money to bribe your way into Lagos since you won't be taking your passport or identity card. I will take care of the repayment of your scholarship. Nothing will happen to your family; I know you have them in your mind."

"But Sir, you've had a nice time until the hour that you did this. You have butchered this lovely thing even though her heart was full of sin. It is not your birthright to kill her. Then you are asking me to cover it up."

"You reap what you sow."

The M.D. slowly moved towards me with the cigar in one hand and the knife in the other. Holding my neck and lifting me up from the carpet, he choked me. I pleaded with him, and he let me go.

"The company is supreme, boy," he said. "Listen to the deal I am striking with you. I like you and, moreover, you are a very brilliant man; that was why I brought you along. I could have knocked you down without being noticed. I could call at my hotel early in the morning saying that my wallet had been stolen by you and, since yesterday night, I have not seen my car."

"But people saw you entering it," I said. Cold came over me and I shivered like a baby.

"Make up your mind, boy. Do it quick. I am listening, my dear. I won't do anything to harm you. I know very well what you will do, but you are scared. The ball is in your court. Do you accept the offer? I will give you enough money that by the time the police come after you, you will be long gone."

"Are you sure it would work? Why did you pick on me? Why me?"

"Your name will go down in history. I am trying to make life easier for you but, instead, you are trying to be difficult and stubborn."

"They will know you did it. Your fingerprints, and the type of cigars you smoke."

He laughed.

"Oh, poor chap," he said, raising his hand. "Look, I am wearing light gloves. As for the cigar, this is not the brand I normally smoke."

Little wonder.

"She knows, you know, and God knows I did it. Now, it is between the two of us. You don't understand," he said, smiling. "She was a prostitute of international repute who shuttled between Accra and Lomé. We got to know each other at La Réve in Accra. She became my girlfriend. This was the very first week that I arrived, and very soon, she became pregnant. Knowing very well who I was, she refused to abort it. She came to my house while I was away at work and made away with my cash. She had a boyfriend who pimps for her, and she feeds him with my money. I am a very generous person. For a long time, it has been my weakness any time I see ladies of class.

"Last night, I saw her at the club. She tried to be smart, but I was rather too fast for her. I told her everything was over."

He went over to the wardrobe.

"Look at these. A man's shirts, trousers and shoes," he said, kicking out some of the shoes. "They live here as a couple. That was why she told me to come up the stairs at the rear."

"Oh, I see. Now I understand. And now you want to put the blame on me. Very soon you will be arrested and prosecuted. It is imminent. Don't think you can get away with it. What about her boyfriend? Don't forget the chap she spoke to."

"Kid, I know what I am doing. You are my only problem. Now, if you don't budge, you'll be forced to. No one knew she had brought me to this place. Whilst we were coming out of the door, a guy came to meet her, demanding his money."

"Which means he had already paid to take her home."

"Don't I know it? Her type of business sells like hot cakes. There are only a few like her up there. I offered more than that guy."

"I see," I said, nodding my head. "You had this dirty plan. That was why you offered more."

"After emerging from the club, those two also came out and hurled derogatory remarks at each other. Within the blink of an eye, they were locked in physical combat, which attracted many people. She left to settle. I knew the battle was aimed at me. I was seen entering my car alone."

He went back to the wardrobe and pointed at some men's clothes.

"I bought all these; she told me that guy was her brother. He shared her with me. Once I got to know her, I realised she had been doing that kind of thing right up till the time I caught her red-handed. She thought she could outwit me."

For a moment, no one spoke.

"Okay, I will take the offer."

I saw his face change and he breathed out. The tension over him had left. He went to sit on the stool.

"Jerry."

"Sir?"

"I hate to thank you, but I am being forced to do it. You have saved yourself and me from committing another murder."

He took out his wallet and, with his left hand, gave me some money. I took it with my left.

"This will take care of you," he said, looking at me.

I did not count it, but I knew it was a lot of money.

"It's already daybreak. You have to get to the border as quickly as possible. Drive my car to the border. There are roadblocks on the way; do not argue with them, it is money they want, so just give it to them. At the border, you leave the car at the car park."

He gave me a duplicate key and collected the original from me.

"When you get to the other side of the border, you ask for the train going to Lagos. Hurry, so that you leave with the first car. To cross, you will have to bribe your way out since you don't have any ID on you. I will give an incorrect description of what you are wearing."

I moved towards the door.

"Hurry and get lost. Go through the elevator."

"You'll never get away with it," I said, with my back to him.

"Forget about that." He came over to open the door.

"One day, the truth shall come out," I said, protesting.

Chapter Five

Following his instructions, I got to the other side of the border and was in the first car that left for Lagos at six-thirty. I rode on a motorcycle to cross the Nigerian border since I had no papers. After everybody had come down from the car, I told someone of my plight, and he gave me directions after I told him I was going to Surulere. I did not find it difficult getting to the street I was looking for. A good Samaritan I met at the Stadium bus stop escorted me right to the black wooden gate of the two-storey building where my friend lived.

The following week, I got a job at a restaurant at the top of the street. I was on the morning shift but I did not get to work on time. The previous night, I'd had a breakdown. The manager invited me to his office and asked me the reason for being late.

As I came out of the office, a lady approached me and sat at a table in the corner of the hall. She had a fair complexion, long eyelashes, a green silk dress with plaits and a white belt, bag and shoes. She had a silver brooch fastened to the right-hand side of the dress. I hurried over to her and sat down.

She was in her late twenties with rosy cheeks and her small mouth was glittering like diamonds.

'This is a real chick,' I said to myself.

Even the perfume she had on changed the scent of the whole hall. As I talked to her, I watched in disbelief as almost all of the men turned their eyes to catch a glimpse of her; even those with ladies. As I listened to her order, my eyes were on her slim fingers, with their well-shaped nails nicely painted in pink.

'This must be the work of an expert,' I said to myself.

"A bottle of lager and a plate of jollof rice with fried plantain and extra pieces of cow's tail, liver and kidney."

She stared at me as I left her table. This came to my notice when I turned back and saw her. We smiled at each other. As I returned to bring the food, I had a feeling that something good would find its way into my pocket. I returned to her table with the beer. When I came back with the food, she was halfway through her beer.

As I placed the plates on the table, my eyes dropped, and I realised I had been missing something; it was her bosom. She noticed what I was doing and smiled, showing her white, well-polished teeth. She might have had extra work done on them. Everything about her was gorgeous - the way she held the cutlery, the way she put the food into her mouth, even how she chewed. Even when she drank her water… no, sipped it.

'Oh, my God,' I said to myself, standing at the counter. Whilst attending to my fourth customer of the day, I noticed she had nearly finished. Hurriedly, I settled the bill and went to attend to the lady.

She was writing on a complimentary card when I got there. I put her change with the receipt on the table after I had taken her plate. On returning from the kitchen, she had left, so I took the side plate containing the receipt and the balance.

"She must be a very generous lady," I said. But there was more to come. As I took the receipt, I saw the complimentary card. I smiled and put the money and the card into my pocket and hurried to the toilet.

'I would love to meet you tonight at ten pm in room 101, eighth floor, at the Federal Palace Hotel' was the message written on the back. How could this lady invite me, a common steward? We are strangers. It continued, 'The money is for your transport.'

I was eager to go after reading the note.

My friend's place was about three hundred metres from the restaurant. As soon as I closed the restaurant, I got into a taxi and went straight home. I told him about the mystery lady. He told me to be aware of Lagos ladies and that if I wasn't careful, I might regret it.

I had no home of my own; to go into the yard, I had to play hide and seek with the owner of the house. Why shouldn't I jump at this golden chance?

I lay on my back on the dirty, blue, spotty carpet with a novel in my hand. It was not very good, and I fell asleep. The old table watch on the old, dirty sideboard read seven. By eight-thirty, I had bathed and dressed. By nine o'clock, I was outside looking for a taxi.

She had written ten o'clock, but by nine-thirty, I was in the reception area. The receptionist, a charming young lady, told me I could not go in until ten because she was busy with some business matters.

When the lift got to the eighth floor, I was counting. One hundred. One hundred and one. I knocked on the door.

"Come in," a voice said.

She looked more beautiful that in the morning, wearing tight white jeans, a blue striped shirt and blue sneakers. As for the perfume, it welcomed me as soon as I opened the door.

She gave me a smile, the type that had not been in my life for a long time. She had dimples. She ushered me onto a sofa.

"Are you surprised?" she asked.

"Why should I be surprised?" I replied. "Where does someone like you stay?"

"I have been a patron of your restaurant for quite some time now. Any time you are not on duty is when I come to eat. Yesterday, I was there in the afternoon, and since you weren't around and hadn't stopped working there, I knew you must be on the morning shift. When I saw you enter the office, I went to the toilet."

She came to sit cross-legged on the carpet in front of me.

"I wanted you, but I couldn't make a pass at you. Sorry, what would you like to drink? Wine, beer, brandy, gin, whiskey, mineral water?"

"Beer, preferably Star, very cold."

The order was made.

She continued. "When a woman approaches a man, then she is a prostitute, a very cheap one. I didn't know what your reaction might be but that was the main reason for the delay in the two of us becoming friends."

"Can I smoke?"

"Of course." She got up to fetch me an ashtray.

"Can I have a match?"

"Here, take one. Or better still…"

She struck the match on the box while I quickly took a cigarette and offered her one, which she accepted.

"Moreover, people might wonder why I went for a common restaurant steward."

"But that's my work and I am proud of it," I protested.

"Then I decided that no one would think for me."

She sat on the carpet with her head on my lap. There was a knock on the door.

"Hold on, I am coming."

When she got up to go, she gave me a kiss on the right cheek. The first kiss from her. It was the beginning of the best to happen.

She locked the door behind the waiter. I was returning with my beer from where the waiter had placed it. With no sign that she was coming, she caught me unawares with a passionate kiss on the lips.

"Let's do it again," she pleaded.

My hands went around a curved waist with a shape to see her through a beauty contest. She kissed me, forced her tongue into my mouth, licked my tongue and returned for a job well done. I extended mine into her mouth. I protested when things became unbearable for me.

My lips and cheeks were all painted with lipstick. On my cheeks was a stamp of her lips, I found out in the mirror. She gave me some tissue to wipe it.

"I am very sorry," she pleaded. "Don't know what came over me. You look embarrassed. Don't be; please forgive me."

"Don't say you are sorry, I enjoyed it. Who would turn down somebody like you? This has been my first time with you, so I have to be shy, or don't I? Every bit of it was okay."

"Let's go and have some food at the restaurant. I am hungry," she said, moving towards the bedroom. "Excuse me."

Away from the bedroom, I returned to drinking my beer.

"Can I have a word with you?" This was Elsie asking after she had returned from the bedroom. She gave me a stick of chewing gum after she had already thrown one into her mouth. Elsie put the rest into the red bag she had brought with her.

"Let's talk."

"Can we talk in there?" she asked, pointing to the bedroom door.

"Can't we talk here?"

"Okay, let's do the talking later," she said. "Let's go and have something to eat."

"That would be better."

"Are you a kid, a novice? You are not behaving like a mature person at all. Let's face reality and stop pretending."

She was becoming angry. I decided to leave but it was getting late.

"What do you suggest we do?"

"Since you work in a restaurant, you'll be in a better position to know a good one."

"Stop kidding; use the register of eating houses."

"You have class, good taste and moreover, you are older than me. You should know an excellent place where the atmosphere would be to our liking."

"The Penthouse at Eko Hotel would be good."

"You see, Bacchus is a dancing restaurant."

My friend had already warned me my mind wasn't steady. I didn't know if she wanted to use me for selfish ends. Only God knows.

"Do you like Chinese?" I asked.

"Bacchus would be okay," she said, putting on her shoes. "The atmosphere is exotic, and their food has taste."

"You're sure of a place like that?" I asked, teasing. "Let's go to a place like that."

We finally went to Bacchus on Awolowo, Ikoyi.

Sunday worked at my place. He was fired for being snobbish to a customer. Dark in complexion, tall, and with a flat tummy, he was always smiling. We didn't believe it when we heard he was snobbish to a customer. Between his upper lip and nose was a well-trimmed, shiny black moustache.

As he approached our table, surprise was written all over his face. Knowing very well that he would be on duty, I had chosen Bacchus.

"Good evening, madam," he said.

"What about me?"

"Forget it. I am only speaking because you are in the company of this charming lady."

Elsie looked at our faces.

"Good evening, boss," he said, smiling. "It is a great honour to welcome such a charming lady to this place. It is my pleasure to do so," and he bowed.

"Thank you for your compliment about my charming lady. Oh, by the way, Sunday was a co-worker before coming here for better pay. Sunday, no jokes."

She moulded the chewing gum she had removed from her mouth into a round shape, threw it back into her mouth and finally into the ashtray on the table.

She ordered two shots of brandy, ice, a bottle of Coke and a very chilled soda for me. Prawn cocktail, fried rice with roasted pork and vanilla and strawberry ice cream over cake with nuts for me, and vegetable salad and ice cream was her choice.

"You have better taste than me. We can wash the food down with some wine," she said, looking at me while she brought out a packet of cigarettes from her bag. She smiled as she looked straight into my eyes, and I forced a grin.

"I am sure you are thinking of what I am not."

"Oh, why do you say that? It's just that I am new to your friendship. I just don't understand. Should I call it from grass to grace?"

"If you like," she said, pouring some Coke into her glass of brandy and ice that Sunday had brought.

"Cheers," she said, raising her glass for a toast. A clinking of glasses followed.

"To our health and new-found friendship; may they grow from strength to strength…" I said.

No word from either of us, then I burst into laughter.

"What do you mean? Do you think I am out of my mind? I am aware of everything taking place."

"You won't believe me; all I have been through, sleepless and lonely nights. If you know and understand me, I don't think you have any feelings for me."

"It would be wicked of me to do that. What's on your mind? Your conscience is disturbing you. What are you up to? Do you know what's on my mind?"

"What's on your mind?"

"I can't tell you. It's too early to say."

"Things like this happen once in a lifetime. This world would be peaceful, nice and exciting if we all stopped pretending. You don't understand my feelings."

"You can stop pretending."

"I am not pretending," I said, confidently. "It's just a matter of time."

"Okay, let's forget about it."

"Your name."

"What about my name?"

"It sounds strange; it's foreign."

'They might have told her where I come from. This might be a trick,' I said to myself.

With her hand on her glass, she examined my face like a doctor looking for a hidden sickness.

"You are Elsie and I am Jerry; both sound foreign."

The first course arrived. By the time that had finished, the main dish would be on the table. We would need Mateus Rosé, very chilled.

"Go and bring the food," I said sharply. "What are you staring at? Don't make up your mind to try anything silly." I got up and grabbed the collar of his shirt.

"Jerry, cool down," Elsie pleaded.

Straightening his shirt, he left talking to himself.

"Do you have a husband?" I asked inquisitively. "Let's continue the conversation before that rascal came in."

"I have, but I can also say no."

"Elsie, don't beat around the bush; lay down the facts."

"You should know by now, if I have one, I wouldn't be sitting here with you."

"Is he dead? Are you divorced or what?"

"He is non-performing, does not function."

"Yes, yes, continue, we are getting somewhere."

"We can't communicate. He is physically dead, no movement, blind. My husband can't satisfy my desires; he can't perform as a husband. For some years now, I have been living with it. Look, Jerry, don't spoil our first outing."

She bowed her head in a pensive mood.

"I am very sorry for his plight."

"Thank you for caring."

"Any time I see you at the restaurant alone, I find it difficult to find an answer to why a spectacular woman like you is walking alone."

"I have had lonely nights," she said, turning her head away. "Don't blame me. I needed someone and I found you, so let's make the best of it."

"Do you mean it?"

"Yes, I do." I walked over to her and delivered a kiss on both cheeks.

"Thank you," she said, smiling.

"Nobody is perfect," I told her. "Almost everyone in the world pretends one way or another. Sometimes it helps, and sometimes it brews trouble."

"Who is pretending? You or me?" she asked. "Jerry, the first time I came across you, it was like I had been relieved of a burden."

She suddenly stopped talking as the second course arrived. Sunday left with the empty plates from the first course.

"As I was saying, you don't know the agony I had to go through after I had seen you. I tried to forget you so many times, but the more I made up my mind, the more my love for you grew. I wanted to talk to you. You don't know how I had wished to talk to you sooner."

"Don't worry," I said, "now you have got me, what do you want to do with me? Think you are now satisfied?"

She opened her mouth to speak, but nothing came out.

"Have I said anything bad?"

"Oh, no. I am listening to you."

"On the first day, if I'm not mistaken, when I saw you, 'Oh my God' I said to myself, 'this is a fine specimen and a splendid lady'. It is not every day that someone like you dines at the restaurant."

She was busy with her cutlery and I wondered if she was listening to me. My cutlery began to make frequent journeys to my mouth while I watched her. Then, she broke the silence.

"Why do you have to work as a steward?" she asked.

"You wouldn't have met me if I wasn't working there. I am qualified to work as an accounting officer."

"Then what's stopping you?"

"I have neither a working nor a resident's permit."

"But can't you arrange for them? You can't get them officially but through the back door."

"One has to be careful of what one does. The swindlers are always around to make a fool of you."

"By the way, what brought you to Lagos?"

I opened my mouth and then paused. Why should this question come out at this moment? A wrong question for this moment. It would make my appetite disappear.

"Lagos is a place I have been longing to come to. I have heard different stories about the city and its people. They say it is a goldmine, both socially and otherwise."

"You left your decent and respectable job at home to become a steward here, so you must be crazy."

"Yeah, that's why I am sitting in front of you."

"No, I don't mean that," she said. "How can you say such a thing? If I have offended you, I'm sorry."

"Okay, forget about it. Now, back to why I came to Lagos. I went to study abroad on the ticket of the company I worked with. After my study, I had to work for them for five years to pay back the money spent on me. As the economy was not as flamboyant anymore, I felt the pinch. What forced me to come down was when some of my juniors returned with stereos or gaming equipment, and some with second-hand cars. I am better educated than most of those guys."

"So, you absconded?"

"Yes, chop-chop. No papers - I just had to grease palms all the way." I drank some of the wine and began the fight with my dessert. "But every misfortune is a blessing. Don't you agree with me?"

"I do," she said, nodding. "It would have been better to bring your passport because of security reasons."

"We came to Lomé in a group. With a group, the passports had to be with the leader."

"What if you are arrested and bundled back home?"

"It would be unpleasant for me; a shame."

I had not eaten half of the dessert when I realised I had no more space to accommodate the rest.

"It's been a nice meal."

"Very delicious." However, it would cost a lot.

"I think the footing of the bill would be nothing to you," she said, teasingly. "Let me call it a sumptuous meal."

"I know you would not like to disagree with me in public."

"What we've just eaten is the equivalent of a month of your meagre salary."

"You now know a lot about me, more than I know about you. Let me hear about you."

She laughed and this made almost everyone sitting around us look round. I know many wanted to but because of the opposite sex complaining, they did not.

"There is not much to say, just that I had a rough and miserable marriage. You are forcing me to tell you what I have kept secret and tried to forget; I fell in love with a gentleman. At that time, he had just graduated and had a good job with reasonable pay, a house, and a car at his disposal. Six months later, we were engaged, and the wedding was fixed for the summer of the following year. Before I met him, there was this grown-up man who wanted my hand in marriage, generous, always well-dressed. He always shopped in the same supermarket. I did not have any love for him anymore, besides, he was the same age as my father, and had a daughter my age from his first wife. She drowned in the lagoon when their speedboat collided with a ferry.

"Before summer, I lost my fiancé. We were returning from my in-laws when the men of the underworld struck; by then I was five months pregnant. I saw him dragged out of the car and shot several times in cold blood. He slumped forward and died. If you were in my shoes, what would have been your reaction? I fainted. The following morning, I found myself in a strange place, a hospital. I had miscarried and lost my husband and the car. I slashed my throat, wanting to die, but I was stopped."

She pointed at the marks of the stitches.

"My dreams were shattered. The doctor said I would not be able to give birth. Oh no, why me?" She began to sob. "Don't spoil the fun. At that time, I felt I did not deserve to live. My fiancé had wanted to take another route, but I insisted, and he was attacked. It was my fault."

"No, don't say that. It would have happened if it had been destined to happen. I am very sorry."

"I finally gave in to the sugar daddy," she said, wiping the tears.

"Why?" I asked, lighting a cigarette.

"Within a year, we got married," she said, fidgeting with her fingers. "I did not know what to do with myself. After he was buried, life meant nothing to me. I stopped working at the supermarket. Some months later, I noticed I had changed. Always crying, I would lock myself indoors for a day or two. I finally realised he would not come back. People were sent to persuade me to marry him. Two months to the day of the killing, he took me to the altar."

"What was the reaction of the public?"

"That's a good question," she sipped from her glass. "What do you expect? Rumour had it that he had sent thugs to kill my fiancé in order to get me and all sort of trash."

She yawned.

"It's getting late; let's go."

"I have had bad times. Imagine on the eve of our second anniversary, there were rumours that I was dating a friend of my fiancé. He threatened to divorce me."

"Was it true?" I cut in.

"How on earth can that be true? It was the work of those wishing to destroy me. Five months later, he was involved in a ghastly accident. Losing his eyesight, the shock made him dumb, and he broke his spinal cord. It was a horrible sight; you wouldn't have dared to look at it twice. At first, he was pronounced dead but survived. It would have been better if he had died."

"Don't worry, God's time is the best."

She felt bad about it, but why should she leave him and come to live in a hotel? That was what I did not understand.

"One day, you may just get up from bed in the morning and find him walking. Believe and trust in God. He works wonders in many ways."

"How many years more do I have to wait?"

"But why are you living in a hotel? What would people say about you?"

"There had been two fires in our house. The second one was intentional which meant the first, too, may not have been an accident. It was a deliberate attempt on his life. He got partial burns, not serious. He is now in Europe. I refused to live in a different house while the burnt one is being repaired. This happened while I was on a business trip to America. I had to cut it short and rush home." She buried her face in her hands.

I knew it was because of his money. The age barrier would tell since she was doomed not to have children; the money would be her children.

"Elsie, you know that people raised their voices against the marriage. What about if someone saw me in your company? You know, as a figure in the public eye."

She cut in; "Am I not a human being? Those hypocrites, don't they do the worst? They preach what they do not and can never do in their lives. Don't I have feelings? Let them say what they like," she said, surprising me. "I just don't understand some men who trust their women to tell them every damn secret about them. In the long run, they regret it."

Looking up at the ceiling, she smoked her cigarette while I sat pondering over what I had just heard.

'Am I safe in her arms?'

"You have to understand me. I am not wicked or callous. Even nuns do take on boyfriends, like the Fathers of Roman Catholic churches keep their secret girls. If I were you, I would be in a sober mood. I could have kept you in the dark by refusing to tell you. I hate keeping things that hurt inside me."

I felt a cold chill run through my body. She just wanted someone to satisfy her; it certainly wasn't love. She might have heard about me and traced me to the restaurant. Nevertheless, I would stick with her.

But her husband was my main concern. Thinking of him had now become routine in my brain. It was very sad, but I knew she was pretending.

"Don't you think my life would be in great danger when our secret love affair is uncovered?"

"Our relationship is not even a day old and look at what you are saying. Are you not a man?"

"I am also concerned about him. It would do him no good to hear of our affair, even though he had been warned."

"Forget about it. I know how to handle everything. It seems you are showing too much concern for him. What has come over you?"

"Don't you think that's going too far? You belong to another man and I am stealing a little bit of you."

She forced a smile.

"I think you like your job as a steward, don't you?"

I nod.

"Who would get a lady like me and toy with her? Even people with money come after me but I don't want their money. I need some affection. It seems you are under pressure. I don't want that. Let's forget it; it's all over."

She drew her seat back to get up. I now realised the grave mistake I had made. Her husband's plight shouldn't have been of great concern to me. He was almost dead; look at her sitting in front of me while he lives in agony.

She turned her eyes away from me, put the cigarette into the ashtray and picked up her bag to leave but I stopped her and tried to persuade her to stay. She insisted on going, but with a lot of persuasion, it was all over. My wristwatch showed one am. She drew the attention of the steward and paid for the meal.

With her two hands on the table, she bent forward. "Thank you very much for your company; see you another day. Please go your way and I will go mine. If you are still interested, you can book a date with me at reception."

It was my fault; now look at me. Elsie hurried out of the hall and I followed her. Sunday stood by the counter laughing.

"Tell me what day to come over," I pleaded at the entrance to the restaurant.

"Say that again? You are not serious, so I will call it quits. Since you don't understand me, let's forget this relationship. You are just a useless man. If I had known... Just get out of my way or I will call the police to have you thrown out."

I was in a fix. How could I let her slip through my fingers? If I lost her, it would affect my whole life. Elsie did not understand me. She went to get into the car but I blocked her.

"Should I call the police?"

"For what? Hold on, forget about all that happened. We need each other. Cool down and let's go. You brought me here, so why do you want to dump me here?"

We drove in the car together. She drove in such a way that at one point, we were chased by a police patrol team.

Elsie began to weep as soon as we were behind the door of her hotel room.

"Jerry, I hate you. When I saw you, it was like I had found my type, but no, you are the wrong one. Oh, why? Why me? Nothing goes right for me in love."

She threw everything that she could lay her hands on, held my shirt and pushed and pulled me, calling me all sorts of names.

I released her hands and hurried to the toilet. She followed me, throwing things at me even after I had closed the door. After showering and cooling down, I went out. Elsie had removed her dress and was sitting on the bed in her white panties and brassiere. Since we were all pretending, I went straight to her, kissing and caressing her. She sighed while I licked her after I had removed what blocked me from getting to the two most sensitive parts of her body.

I worked on her from her thighs up to her fresh bosom with pointed nipples, then back down to the stomach and beyond it, occasionally pulling the hair with my teeth. As I licked her, she yelled for more. While I licked her, my fingers were fondling her hard nipples. She cried out as I penetrated her. It was sweet and tight. As she jerked, I pushed and she held me, crying and calling my name for more. Before I ejaculated, she had climaxed twice. Before daybreak, we had three more rounds of love-making.

At seven o'clock, I was still on the bed, naked, and I should have been leaving at that time. She ironed my clothes with a small travelling iron while I took a quick shower. I had almost finished drying myself when she came in. Before bathing, she had to wash her pants, and while she did that, I climbed into the bath and penetrated her from behind.

"Jerry, aren't you late?" she asked.

"You asked for it," I told her.

In a taxi on my way to work, I felt sorry and pitied her husband. He had been missing a sweet apple.

When she walked out on me at the restaurant, she had forgotten her brooch which, mistakenly, she had forgotten to pin onto her dress after using it to remove dirt under her fingernails. I had quickly picked it up before following her. At the hotel, I hid it in the toilet. Pretending that I needed to pee, I had gone back for it.

Chapter Six

After work, I went to a friend who knows some big-time dealers in silver. John was a full-time pawn broker who resided in Ajegunle in a one-room apartment.

Their room had its main entrance on a busy street and between their room and the street was a gutter which was dug some years back. John's girlfriend cooked in the sitting room and washed just outside the room. Next to their room was the toilet, which stank and was an eyesore. If the wind blew into the room, the stench it carried into it was drenched in booze. Worst of all, his only window was behind the toilet.

He was advised by his friends to leave that place but he refused. Who did they think would want to come and live there? Okay, he should have let some people clean the place - no way. Do you know what he did with his money? Gambling and women; he had a soft spot for the fairer ones with big bosoms.

Cigarettes would be first, and drinking, he was excellent at doing that.

I got onto one of the Ijora-Ajegunle bound buses opposite. As a matter of urgency, as you are aware of the conditions in my place of sleeping, the bus was overcrowded and I had to hang on to the entrance behind a uniformed soldier. The passengers were packed like sardines, but still, the conductor, a young, black man about twenty-two, kept on shouting for more passengers. I wondered if he had any respect for human life.

The passengers challenged the conductor when he shouted for people to enter and sit when he knew very well that there was no breathing space. Twenty metres from the bus stop, the driver stopped when two men and a girl waved. He got up, asking the passengers to move forward. Since he had stopped at the foot of the bridge, he slowed the movement of the other vehicles.

If he had known that he was being watched by two traffic wardens (Majamaja), he would have used the bridge near the stadium. The bus was signalled by the two traffic wardens to stop.

The lance corporal directed the driver where to park while he stood in front of the motor to stop the driver from escaping. The driver obeyed and came down pleading, and lay prostrate on the street.

"Please! Please!" he said from the ground.

"Where are your particulars?" said the Majamaja.

He got up when he found out his pleading wasn't working.

"Ah, Oga, I beg now," said the driver, moving closer. "I will see you," he continued.

The driver knew he was at fault. But why tell the warden he would see him? It was the drivers who had made him corrupt. I didn't blame the drivers. The vehicle didn't belong to him and he had a family to feed. When the case arose, it would not go to court on that day; maybe a day or two after. If he was unlucky, the case would be postponed until the next week and he would be detained till then. The employer of the driver might sack him since the bus was at the police station and there would be no money for the family.

He finally went to the bus, raised his seat, took out his licence and put five naira in it. Then he went back to give it to the warden. As he went through the paperwork, I noticed the warden's face change. He smiled and moved to the bonnet of the bus, then to the driver, and handed the document over to him.

"Next time, be careful. Everything is alright."

"Thank you, Oga."

He drove off, making four stops at Alakas, Iporiri, Costain and Brewery.

At Ijora, it was a real tug-of-war; only the fittest entered at that time of day when workers had finished. On all the buses that arrived, the conductors shouted at the top of their lungs for passengers and called out destinations that they were headed to. There were the Danfors, VW passenger buses, Nissan E120s, Mitsubishi, Toyota taxis of different makes and, of course, the big Molne buses.

In less than ten minutes, I got a seat in a Nissan E120 going to Ajegunle. It would have been easier if most of the big buses heading for CMS Edumota, Tinubu and Obalende went to Ajegunle.

Some of the passengers would rush to any vehicle that arrived as if embarking, but no, they rushed to rob the poor workers of the few kobos he had sweated for. They robbed from beautiful, charming ladies and nice, handsome-looking gentlemen to neatly dressed rascals with their own type of dressing. Children were clamouring and rubbing shoulders to enter, while older people were struggling too. The insane were also around, who terrorised the passengers by chasing them or throwing things at them. Sometimes, just their appearance would terrify people, especially the sophisticated ladies who would scuttle away.

Because of my gentility, it took a long time before I got a bus. Since workers had finished at their various places of work, there were a lot of vehicles on the street.

John had a girlfriend called Monica, who was fair in complexion. He liked the fairer girls. She was a teenager, in her final year at a famous girls' secondary school.

Her parents were very strict and disapproved of the relationship between John and their daughter because he was married, was many years older than Monica, and had a questionable character. Every day, when she had finished school, her first place of call was John's house. Wherever he was, or whatever he was doing, he would return home when she arrived. You might ask where the wife would be when Monica came over. She had a permanent afternoon shift as a receptionist with a modelling house.

Monica opened the door when I knocked for the fifth time. She was singing a very popular song among students.

"Monica, stop murdering that song," I said, entering.

"Is it any of your business?" she asked as she sat on John's lap.

"Forget it." That was John.

We shook hands.

"Afternoon, John."

"Afternoon."

"Monica, afternoon."

"Don't greet me," she said, going into the bedroom.

The road from the bus stop to the house was so bad that passenger vehicles refused to use it. So, I had to trek about two hundred metres under the hot and burning sun. The room was hot and the old table fan, instead of blowing cold air, blew out hot.

He apologised for the hot atmosphere. The air conditioner had broken down a day before. You would be surprised when you entered the room; very tidy and the setting was perfect. One would have thought that since the surroundings of the house were dirty, it would have been the same inside. The walls were painted green with a white ceiling. The armchairs and sofas were cream, with a green carpet. On the black and white room divider facing the entrance of the room were electronic gadgets; modern and updated ones. There was a video recorder, a computerized turntable, an equalizer, an amplifier, a cassette recorder, and on the top shelf was a radio set. In the middle was a twenty-four-inch television set. In every corner of the room were big loudspeakers. Different types of glasses, ranging from wine, sherry and small glasses, were displayed in a white sideboard. Assorted brands of drink were kept in the locked side of the sideboard.

John whispered into her ear. Since the two handkerchiefs I carried were wet, I placed them on the arms of the chair on which I sat for them to dry before I left.

"What will you have?" Monica asked, with her hand on her hips whilst she bowed.

"Brandy on the rocks."

The two of them drank it neat while I settled with my brandy on the rocks.

"Forgive me for not being able to see you for a long time," I apologised, sipping my brandy.

"It's okay."

"My work and, most of all, the accommodation problem as you already know." I paused and looked at his face.

"Monica, could you please excuse us for a minute? I want to have a tête-à-tête," said John. Monica left, frowning and hissing.

"Do not be offended," I said. "It is business that has brought me here today," I said after she had gone into the bedroom. John poured himself another shot of brandy.

"Before I go on… Some time ago, there were rumours that you snatched a bracelet from your sister-in-law at a party."

"It was the first time I had done something of that sort."

"But why did you have to do that?" I asked. "You have added more dirt to your already soiled reputation."

"I know, Jerry, but I could not turn my eyes away. It was too tempting. A combination of gold and diamonds; no way. If only I had not been seen. I had heard of the bracelet, the quality and price; I had my eyes on it for a long time. In this world, when you are playing a game, it's either lose or win. That's that, so forget about it."

"You shouldn't have taken it considering she is your sister-in-law."

"Being a sister does not arise. I have to eat and feed her sister. With all her money... Don't make me say things. I took every precaution not knowing that the demon was looking at me."

"How much would you have got? Was it worth more than your reputation?" I asked him.

He bowed his head.

"I know; it has happened already. After all, it is my own life," he said, shrugging. "It would have been a clean and perfect snatching that night. The place was crowded, there was a lot to eat and drink, a good band and music to dance to. The crowd was gay. No one would have that kind of chance and let it slip away just like that."

"Okay," I said, bringing out the brooch from my pocket. "In my pocket is a diamond that would make your eyebrows raise or stand like the long prickles of a porcupine."

He wanted to grab it when I took it out, but I was smart.

"Sit down! Didn't I tell you?"

I gave it to him in a more civilised way and he grinned.

"Monica, come and see," he called with his sonorous voice.

"What is it?" she asked, charging in like a bull. Monica came in wearing only her white brassiere and blue underskirt.

"Look at this," he said, handing it over to her.

She opened her mouth wide in surprise and took it. She sank into the sofa by my side, motionless, staring at it. Suddenly, she stood up.

"Let me test it."

I held her slip, "No way! You can't go in there with it."

I got to my feet and refused to allow her to take it into the bedroom until she handed it to me. There was absolute silence in the room. She looked at John's face and then mine. She took a cigarette from the packet on the room divider, lit it, and disappeared into the inner room. John broke the silence after she had gone.

"Don't let this embarrass you; it's nothing to her, she has gold fever," he said, scratching his back with difficulty. "Man, I have seen this type of thing before."

"You are right; when she sees things like this, her eyes move up and down; she really fancies them."

"Do you want to get rid of it?"

"Yes, that's why I am here. How much is the price?"

"How much do you want for it?"

"I thought you'd be in a position to tell me; that's why I came here. Be serious and stop dancing around it."

"Okay, leave it till tomorrow."

"No, never. When I leave here, it's going with me."

"Are you a woman?" he asked, teasingly.

I wrapped it back up and put it back into my pocket.

"John, I must be going."

"Jerry, hold on, I am coming," he said, getting up. "Hope you'll not leave."

I was placing the needle onto a record I had just put on the turntable when he appeared with a box guitar.

"Let me play you some music to cool you down," he said, resting on the side of the room divider. He did not smoke but the girl smoked heavily.

"Monica, I have told you to stop smoking," he told her as she came out for another cigarette.

"You can go to hell. I am not going to stop." She drew the curtain and went in.

"Don't mind her. She wanted some sex this hot afternoon, but I refused. A classmate just left before she came in," he whispered into my ear.

"Before I leave, I want some advice from you," I said, as I lowered the volume of the amplifier. "Last night, I was out with a lady of money. There was a misunderstanding between us. As she was leaving, I spotted it on the table and smartly put it into my pocket. Later on, having left the restaurant where we had gone to eat, we carried on getting to know each other. She did not ask of it, but my conscience told me it was a plan to test me."

"Man, this is your chance. You are lucky. Throughout last night, you were with her and she did not mention it?"

"But…"

"But what? Don't be so stupid as to return it to her."

"I will talk to her about it; she might ask me to take it."

"You've made a big catch here, so don't let it slip. Chances like this come once in a lifetime. This is something I am looking forward to and I would suck her dry."

"Because of what you intend to do, it will never, and I repeat, never, come your way."

"I am planning to sell it then split. She knows a lot about me. Last night, I told her a lot about me."

The ice in the brandy had melted. I drank everything in one go and bade him farewell. He escorted me to the door.

"You can come back after you have tried other places," he said, shaking hands.

"I am coming back tomorrow. The same time."

"You have let him get away with it," I heard Monica shout at him. "Don't you know I need to buy those shoes that girl wore yesterday? Are you crazy?"

The door was slammed; I shrugged and walked away. If business is good, he'll take her shopping and buy a portmanteau full of clothing for her travel to the Yankari Game Reserve. I hear she likes the warm spring, so almost every month, they travel at weekends. I wonder how someone like Monica can travel and still cope with her studies.

John knew she had extravagant tastes. I knew he couldn't marry the girl, and neither would he want to. It was only fun; she knew he was a spendthrift. Things were not as before; he was keeping a low profile. If he was totally broke, Monica would say bye to their much-talked-about relationship.

Chapter Seven

When I got to the bus stop, I looked tired, and stood with my arms akimbo, pondering about the next move to make.

Four ladies aimlessly crossed the street towards me, conversing between themselves. During the daytime, it's always a busy street but in the dead of night, it would be a ghost street. On rainy days, it was difficult for both vehicles and human beings to ply it. In the morning, the street was lively with all sorts of people going to their various workplaces. In the morning, a bevy of sophisticated ladies would troop onto the road from their homes. The latest makes of flashy cars also added some colour to the area. Any time I found time to go to John's place, I took some time to see things for myself. Even in the afternoon, I would stand in the burning sun, and from my pants to my shirt would be wet as if water had been poured on me.

The room in which I lived with my friend had no mosquito net. At night, the room became so hot that even the fan gave out hot air. One was then tempted to open the louvres but if you dared do it, you would have a bad time with mosquitos.

Sometimes, when the room was hot, I would lie naked on my back gazing at the dirty white ceiling which had not been painted for a decade. Fanning myself with an old newspaper, I would shift my mind from my problems to listening to some music from the next room.

In the room was a long, old sideboard brought from the store. We had always made the room look tidy by trying to sweep every morning and dust the room. Under the double louvre window was a double steel camp bed. It was so noisy – even sitting up or trying to rise from it would make noises.

The paint on the wall had almost washed off. We pasted pictures cut out from magazines on the dirty spots. Beside the area where clothes were hung was an old writing desk with old newspapers on it.

A dirty red carpet with cigarette burns and chewing gum on it lay between the bed and the sideboard.

The odour of cigarettes and liquor was what would welcome you as soon as you opened the door. If I had a girl to sleep with me for the night, the occupant of the next room had to go elsewhere and when he brought home a catch, I would have to go. If you were really unlucky, you had to sleep in the corridor, a guest of mosquitos, cockroaches and mice.

She knew I had little money so there was no need for me to do something that would later give me a headache. I manage to smuggle, with the help of a workmate, a bottle of White Horse, a packet of roasted groundnut, a packet of the cigarettes she smokes, two bottles of mineral water, some pieces of fried meat and four meat pies from the restaurant. This had been possible after promising a hand-out to my colleague.

I did not expect her to ask for food in my house, but if she did, offering a meat pie and fried meat wouldn't be so bad. The guy in the next room gave me his cassette recorder with some cassettes, which I put on a small cupboard by the side of the bed. After I had eaten a pie and two pieces of meat, I washed it down with a bottle of mineral water.

I hurriedly had my shower since time was passing. With a sweet-smelling powder under my armpits and some over my chest, I lay on my back on the bed with two shots of the whisky I had brought in a glass on the cupboard. There was a nice song from the cassette I had borrowed. I lit a cigarette and gazed at the dirty ceiling with staring eyes.

Twenty minutes later, after I had finished the two cigarettes, I heard the illiterate gateman shouting my name. I rushed out.

"Somebody do look for you," he said as I came out. I told him to lower his voice and beckoned for him to come closer.

"Na woman, fine one."

"Okay," I said, putting my hand into my pocket and offering him a note.

"Thank you, thank you," he said, grinning.

"Make you bring am inside," I said.

I hurried into the room for a final check. It was exactly six pm. As she approached me, I welcomed her, smiling. I hugged her, a big one of course, and we entered the room. We kissed passionately behind the door. When she sat on the bed, it did not make a noise because I had cut up paper and put it under its legs. I gave her some old magazines and offered all that I had reserved for her. We conversed and Elsie told me she was renovating a place up-country to be used as a restaurant. She would offer me the post of supervisor. I was happy but it was short-lived when it came to my mind that most of the people in Lagos have sugar-coated mouths. Throughout our conversation, she neither asked me about the diamond nor said anything about it.

She left around nine after we had had a nice time. I could not see her off at the gate since my friend's master was in.

The husband had arrived home. There was no way I could see her. I planned a strategy to phone Elsie and let her know I had the brooch and then explain to her how I came about it.

The following morning, by greasing the manager's palm, I obtained permission. From the restaurant, I went straight to Igbobi to phone her. By the time I got to the telephone booth, there were about six people waiting in a queue. I had no option but to join it. Thus, the long wait began for the next one and a half hours that I was in the line.

The operator asked me to wait for ten good minutes after it got to my turn. Her next move, after the ten minutes, was to ask me to replace the receiver since the line was busy. Exactly four minutes later, I picked up the receiver when it rang just once.

My decision to let her know about my having the brooch was a painstaking one.

"Hello," I said.

"Hello. Good afternoon, this is Elsie."

It was her voice, so I paused for a moment.

I needed some money, but to let her know about it, I just didn't know what would happen. To have left it to John would have been the most stupid thing in my life. A passport and a ticket were the things I needed. To regularise my papers and stay on was a cover-up. If I was put in the newspapers and a ransom so big hung around my neck, some kind of bastard would trace me. Even the restaurant was a dangerous place to work. I had put on weight and grown a moustache and beard.

I remembered a story I heard of a labourer who came across ☐50,000. He alerted the manager who I heard was white. He gave the man the boot outright, telling him that he did not need money.

She spoke with some uneasiness in her tone as if there was someone standing by her who she wouldn't like to hear what she was saying.

"Do not be angry, Elsie."

"What is it? What do you want from me?"

"You forgot your brooch on the table the other time when we went to the restaurant."

"I don't get you; speak louder."

"Your brooch," I shouted.

"Where is it?"

"It's here with me."

"Where did you get it?"

"You left it on the table at the restaurant during the time you walked out on me."

"For God's sake, why didn't you tell me before? Why did you do that?"

The booth was in such a condition that staying in it was unbearable, but it was private and confidential. No one would hear. It was really hot and uncomfortable.

"I didn't know you had it. That morning, when I found out that it was missing, I gave the restaurant manager hell and did the same at the hotel," she said.

"How will you get it?" I asked. "Or do you suggest I come over to your place?"

She shouted at her end. "No! A big no."

The burnt house had been reconstructed. I paused.

"Hello, Elsie? Hello? Hello? Can you hear me?"

"Yes, I can," she answered. "I am thinking of my next move. It would not be right to come here. Neither can I come to you."

"I want to see you, so you try and come to my place this evening."

Those in the queue knocked on the glass for me to hurry.

"I can't promise," she said, "but I will see what I can do."

"See you; bye."

Chapter Eight

It was three-thirty-two on Thursday when I came out of the restaurant. I had closed for the day. It had been a lucky day for me; with a smile on my face, I counted the tips I had in my palm on the terrace. After counting, I hurried to the locker to change my uniform and split. John, on his way to my house, spotted me at the entrance to the restaurant.

The taxi stopped a few metres ahead and reversed. He demanded one naira from me to pay the cab driver.

"Do you still have it?" he asked on his return.

I did not answer.

"Or have you given it away?" he continued.

"I have not, but I am not selling it. You know it does not belong to me. She is coming for it tomorrow. She would have been here yesterday, but she couldn't make it."

"Look, man, don't be a fool. You'll get a good deal for it."

"No, forget about your good deal. No, I am not," I insisted.

"You are an example of those who give out everything they have because of women, even to the extent of murder."

"Not me, rule me out," I retorted, shrugging. "You can't force me. I promised to come yesterday, but since I decided not to sell it, that was why I did not turn up as promised."

"This is your chance because she took you out. Do not make a mistake by returning it. Your so-called lady you told me is rich, so why?"

I turned to walk away but he held my arm.

"Jerry, tell me if I am going too far," he said as he moved closer to me. "You are aware that the husband is fighting for his life. No one knows when he will be defeated by death. The chances of surviving are very slim. How do you feel going about with a married woman?"

I folded my arms and listened intently. He put his hands in his pockets.

"As someone older than you, I am advising you to sell this thing, stop seeing her and do something for yourself. After all, there are girls of your age who are single. You are cursing yourself by going about shamelessly with a sick man's wife."

"What about you?" I cut in. "That chicken girlfriend of yours - do her parents recognise you? Tell me, can't you see the stone in your eyes?"

"But I have no stone in my eyes," he said, touching his eyes.

I laughed.

"What are you laughing for, you useless man?"

"What I just said doesn't mean you have it in your eyes. Paddle your own canoe and leave my life for me. Neither you nor anybody else can run my life for me."

"Okay," he said, removing his left hand from his pocket. "I know your problem. She goes out with you well-dressed, beautiful and charming, but with the money, you can do something for yourself; go places. You can have a girl who you love, see her always. I mean, anytime you feel like it. A girl by choice not by chance. She is a lover by chance. She can slip through your fingers at any time, unexpectedly. Let me call your friendship one of darkness."

"Please, thank you for your advice. Go away and leave me alone. Do you listen to elders who have advised you to stop disgracing yourself? You bring shame to your family. That chicken of yours, you can't stop with her because, as you put it, she is beautiful. Please leave me alone before I call the police."

"Look at you. Have patience; you don't need to be angry," he said politely. "I have strong connections to get you work, a decent job topped with good pay. Let's make a deal and forget about her. She can't come to your house. You have an excellent C.V. You don't have to do this kind of work. With decent employment, you can get yourself nice accommodation and a girlfriend of your own."

"Thank you, Mr Adviser. Your idea is not bad, but I am not giving it out. Since I am not the owner, I am forbidden to sell it. Moreover, I have told her to come for it."

"Do you know something? What about if she takes it and stops seeing you? Then you'll lose it all."

"It does not matter; such is life," I told him. "Forget about it. Talk of other things."

He looked at me steadily.

"One day, you'll bite your fingernails and regret choosing a married woman instead of making money."

I chuckled.

"The worst is yet to come," he continued. "May God forgive you."

"You can do what you like. Go to hell," I said, losing patience. "I would rather pray for you; everything about you is unholy."

I knew he was making a point, but I had told her already.

"In case you change your mind, which I know you'll do, let me know as soon as possible," he said, dejectedly. "But if you don't, it's up to you. I'll leave you to your fate."

He turned and walked across to the other side of the street. A blue Range Rover missed him by two steps. He was lucky, else he would have been crippled, given the speed at which the vehicle was moving to beat the traffic light and the screeching noise of the tyres when the driver applied the brakes.

Chapter Nine

The non-functioning table lamp stood on top of the old sideboard, lifeless. For her second time coming to my place, I borrowed a velvet throw from the guy next door. All the photographs of ladies' cats in round shapes I pasted on the wall neatly. I swept the carpet several times and, with the sharp edge of a penknife, I removed the chewing gum. I did it all to impress Elsie and nobody else.

At my request, my friend brought me some forget-me-not flowers from the next house. He stood at the doorway teasing me as I adorned the room with them. The room had come back to life once more.

From the shopping centre, I bought some snacks and mineral water and a card wishing her many years of friendship together. I was in high spirits once more after my admonishing of John.

I put on the new cream safari suit I had bought with last week's tips. It was well-ironed with straight lines like a soldier's uniform. I polished my white shoes and began to wait. Any footsteps I heard approaching, I would look through the curtain, stretching my neck like a turtle. I became worried as time went by. Seconds turned to minutes, which turned into hours, and then finally became a day. I shuttled between the room and the corridor till I lost hope.

With a cigarette in the fingers of my left hand, I settled into the old armchair. It wasn't easy for me. I went to the toilet. As I was urinating, a big fly landed on my left cheek. My hand went up, wham, but the fly had gone and my palm settled on my flesh while the urine spilt on my trousers. What had happened to her? Again, tomorrow, it would be the same excuse. After all, she was somebody's wife.

Whilst calling my friend to bring me some cold water, I heard the steel gates open. My heart began to beat like the drum of the town crier. Then I heard someone running. It was the security man. He announced her arrival and I asked him to usher her in as quickly as possible. I hurried to the room to have a last look at myself. I heard the sound of high-heeled shoes coming and I went into the corridor to welcome her.

She was glamorous and smiling. Her red and white checked woollen plaited skirt topped with a red silk blouse made me ogle. She had on a pair of white shoes with red dots and a red bag along with a white scarf with multicoloured dots. A combination of red, blue and white earrings and a thin, gold chain made her look so colourful.

For the first time, she had her engagement and wedding rings on. Her makeup was perfect and toned in with her dress.

"Oh, my God," I said. "Look at that. Elsie, I told you the other day, you are irresistible."

She gave me her hands. As I touched her fingers, she felt the rings and her face changed.

"I forgot to –"

"Don't worry, I understand," I said sharply. Quickly, she removed them and, looking away, put them in her bag. We paused till we got inside. Behind closed doors, she touched my chest and extended her hand and touched that part of my body with her slim fingers.

"Have you noticed anything?"

"Of course; this is unusual. Are you sick?"

I grinned.

"No, because of you," I said, scratching my back. "I thought you had another excuse for not coming."

She moved forward and placed her hand on my shoulder.

"Don't worry, everything is going to be alright," she said, looking straight into my eyes. She kisses me. We kissed till we fell on the bed.

"Hold on, Elsie, an intruder might come in." After locking the door, I went to her. Elsie had gone to sit on the armchair. She looked around as if she had not been in the room before.

"I am impressed with the change in this room. Strange things have found their way in here."

I went to the toilet again.

Elsie hid behind the door so that I could not see her. My eyes jumped. If you were in my shoes, what would happen to you? As I tip-toed to look under the bed, she jumped out and grabbed me from behind.

Oh, my God, if not for my being strong, I would have peed my pants!

"Elsie, it is not funny. Don't laugh."

She kept on laughing.

"Don't be stupid, it is not funny," I shouted at her.

"Jerry, mind your tongue," she shouted back.

"I am sorry," I apologised.

"Jerry, I didn't mean any harm. Please believe me."

I pulled the armchair towards me where I was leaning on the sideboard. She sat on the arm.

"Elsie, why don't you arrive on time? You look like someone who does not honour her promise."

I dropped the end of the cigarette I was holding onto the carpet and stepped on it. She looked at me, then at the carpet. I got the message and quickly cleaned it with a tissue, but the ash stain stubbornly refused to go. She forced a reserved smile.

"I am serious. Do you think I am mad? This is the second time you are coming to me, and, for the second time, you are late. The day I came to your hotel, I was thirty minutes early because I needed you. Are you taking me for a ride?"

"Jerry, don't say that," she said, moving closer. "There were some visitors who had come to sympathise with us. I got away with a flimsy excuse."

I sat motionless, looking at her and pondering over what John had told me. I was stealing from someone's house. If she belonged to me, I could see her any time. John was right but…

"What's on your mind?" she asked, taking one of the flowers from the sideboard. "It's going to be alright."

She gave me the flower.

"How soon?" I asked.

If she had known what was on my mind, it would have been very unpleasant.

The wind hardly blew towards the window, but when it did, fresh air entered. At that time of day, it was impossible for that to happen. All of a sudden, she stood up, looking at the photographs on the wall.

"I know this girl," she said, sorrowfully pointing to her. "She was robbed and raped to death by an unknown person. Up till now, the police have not found out who did it."

"This world is full of wicked people," I said, moving closer to her. Karma would one day catch up with that person.

"What about your query?" she asked.

"This is Lagos. It's all over."

"When you are alone here, how do you feel and what do you do?"

"I enjoy reading magazines, novels and newspapers. Interesting international magazines," I said as I moved to the desk with the papers. "Do you also like reading?"

"A lot. Sometimes, when I am free, I can read without eating for the whole day."

She moved over to the desk, took out one of the magazines and, out of curiosity, turned the pages one after the other.

"I fancy this house. The architectural work is nice," she commented.

I moved to her side and placed my left hand on her waist.

"Yeah, I also like it. Very nice work."

"No wonder," she said, "it is situated on a street in Beverley Hills. Hope you've heard about it. Most of the celebrities reside there."

I spread the snacks on a plate on the sideboard. She declined to eat but had some brandy. Elsie left the brandy and came over to me.

"Are you sure?"

"Yes, forget about it. It's you I want to eat. Eat and give it to me," she said, as she put her hands on my shoulders. Then, all of a sudden, she moved back and glanced at her beautiful watch.

"I must leave," she said, going for her bag on the bed.

Startled, I folded my arms and leaned against the old sideboard. She gave me a kiss and was about to open the door but stopped and turned to me.

"What about the silver pin? It nearly slipped my mind."

With no word from me, I went over to the bed and drew my travelling bag out from under it. Without looking, I gave it to her. As I squatted beside the bed, I began to ponder over what John had told me that afternoon. To come to a conclusion that she would always find an excuse for me would be premature and uncalled for.

She opened the door to leave whilst I sat on the bed. She closed the door again and came over to sit by me.

"Oh, darling. Why have you all of a sudden gone dumb?" she said, unbuttoning my jacket. She began to fondle my nipple which made me laugh. "You have to understand, I have to go."

No word from me.

She put one leg on my lap.

"Elsie, darling, I do understand. But can't you risk just a few minutes with me? I need you."

She got up.

I pulled her by the skirt.

"Please don't leave me. I need you. You are more precious than anything else on this earth."

"Go on, I am listening to you."

I went for the brandy she had poured into the glass.

"Jerry, we have to be very careful. As I am important to you, so you are to me."

"Elsie, we have just begun. It is said that we must make hay while the sun shines."

She gave me a long kiss, tickling me.

"When are we going to see each other?" I asked as I lay on my back.

"You still want me to come here?"

"Why not? If you can't come here anymore, it would be better to meet at a place that is more convenient. I wish I could see you every minute. Let me know when next I am seeing you and where."

"When we are seeing? Is that what you mean?" she asked, teasingly.

"Let's be serious."

"The relatives, friends and business associates troop in every minute," she said, sipping from her glass. "I don't know what kind of mess I have got myself into."

"Elsie, what are you doing about it? Just tell me when I'll see you."

"This is how I have been living with him all year. Since the accident, everything has changed. My life, I mean, everything about me. My driver is a distant relative of my husband. Do you know how I came here? The driver dropped me at the hairdresser's place, then I went through the back door and across a building site. The driver is waiting outside the salon. They are always spying on my activity because they say I married him because of his money."

"Elsie, I understand your feelings but –"

"What did you say the other day? You have to sympathise with me. Stop being selfish. In the house, I am always lonely. I have everything but not happiness."

"Forget what I said the other day. You have to reason with me. There are always a lot of complications when love is still young, so let's make the best we can out of it."

"The little time I have spent with you means a lot to me. I am happy here, but at the same time, I'm thinking of what it would be like at home. Just wait; patience will make us succeed. I fell in love with you the moment I saw you. But for him, it was because I needed company. I have myself to blame. Time will tell."

"Listen to me, it would not be proper to call me on the phone. The phone has an extension upstairs but it is not safe to call me in the house. Please, please. I will see you as soon as I can, when it is safe."

"Okay, don't worry," I said, managing a sardonic smile. "Just try and make it soon."

"Sure, dear. Let me go."

She kissed my forehead softly.

"Hold on and let me feel you."

"Oh, my God," she said, "you are very difficult. Let me go. Time is passing. Try to understand."

"Elsie, I do understand you, but it is very difficult for me. Can't you stay for a while?" I asked, teasingly.

She opened the door and hurried out. I stood behind the door with my face buried in my palm.

'When am I going to see her?' I asked myself. I couldn't even hear her voice, so sweet. 'Not now,' I replied.

"Since this world is a wonderful place, I have hope that anything could happen. I have hope," I shouted.

As the days are born young, live to grow and die old, so will our love grow old.

Chapter Ten

I went about my stewardship job with the hope that she'd call at the restaurant. Even when I was not on duty, I would hang around. Those days, I was receiving a lot of tips and for me to avoid thinking and wondering about her too much, all the money was spent on drinks, so I was always tipsy.

A week had passed without seeing her. Then I got this feeling that since she had the telephone number of the main building, she might call. I couldn't wait any longer. If by tomorrow, she had not phoned, I would have to take the risk. If she called and my friend's master and madam were at home, she would have to drop it.

I didn't think she would take that chance when people were in the house. There was a lot of money involved with her husband. My not seeing her had set our love affair back. Every day, I woke and went to work with high hopes that she would call, but every day, my hopes were dashed.

Any time I heard footsteps I would come. At the restaurant, when the door swung open, I would have hope. I always wished it would be her.

Every Tuesday was my day off, so I would sleep and stay indoors till eight o'clock in the morning, wash and then go to a nearby canteen to eat. It became a routine for me. Always, I settled with a plate of rice, fried plantain, some meat and fish, followed by a bottle of Fanta or Coke. A cigarette from my favourite brand was my dessert. On my return, I would have purchased the day's newspapers. I would open the louvres and draw the window blind to one side for some early, fresh morning air to enter while I lay on my back, bare-chested, reading.

On that Tuesday, I had gone about my usual routine, returned home, and settled with the dailies. I heard someone shout, "Thief! Thief! Stop him!" outside.

I rushed out, but before I reached the steel gate, there was a gunshot and a long and painful scream followed.

'Oh, my God,' I said to myself. 'When will these faceless armed robbers let us have peace of mind?'

Later, I learned that about four elegantly dressed men had gone into the house adjacent to ours and driven out the gold metallic 200 Mercedes being washed by the driver. He was silenced with a big cut on his head. A young man in the house saw it from the sitting room, rushed out, and was shot in the elbow.

It shook me so much that when I returned to my room, Elsie and the robbery had disturbed me a lot. From the old ones, I picked a magazine to glance through, but it did not erase what I had seen. I lit a cigarette but after the first puff, my next action was to put it out in the tin lid I was using as an ashtray.

I bowed my head, took a deep breath and thought for a moment. Then, I realised that of late, I had not been myself, drinking and smoking a lot.

I stayed in the room until noon, expecting either a call from her, which my friend would let me know about, or that she would appear in person.

I was stroking my nose just after noon when I heard quick footsteps approaching. I rushed out but it was in the next compound. As soon as I had returned to my seat, I heard the steel gates open and rushed out again. It was not her, but my friend, on seeing me,

135

opened his wide mouth with thick lips to laugh at me. He teased me till one of the eggs he was carrying fell and broke. Then, silence took over. It was my turn to hurl abuse at him, but when I noticed it, I regretted it and apologised.

The disturbing noise of sirens woke me late in the afternoon. Reluctantly, I picked up a romantic magazine which I had bought in a bookshop some days back, then I went back to sleep once more. The book was beneath me when I woke.

After I finished bathing, I had not even dried myself when I heard a sweet voice like Elsie's. With the towel around my waist, I rushed out. It wasn't for me but for the main building. Back in the room, my stomach demanded some food, but my appetite wasn't there.

Sitting on the bed with my back resting on the wall, I began to think about what my friend John had told me. If I had sold the brooch, by now, I would be in the money with my own kind of woman. Even if she did not love me, with the money, she would bow to my orders.

For a long time, I had not thought about her husband, but now I hated him. I did not feel pity for him and wished he had died. The sympathy I had for him had disappeared and he was now a pain in my neck. It was him who was blocking me, depriving me of my happiness.

After I had returned to work the following day. I waited but there was no sign of her, and, in my absence, there had been no call. I went through this for another three days. I became isolated and lonely. At work and home, everyone thought I was sick. When I told them that everything was alright with me, they didn't believe me. Even the manager had wanted to give me a few days off with pay, but I stood my ground and insisted that there was nothing seriously wrong with me. I was just depressed and nothing more. I could not lose her and the brooch at once. It was not possible.

With no food and always alone, I looked like a sick person. Truly, I was at heart; my brain was doing too much thinking.

On the fifth day, the manager asked me to change or I would be kicked out because the customers were complaining about me not being lively. On my way back from work, I found a local shop and bought some of the local gin. In fact, I filled my body with more than it could take. Back in my room, it was like I was being tortured. In all my years, I had not had that kind of experience before.

My intention was to get drunk and call her on the phone to tell her everything I was feeling inside me. Unfortunately for me, on getting to the house, there was a visitor in the hall.

It was when I began to vomit that a tiny sound of knocking got my attention. The situation I was in did not allow me to get up and open the door. The visitor decided to knock at intervals. Since I was sitting far from the door, I had to crawl like a baby, but even that was a task for me. I fell and slumbered after I had turned the key to unlock the door.

It was late in the night when I woke up. I raised my hand to glance at my wristwatch, but it was not there. 'Oh, my God, what have I done to myself?' I tried to switch on the light. On the bedside table was my watch on top of a piece of paper. It had just gone past one am. I quickly took the paper and tore it open as it had been stuck.

I looked at my friend who was sleeping peacefully. I felt weak and tired. I needed some water, cold, of course. I sat at the table and began to read.

'Darling,

I was here, but the condition you were in was disgraceful and it was too much for me, and I had to leave. You really were out of your brain.

Hope you'll forgive me for staying away for so long. Was it because of me that you got yourself into this mess? Please forgive me. See you tomorrow.

Bye, and take care.'

With a clenched fist, I hit the door, waking my friend.

"Stop disturbing me, Jerry," he said, yawning. "No one got you into this mess; it was your own stupidity. She was here. The whole room was smelling. Elsie wiped up the rubbish you vomited and went out to buy the deodorant on the sideboard."

He pointed at it. I grabbed it, kissed the tin, and wrapped my arms around it. Without a word, I went out to drink some water. I battled with sleep before I finally gave up.

Chapter Eleven

It was after twelve when I woke up feeling weak and hungry. My reporting time for the afternoon shift was one pm, so I hurriedly had a quick bath. I felt as if I had engaged in a fight the night before. Never in my life had I felt like that before. It had not been all that smooth.

Elsie was on my mind. She had stained my blood and I couldn't bleach her out of it. Nothing was going to stop me from seeing her, even if I had to go down to her residence. Without her, I had a bleak future. I knew I was stealing someone's woman, but she was driving me crazy.

A tipper truck screeched to a stop a few steps away from me. It was then that I realised I had wandered into the road unaware. I would have been killed, just like a goat.

As I pushed the black wooden gate to enter the compound of the restaurant, I got the feeling that she would surely call there.

I went to sign the register, but it was not in its usual place. In the manager's office, he told me I had been given the boot and asked me to come for my salary tomorrow. Without saying a word, I opened the door and slammed it on my way out because it did not come to me as a surprise. Ignoring everyone in the hall, which was full to capacity, I hurried out into the sun.

As it was a very sunny afternoon, I got into an 505 Peugeot taxi, which made the distance to my house less and saved me from the scorching sun.

The guard informed me that I had a female visitor and went on to tell me that it was Elsie. I pushed the door wide and rushed to the boys' quarters. Even though I felt weak, on hearing that she was around, I became strong once more.

There she was, sitting on the bed, wearing a maroon round-necked dress with tiny white circles in big blue triangles, a large white leather belt, and white sunglasses raised to her forehead. She also had a white handbag and white and maroon shoes embellished with ornaments. The makeup was as usual. She jumped and embraced me with kisses. I carried her in my arms and kissed her, then majestically, I moved to the bed and placed her on it like a loving mother puts her newborn to rest. She smiled and covered her face with the magazine she was reading when I came in.

With a smile shown all over my face and arms akimbo, I gazed at her. There was silence until she opened her mouth after uncovering her face.

"Jerry," she called, smiling.

"Hello," I replied, going on my knees beside the bed.

"I hope you have forgiven me." She removed her sunglasses and put them on my face. "You make a nice model," she said as I stood up and went to the mirror and adopted a nice posture. With my thumb and forefinger, I held the glasses at the midsection, removed them and put them into her handbag.

I locked the door and went to sit on the bed beside Elsie. I pulled her toes after I had removed her shoes. She screamed.

As the scream died away, there was a knock at the door. Some time ago, it would have sent me rushing. I refused to reply to the knock; after all, she was with me. The knocking became louder and louder.

"Who could this devil be?" she said.

I was sure it was not my friend or the guard. Her face changed when, for almost three minutes, the intruder kept knocking. Sluggishly, I stood up, moving towards the door. She beckoned me to wait, picked up her bag and shoes and went behind the door. As you know, with the riskiness of our affair, we had to take precautions.

I unbuttoned my shirt and put on a heavy, sleepy face pretending to be just out of bed. I opened the door halfway and drew back the new multicoloured curtain a little.

I asked Elsie to hold on and after putting my shirt on, I went out. After all, she did not belong to me. I locked the door and told her I had a very important place to go, so she should try again next time and I apologised. She did not believe me but she had no choice but to go out with me. Out of the gate, I got into a taxi. About twenty metres away, I asked the driver to stop with the excuse that I had forgotten to lock my door. I jogged home and gave a strong warning to the guard to be very careful of people he allowed in.

She was still behind the door when I opened it. With a twisted lie, I was able to convince her that there was nothing to worry about. Whether she believed it or not was her own business.

Elsie apologised for not being able to come and see me and I also apologised for last night. Her excuse was that her husband was seriously sick and with the nurse and doctor always around, she could not go out. Even business was put aside; life is more valuable than money.

"His people," she began, "they think I have been seeing somebody, but there is no evidence. They know that when he dies, most of the property will come to me. It is jealousy and envy that disturbs them."

"Elsie, my dear, I thank God that you are around. You do not know what I have been through. I had even made up my mind to call your house, or even go there."

Stretching myself vertically on the bed, I extended my hand to her. She came over and sat by me.

"As for now, it's all over," she said, as she drew invisible lines on my face. "The other night when I was here, I felt very embarrassed. Let this be the end of it. Never let me find you in that mood again," she said as if talking to her son. "Jerry, I could no longer wait to see you. With the excuse that I was going to see the family lawyer, who had not shown his face for the previous week, this was my first port of call before I went there."

"Elsie, something is biting my back." I removed my shirt for her to scratch my back for me.

"Today's excuse - I just don't know how they would take it," she said as she tickled me. "It does not taste good in my mouth. I am tired of staying in that house; let them go to hell."

"Did I hear you say that?" I asked and turned around. "Let them go to hell?"

"Yes, that's what I said. I am really fed up with all those old men." She got up, took a few sluggish steps to the old sideboard, and rested on it, facing me.

"I am always happy when I am here with you."

I noticed her face and voice change.

"No, no," I said, "don't spoil the fun. It was all because of you. I could no longer bear thinking of you.

I thought it would help, but unfortunately, you came to find me in the mess."

"I understand you, my dear."

"You have to," I said as I raised my legs onto the bedside cupboard. "In the night, I saw the note and the messy situation in which I lay. My friend even told me you cleaned some and bought the deodorant. I am very grateful."

She opened her mouth to say something, but I cut in quickly.

"Don't say anything," I said and got up. "Elsie, dear," I continued as I stretched my hands to reach her shoulders, "I know you would be ashamed of me with my friend around, even going on to ask yourself questions without answers like 'why should I indulge myself with this useless man?'"

"Forget about that. It never occurred to me; never came to my mind," she said, drawing an invisible line on my chest. "You are all I need to be happy. If not, why would I leave my lavishly furnished home and come here? What disturbs me is the limited time we have together."

"My dear, today you have to stay a little longer. It's on my mind to get a nice and decent place for myself, so, any objection? Your input is welcome."

"No," she replied, nodding.

"But my problem is…"

"I know," she said, smiling. "Funds would be no problem. To tell you the truth, I don't like this place. Your street is a busy one and anybody can see me entering not once but many times. Act fast."

"But can't you leave him now?" I asked, pretending as if I was not sure of what to say. "According to you, he does not function; he can't perform as a man. If you were in his shoes, he would have got a new wife or a score of girlfriends, so why waste your time on him? After all, you did not force him to marry you; he did."

"I see. I can now see that you are serious. This is what I have been waiting for and thinking about. If you had given me the backing and encouragement a long time ago, I would have known what to do. Now, any time you see me you want sex."

"You say I always want sex; don't you enjoy it? Who would get you and let the charming lady slip through his fingers?" I asked, teasingly.

"But what would the world think of me?" She closed her eyes. "I mean, the two of us! We have to get away from here with enough money to keep us for a long time."

"And what are you waiting for? You know all this, but you've done nothing about it and you'd rather sit with that almost dead creature," I said, turning away from her.

"This is something I have kept to myself and never told anybody. You know it was because of his money; he is old and it is a shapeless frame on which his body is built. Oh, God, forgive me. When he kisses me or has sex with me, I don't have feelings; I don't even think he loves me. He just wanted someone gorgeous as a wife. I shut my eyes to the world and accepted him but he has treated me so badly. Not a tiny drop of love do I have for him, but his present condition makes me feel pity for him. What happened to my fiancé made me marry him."

I stood motionless listening to her.

"His friend approached me to have an affair with me but I turned him away. They don't understand why I married someone like him. Some think it was because of his money, which is true. They lure me with money, even when I go on business trips alone, but I don't give myself to anybody who comes rushing because they say I am beautiful and all that. It can't satisfy me."

The look in her eyes, the clothes she wore, and everything about her made her look like a fairy.

"When have you planned to get your own company?"

She raised her head and stared at me.

"You think I am a fool, don't you?" she asked, hands akimbo.

"No, don't misunderstand me. I only wanted to know."

"You want me to tell you?" She moved over to the chair.

"If you like."

"Okay," she said, throwing her hands up and nodding her head. "I have shares in some companies and others are owned solely by me. These are not known to him. You know I have to be very careful else it could cause trouble and people would tag me as the unfaithful wife. Plans are in the pipeline to build my own house. Already, his people and some friends do not agree with me; they see me as a gold-digger. Every kobo I am investing belongs to him, and so it has to be step by step, but for how many years is he going to stay alive?"

There was no answer from me.

"Just a few more years," she answered herself. "Or what do you say? Don't be in a hurry. I do not want to be disgraced so that when I am passing, people would point fingers at me, and I would bow my head in shame."

"Do you mean you want him to pass away?" I asked, surprised at what she said. "Do you know how long he could stay alive? Maybe modern science and medicine can make him strong again."

"What do you want me to do then? Suggestions, if you have any."

"Why not do something about him? It's no joke and I mean when I am saying. You could jolt or jostle him with force, and it would have a great effect on him and could kill him. After all, you do not have any children with him. Wait for a few weeks and then move out of this town or even to another country."

"How are we going to live abroad?"

"Do not tell me you do not have an account abroad. You have been transacting business abroad for a long time, so don't tell me you don't have one. Okay, if you don't have one, we can work it out. Ladies like you can sign cheques for fat money abroad. You of all people will have connections, so don't tell me you don't have. Say you don't have and I will knock your teeth out," I said, teasingly, raising my fist towards her face.

She laughed.

"Don't laugh; this is no time to joke."

"You think it's easy to work with him? Even the money I get here, if it had not been for this accident, he would have detected it, but abroad, it's no joke."

"So, do you mean you would wait until he kicks the bucket? Then you'll wait forever."

"All of his household and most of his friends, as I have already told you, do not agree with me and are suspicious about my marrying him. The moment I leave…"

I cut in. "The moment you leave, what would happen?" I retorted.

"If I do not leave in an honourable way, they would find all means to retrieve everything I got from him;

even some of my friends can betray me. So, I have to tread softly so as not to cause any trouble."

The noise of a thunderstorm was heard in the room. She looked at her watch.

"I must go; it is going to rain." She hurried for her bag and put on her shoes, then went to the mirror to retouch her hair and makeup.

"Elsie, can't you stay with me till morning? It's going to rain."

There was no reply from her. Instead, she was busy with her retouching.

"Elsie, would you stop what you are doing and answer me?"

She did not even bother to reply.

"Since you are prepared to stay with him, I think it would be better for you to stay at home. I don't want to see you anymore."

I opened the door to see her out. Instead of answering or walking, which I could not stand, she walked over to the desk and picked up a magazine.

"Elsie, would you answer me or do as I say?"

She jumped to her feet.

"Jerry, I think you know who you are speaking to. You'd better mind your words and how you talk to me. Is it because of this poky room? How can three of us sleep in this small room? If I am in love with you, it doesn't mean I would lower myself to sleep with two people in this small thing."

I controlled myself not to say anything.

"Are you not interested in me?" I asked as I walked over to her.

"It is me who should ask that question, not you. A few seconds ago, you opened the door, asking me to walk out. I would have, but I feel pity for you."

"What do you mean you should be asking that kind of question? I am asking you to stay, but you are refusing so that you can go to your so-called husband."

She drew the curtain aside.

"Have you seen the weather? It is raining heavily."

"Forget about the rain. I want to have a more serious affair than this. Or are we going to live like cat and mouse forever? You better change your gear into a more serious one."

"I know," she said, waving her left hand.

"Don't just say you know. If we don't plan well, the moment you notice the money isn't coming like before, you'll walk out on me for a better person. You'll need new dresses, cosmetics, and things to make you more beautiful. To live without enough money would not be easy for you. Your taste, I am jobless and would have to depend on you."

She turned her back, sobbing.

"Why should I do that to you? What do you take me for? I understand and know it would be difficult for us, but not so difficult that I would think of deserting you."

I moved over to her.

"Jerry, I love you and promised that nothing like that would happen."

She caressed me and kissed me passionately.

"Elsie, it's okay, everything will be alright."

"My dear, I am serious about what I am saying. I think it would be better to stay with him while he lasts. But I have to see you always. Yes, I have to see you."

She drew herself up.

"I have a plan. The driver in the house is leaving. It would create a vacant post which you have to occupy."

"That's right; it would work. This would give me the opportunity to see you always, then we can be ourselves when I am outside. But we have to be careful not to make people suspicious."

Chapter Twelve

She stood in front of me looking worried and like a dejected fellow. She moved over to the sideboard and poured herself some brandy. She drank it all at once, her face twisted and eyes closed, then swallowed and shook her head. She brought out a packet of cigarettes from her handbag which was hanging on her right shoulder. She removed a cigarette and stretched her hand for me to take it. I went to bring a matchbox from the drawer. On my return, I saw her lighting hers with a glittering lighter. I put mine between my lips and she lit it for me. After putting it back into her bag, Elsie brought out a packet of chewing gum and offered me some. She removed the cigarette from her mouth and exhaled.

"Jerry, I hate to go but I have to leave."

"What!" I cut in.

"But it's getting late."

"You can't leave me like this. We haven't even finished talking about the work and when next we are going to see each other."

Holding her two hands, I pulled her towards me and kissed her, but pushed her away all of a sudden to look at her face, whether she liked it or not. I did it because whilst I pulled her towards me, I noticed her drawing herself back. She looked at me; the tension in her eyes was great.

"Oh my," she said, putting her head on my left shoulder.

She unfastened the bottom of my shirt and began to caress my hairy chest and went on to fondle the nipples of my manly breast. So that she did not crumple my shirt, I talked her into removing it, which she did. Leaving her blue pants and white brassiere on, the locket on her tiny chain rested between her standing breasts with pointed nipples. After finishing with my buttons, she undid my zip too. Then my trousers went down to my knees, then to my feet. I released the hook and eye behind her brassiere and removed it.

I turned to move to the bed but changed direction and went to the door to make sure it was locked. I knew

I would be causing my friend a lot of inconvenience but what could I do? It would not be a surprise if he asked me to move out one day, but I hoped he would not.

Since I wanted a quick one, I removed my pants and sat at the edge of the bed with my 'boy' angry, swollen, and restless. Elsie removed her brassiere and pants and came to sit on me. I began fondling her nipples. She wriggled in excitement whilst she toyed with my thing.

After some time, she walked over to the sideboard and bent, with her hands wrapped around its edge. She asked me to come over, which I did quickly. I entered her and began to push while I fondled her nipples. She took part by wriggling her waist. When she noticed I was about to come, Elsie turned quickly and grabbed my cock into her mouth and sucked.

After she finished, I moved to the bed and lay on my back. Elsie came to me and started working on my prick, then, after a while, we changed places. I, in turn, sucked and licked her. Screaming, she asked me to get into her, which I did quickly.

"Ah, ah, push, push hard. Give me more, please. Please, don't come, hold on," she said, wriggling and groaning like someone in pain.

Twenty minutes later, we were lying on a piece of rug in front of the old sideboard. She was naked, while I wore a piece of cloth around my waist. Elsie ran her slim finger down my chest.

After finishing the cigarette, I removed my wrapper and threw it into the air, laughing. I climbed on top of her and, with my knees, threw her legs apart. It took her unawares as she had already closed her eyes and was dozing off.

"Oh no," she pleaded. "That's enough, please don't. I have to go. Let me go."

I smiled with excitement. I put on more pressure and pushed, pressing her hands down. She groaned and sobbed with tears running down her cheeks like a kid. I licked the tears with my tongue.

"I asked for it," she said, sobbing. "If I had not given in to your plea, but it's too much."

She made a lot of effort to dislodge my penis.

"No, no, Jerry, you can't do this to me."

With my tongue, I licked her nipples and her ears, and she finally gave up. I gave her a good fuck, which she later admitted was nice.

Quickly, she got up to dress like a student late for school. I lay on the bed naked with my head on the two pillows, a cigarette in my left hand and a glass of brandy on the cupboard.

"I am going to make arrangements for you to work in the house as a driver," she said, whilst retouching her hair with a tiny blue comb. "You have to do it or I will stop seeing you," she said, looking in the mirror, but quickly turned like an actor rehearsing her part. "Never, and I repeat, never phone or come near my house till I call here. Is that clear?" she said, with her finger pointing into her right ear.

In fact, I became uncomfortable when I thought of stealing and eating someone's wife and then going to live in his house and eat his food. Oh God, forgive me. It really disturbed me, but I had no choice. All those little girls who befriended me, I paid them, but Elsie paid me for making her happy. I have her body and everything free of charge.

"Tomorrow, I will talk to the people who sew the uniforms for our staff. In the afternoon or evening, you can go to them, and they will take your measurements. Give me my bag," she said, pointing at it.

"You would make a good goalie for the national team," I said after she caught the bag I threw to her from where I lay.

She scribbled something on the back of a business card, came over and handed it to me.

"They will tell you when everything is ready. You are to start the work as soon as everything is ready. I am sure by the end of the month it will be ready. Get ready."

She put a finger into her mouth and stared at the window.

"Ah, I forgot. Since he is sick, there will not be much work for you, so you'll help in carrying him."

This did not go down well with me.

"Any objections?" she asked when she noticed my face change.

"Oh, why do you ask? It's alright, I handled my grandmother alone when she suffered a stroke, and I did it well, so I see no reason why I can't do that for you."

"It's not going to be a regular routine, but when you are around," she said as she opened her handbag. She brought out a bunch of notes and, with a smile all over her face, handed them over to me.

I took the bunch in my right hand and pulled her with my left and she fell on me, protesting.

"No, no, you'll spoil my hair and makeup." But she allowed me a kiss. "Now, I have to leave. The rain has stopped," she said, getting up. "Jerry, you've made me very happy tonight and I am leaving you with mixed feelings. If I had my own way, I would stay with you."

I noticed that my 'Tom' was responding to my feelings, so I wrapped a piece of cloth around my waist.

"This will take care of you till you come to start work at the house. When I call the tailor, I will leave a message for you if the need arises. Do not shower your money on your little chickens," she warned.

"Since you want me to do the job and this will bring us together, I'll do it. But I hate being pushed around and people interfering with my work. If the workload is too much and it becomes unbearable, I will call it quits. I promise that I will be careful and do everything I am asked to do diligently."

"Your room will be in the boys' quarters, facing the Kuramo Beach. It is made up of two bedrooms, a kitchen, bathroom and toilet. It is secluded from the main building. You'll have your privacy when you close."

With kisses on both cheeks, she left me. 'This must be some sort of lady,' I said to myself as I stood staring as she closed the door.

With some money in hand, I had a bath and put on black trousers, a cream shirt and jacket, and black shoes. I removed some of the notes Elsie had left for me, bade my friend farewell, and sneaked out.

Chapter Thirteen

Outside the gate, I breathed the air of freedom once more; it had just gone past nine. My head was bowed, looking at my shoes when I heard the horn of a car. It was a taxi. I signalled and it stopped right in front of me.

"Kalakuta," I told the driver.

"One-fifty," he called.

"One naira."

"Okay," he replied.

He was fifty kobos short and since I was alone, he might refuse to go there. Moreover, since it had rained, the road would be bad. At the stadium, he picked up a female passenger, fair and cute with a spotless, robust face. She changed the odourless atmosphere of the taxi with the perfume she had on.

At the bus stop popularly called Barrack because of the Police Barracks there, about a hundred metres to Ojuelegba roundabout, a young man with thick lips, dark in complexion, and clad in a grey safari suit got into the car.

At the roundabout, there was a slight holdup caused by a herd of cattle being driven home after being lucky to escape the butcher's eye. As I stepped out of the taxi at the junction of the road leading to Kalakuta, I was welcomed by the wind which had cooled after the rain. Since it had rained, I thought the streets would not be crowded with body-sellers and their buyers. Some of the streets in front of the houses are not tarred. In the rainy season, they become so bad with big potholes that no drivers like to go on them. There were men of all ages who had come to taste the forbidden pleasure of the sinful area. One could buy drinks of all types, from the local to the foreign ones, even those which were banned. Drugs, both soft and hard, drink, food – all these things could be bought into the wee small hours of the morning.

I noticed that some men strolled from one end of the street to the other to pick from the sea of call girls lining the street. Whether your taste or likening was for slim, fat, short, tall, those with heavy backs, big bosoms or small and pointed breasts, they were all at your mercy. The moment you stood or stopped near one, a healthy smile would welcome you. She would mention her fee, then, if it was too high for you, you could beat it down, but only to what pleased her. Sometimes, when there were not many callers, they would even go to the extent of calling to you or pulling your clothes.

Some of the girls and women were clad in short jeans, tight ones to show their curvy figures, transparent dresses, blouses, round necks and t-shirts. Some of the houses were well-built, others were slums where one had to bend before entering.

Here, you don't have to sit at your door or stand against your window to display your wares, but you have to come to the street. You can see pros with a touch of class, most of them with bleached skin, and others remaining just as they came into the world.

If your service is good and you are good in bed, I bet you'd have a lot of callers who are tagged as customers who would be coming and going out of you and your room. Even if you are with someone, the customer would wait till you come out. Most of these customers pay double the price and some three times as much. When a customer asks for the dress, pants, and brassiere off, he has to pay extra, and extra for caressing.

Sometimes you'd hear the girls calling each other names. Why? Because someone had snatched another's customers. Moreover, if he paid well, then each one would be at the other's throat. If you were drunk, you would not be allowed in because you would take too long to come. If the two of them did not come to an agreement, you'd hear them hurling abuse at one another, at which point, the hostess's voice would be high.

Some men have oversized rods; these people always have trouble with the call girls. When you have trouble and you can pay extra, just put on your clothes and walk out; never try to fight or beat up any of them. Their boyfriends and pimps can deal with you ruthlessly if you try that. They have no love for you; the moment they have your cash in hand, which pleases them, you get your satisfaction.

It is a marketplace for human beings. One can choose.

I walked to the corner of the street and positioned myself by a yellow, two-storey building. With my arms akimbo, I watched a man about twenty-five donning a cream sports suit with two breast pockets. He was fair in complexion, average height, and about forty metres from where I stood. With a cigarette in his fingers, he moved slowly, looking at the girls line up like a team for a football match on a pitch. These kinds of players are not for the field, but for the bed.

Just at the entrance of the building where I stood, he stopped, like an officer inspecting a guard, and wanted to chat with one of the men.

The men stopped in front of a slim, fair lady in her early twenties, clad in white dungarees and a blue t-shirt with the inscription 'I'll satisfy you'. The three other girls in line with her gossiping, dispersed.

"Hi," the man said.

"Hello," the girl replied, smiling.

"How much?" the man asked, moving closer.

"Five."

"Okay, baby," the man said and threw his cigarette into the gutter.

The girl took the lead and he followed like a dog and its mistress. They disappeared into the entrance of the building.

I crossed the street over to a bar and had a bottle of my favourite beer, then left for home. It was one am when I reached home.

The following morning, I was still in bed when I heard someone knocking. My friend had left for work. The fellow knocked for the fourth time, louder than the others. It occurred to me that he was getting impatient and might leave. It might turn out to be very important. Quickly, I jumped out of bed and opened the door halfway.

"You no dey sleep early."

"Sorry, I am sorry," I apologised.

"Peter, Fred, dey look for you."

"Okay, tell them sey I dey come."

He turned to go.

"Wait, wait."

I entered and brought him a ten naira note.

"Allah, go bless you, thank you," he said, bowing. Since I was an illegal tenant, it was wise of me to tip him anytime funds were available to me. He had instructions from me that anytime I got a visitor, he should ask for a name. Earlier on, he refused to do it till I started greasing his palm.

Ten minutes after ten, I was in my faded baggy jeans, red t-shirt topped with a faded denim jacket with patched pockets and white gym shoes.

"Alright," they both said as I emerged from the house.

They made flattering remarks about my clothing.

"Peter, it's been a long time, where have you been?" I said as I shook hands with him.

"Jerry, don't you know?"

"Tell me once more. Is it that bitch of yours?"

"My work. I am even thinking of calling it quits."

"Don't try it; there is no work," Fred advised him.

"Where do you think we can have some fun?" Peter wanted to know.

"Fred, the old usual place."

"Ijora, or do you have somewhere in mind?"

"Okay, let's move on," Peter fuelled my suggestion.

As we were crossing the road to the other side, Fred hailed a taxi. I took the front seat by the driver, whilst the other two occupied the back. We joked and conversed amongst ourselves and it even got to a point where the driver joined in.

Since there was a thoroughfare leading to the hotel, we alighted on the dual carriageway then trekked to the place. At the entrance of the hotel, Fred and Peter decided to see some friends whilst I went straight to the spot.

Entering the hall which houses the bar in the hotel, I stumbled, but a gentleman sitting at a table next to the door came to my aid. He turned out to be a friend who I had not seen for some years since I came to Lagos. At the table with him was another gentleman and a lady who frequented the spot. We exchanged greetings and pleasantries. The music was so loud that we had to shout. The place was not crowded as usual; had it become boring? Maybe it was too early. By noon, it would be as lively as always.

The dancefloor was not all that big; it would accommodate about twenty couples dancing because of so many chairs and tables. All four walls were decorated with paintings of girls and women in bikinis, with bare breasts, big ones and round with hard nipples. Some drawings showed boys and girls dancing to a tune. One could see the musical notes painted on the wall. There was a painting of the late Reggae star, Bob Marley, and I think the painter did a marvellous job on it.

A drawing of a lady with good vital statistics, with broad buttocks and drooping large breasts and the inscription 'I want a man to dig it to me,' also brought some colour to the place.

Drawings also decorated the ceiling.

Behind the counter was another hall with stuffed sofas. A corridor led to tiny rooms with numbers on the doors that housed the call girls.

After exchanging greetings, I went to the counter to order some beer. Since we were there in number, I ordered three different brands. Each of us drank different brands. While at the counter, one of the guys, with whom I had exchanged pleasantries earlier on, beckoned. As I was moving towards his table, Peter and Fred entered with a girl whom I later got to know as Melinda.

She surveyed the few people in the hall with a cruel smile. I directed them to the table just after the one in the corner where one of the big loudspeakers stood.

Hurriedly, I went to the guy, leaned over and he whispered in my ear. While listening to him, my gaze dropped onto a dark-skinned lady who sat at a table by the door. I winked at her, she shrugged, picked up her drink, sipped it, and put it on the table, covering it with her slim hand.

My friend asked me to buy a bottle of beer for him. With excitement burning in me, I collected the six bottles of assorted beers and took them to our table. The girl, after a lot of persuasion, agreed to take Coke. The waiter, leaning against a decorated pillar in the centre of the hall, moved sluggishly towards our table.

"Who employed this man as a waiter?" Melinda asked, looking at my face and tapping her manicured fingers on the table. Her brows pulled together in a frown as she searched the waiter's face. She had wanted to say something, but I saw Fred step on her foot for her to keep her mouth shut. Instead of the rude remarks she would have made, she groaned in pain, and I looked at him with a cold face.

"Please buy me two bottles of Coke and a bottle of beer." Pointing to where those guys sat, I said, "Ask the one in the grey shirt what brand he would like." I brought out one of the crisp new five-naira notes and handed it to him.

There was a little silence. Fred coughed, his eyes searching from Peter to me. I looked at him, then my eyes moved to the rest of the table. Melinda, who had been leaning on the chair, lit up her face with a smile, closed her eyes, opened them again, and reached into her handbag which was hanging on the back of the chair. She pulled out a packet of Rothmans king-size cigarettes and offered one to everyone in turn.

"Thank you," I said as she extended her kind gesture to me. "It is not my brand."

Fred sneezed and cleared his throat.

"How are things, Melinda?" he asked, leaning forward to draw the glass ashtray towards him.

"My work - I would say the pay is just enough to keep me going happily, feed myself and pay the rent for my flat." She tapped the ash from the end of her cigarette onto the floor. "My boyfriend takes care of my clothing and entertainment."

The two bottles of Coke were placed on the table just in front of her. After he had removed the top of one and was stretching his hand to reach the other bottle, she asked him to only open one.

While the three of us were consuming booze, a girl I had been making passes at, but who had left me disappointed, entered the hall. I noticed her scrutinising the faces of all in the hall from one end of the spot to the other. By the faces some of the men made, I knew they were saying to themselves 'it's me you are looking for'.

Finally, when her eyes fell on me, I quickly turned my head, pretending that I had not seen her. She walked towards our table and, since there was no chair, she pulled one from a set of chairs by the wall.

The noise of the big loudspeaker behind us made the song blaring from it sound loud and harsh. Being a popular tune, almost all of the occupied tables became deserted. The dancefloor, although small, meant the merry-makers managed to dance, clapping while others made cat- and dog-like noises.

Chairs that had been empty were now occupied. The place was so hot that the two ceiling fans could not cope with providing a cool atmosphere for the crowd. Almost all the dancers were soaked in sweat, especially the bigger ones, and some had their shirts sticking to their flesh. The girls with light and tight dresses on, and sweating profusely, displayed their pants to the crowd as they were traced on their dresses.

A dark-skinned woman who looked rotund, with a bottle of beer in her hand and in the middle of the crowd, raised her head in intervals to breathe some fresh air from above. A hairy guy danced with a slim chick who wore a white brassiere with loose straps. Whilst busy dancing, the strap on the left shoulder slipped down. She tried to pull it back up but there was no space to raise her hand. The guy struggled to put it in the correct place when she turned her back to him. He felt satisfied and, likewise, the girl. With a red handkerchief with blue banding, he wiped the sweat from the girl's face and neck and then dealt with his own sweat. By this time, most of the dancers were returning to their seats.

As the song died slowly, another started cutting in instantly. The next was popular too, but not as much as the previous one. Some shouted and others screamed at the top of their voices "Encore!" Some males asked their partners to retire but they refused, while some males also paid no attention to their partners who wanted some rest. One girl, who was sweating profusely, after pleading with her man to retire with her, left alone.

A brown-skinned girl, who might have been around twenty, spoiled the merriment in the hall. We had met her when we arrive earlier on. Sitting at a table by the counter with another girl and three boys, and with a dozen bottles in front of them, some empty, she started rowdy behaviour by pushing and kicking others around her. Some did not take it lightly, whilst others ignored her as she was tipsy. But her partner, who could not bear it, held her at the waist, with her hand clinging loosely to his shoulders. He led her to their table.

At the table, she buried her face in her folded arms which she had placed on the table. Some of the bottles fell, spilling the booze. All of a sudden, she grabbed a bottle with some beer in it, put her finger into it, and shook it. When she took her finger out, the contents of the bottle were forced out, spilling upwards with most of it settling on a guy with a cream beret and white shirt with cream trousers.

He stood up as the booze decorated him and charged to their table.

"What's this all about?" he asked in an annoyed voice.

The girl beside the tipsy chick stood up to plead with him and stuck out her tongue, teasing the guy. Before a word from anybody, he slapped her. He was rewarded with a blow in the belly from the girl's partner. The guy, whose clothes were drenched in booze, came around and a free-for-all fight ensued.

Those who felt that what the girl did was wrong stepped in for slapping the girl because of what she did. Those who did not agree because she had only done it because she was tipsy, came to fight on her side. Bottles and chairs flew in all directions.

An elderly man, who had just entered, noticed blood oozing from the back of his head onto the faded red jacket he wore over black trousers. Since he was already soaked in sweat, he had not felt it till someone drew his attention to it. We were on our way out when the man drew the waiter's attention. I heard someone shouting, "Get the police to stop the fighting!"

I remembered that later in the afternoon, I had to go to the tailor. As directed by my lover-to-be madam, I called at the tailor's place. After the measurements,

I got a promise that the uniforms would be ready the following weekend.

Chapter Fourteen

During that week, nothing serious or important happened, just going up and down to clubs and picture houses with different female friends. The weekend finally arrived, and I went to collect my uniforms. In fact, I did not collect everything since the two white jackets with one pair of blue trousers were not ready. Straight from the tailor's place, I went to my new employer's house.

It was rare to find a man giving another man a lift, especially because it was in the evening. I was surprised when two young men in a blue Volkswagen stopped about twenty metres away. The driver had to struggle to stop because he was driving at high speed as if he was in a grand prix. When the car screeched to a stop, I began to run towards them but as I got to within a few metres of the back bumper of the Beetle, they drove off laughing. The man beside the driver put his head out, and stuck out his tongue, teasing me and waving.

I couldn't believe that a human being could behave like that to his fellow man. Hands akimbo, I shook my head and watched till they disappeared onto a branch of the road. It was now getting late. No one who values his life would stand in that street waiting for a taxi.

Fourteen minutes later, a Datsun Bluebird cab stopped for me. I showed him the address and he beckoned for me to enter. We agreed upon a fare that favoured him. He looked like a wrestler. We had a tough time locating the number of the house. It was my fault since it was dark; it would have been better and more sensible of me to get out and ask. The masculine features of the driver made me think he would drive away, but he proved me wrong. He did not charge extra. Some drivers even go to the extent of hurling abuse and yelling at their passengers to get out of their car.

When we finally found the house, nothing in the area resembled the quality of the building. It was a masterpiece. The magnificent work, I later got to know, was the last architectural work of a well-known architect who had passed away a decade and a half before.

At exactly seven-thirty, I was behind the massive black iron gate, making enquiries from the security men through a small round hole. I was asked to wait, and, less than five minutes later, I was allowed in. There were two security men in long-sleeved jackets and trousers made from a green material. The man I spoke to behind the gate was in his early forties, fair in complexion, tall and slim. The other man, K-legged with a protruding belly. I nearly laughed when I set eyes on him. In his late thirties, his name was Joseph, and the other man, David. These two men were on permanent nights whilst the other two were on days.

The compound was lit so every part of the front of the building was visible. Windows, doors and the walls of the main building were painted white. It was a mini-castle as I used to describe it. It had a little compound in front, occupied with green, green grass, well-trimmed and with assorted flowers lining the walls.

As I went up to the porch, I saw a slim, middle-aged man in some tattered clothes with a shovel in his right hand and a plastic container in the other. He looked at me and I nodded to greet him.

As I stepped into the black and white terraced porch, the door to the main building opened. Thinking it was her, I began to smile, but when it turned out to be someone else, I put on a serious face.

There were flowers of different types and shapes in black and white pots lining the walls and some hanging from the ceiling.

She had been informed of my coming to the house. It was not a difficult task to identify me. Yes, she was expecting me. Clad in an all-grey outfit, she was lying on a sofa. With a magazine in her hands, opened to cover her face, the moment I saw her I knew she was not reading, but pretending.

The woman announced my presence in the sitting room. Elsie placed the magazine on her bosom and looked at me. I greeted her. Whilst she got up, she responded and asked me to follow her to the porch. Hurriedly, I opened the door for her and after I had walked out into the porch, I gently closed it.

She settled into a lazy chair in the corner between two pots containing white roses. A faint sound came from the room. We both raised our heads and I saw a woman move quickly away from the window.

As I talked to Elsie, I noticed the two security men standing near the tiny room beside the gate looking curiously at us. All along, I carried my blue travelling bag on my right shoulder. I placed it on the floor by the table and was almost upright when the gardener came up to water.

Elsie got up and I followed her. I closed the door behind me whilst she went to close the one leading into the corridor.

"In this house, everyone is suspicious of everybody," she said as she moved toward me. "This is the only place we can be ourselves, but we have to be very careful. I think you noticed what happened a while ago."

The expression on her face changed. I felt uneasy and wished I had not come. But I had no other choice than this. Instead of giving me the welcome a lover deserved, look at what she was saying. I turned to face the corridor after she drew up the coffee table and put her legs on it.

"What is wrong, Jerry?" she asked, lowering her voice.

I tried to form a smile, but it did not work.

"I do not know," I suddenly voiced. "It is nothing. Forgive me and forget about it," I pleaded.

Once more, I put my bag down from where it hung.

"I feel fine; nothing is wrong," I said, moving closer to her.

"No, no, not here."

As I was moving back, the door to the corridor opened. The woman entered.

"Can't you knock?" Elsie queried.

"I am sorry, madam. Supper is ready."

"I don't even feel like eating…"

She paused while the woman still stood, waiting for further instructions from her.

"Have you eaten?" she threw the question at me.

"No, madam."

"Please make some food for him."

She turned to leave.

"For my food, leave it on the table. I would like a little bit of it and put my orange juice in the fridge."

Elsie did not say another word until the woman had shut the door after she had gone out.

"I know everything in the house is fine. He has good taste; hence he buys beautiful things that he can afford. He is loaded with bread."

She got to her feet.

"Now, tell me, don't you want to work here?"

I did not answer.

"First, let me give you a quick kiss," I said.

"Not here," she said, smiling. "You must be joking. You must be very careful of what you do and say. The nurse wanted the job because she was a relation and, likewise, the doctor. A close friend brought in someone, but I rejected him. Anybody at all can come in, just walk in and catch us unaware. At this very moment, someone is watching us, I am very sure. All the workers here are nosy parkers in my affairs."

Since the last time she was at my place, I'd had a lot of fun, but I told her it had been sleepless nights for me, thinking of her. If at all, I had sleepless nights because of her bed-ridden husband. She also made me understand that it had been the same on her part and that she had taken to drinking, but since I was now in her house, everything would be back to normal.

She asked me to go to the kitchen for my food and asked the cook to show me my room. As I was about to open the door, she called me.

"Jerry, hold on first. We have to see my husband but first, let me go and see if he is awake or sleeping."

After she had left, I moved to the door leading to the porch. With my head bowed, I leaned on the door. I did not notice her entering or moving towards me. She must have been staring at me for quite some time. I felt the presence of someone breathing. When I looked up, Elsie was standing in front of me.

"I am sorry for all this," she pleaded. "He is awake, so let's go and see him. Be a man, control your emotions. It is very pathetic. Please, please, I am sorry for all this. I would want you to eat before you go to him. I don't want to spoil your appetite for good food, but it is better for you. After you have finished with him, you can go for your food, then go to your room to eat, shower and have some rest. That would be better than to go to the boys' quarters and back again, or what do you say?"

"Which one do you prefer?"

"Okay, let's go in first."

She took the lead and I followed closely. I felt like holding her waist, turning her around and giving her a quick one. But it could be disastrous. The family had their bedroom upstairs, but because of his handicap, he now had his room downstairs, which was the guest room.

The corridor looked neat, decorated on the walls with different photographs of the family and flowers at every door in the corridor. There was also a carpet to match the colour of the walls.

After the second door, she paused and asked me to wait, then she opened the door and entered. I made up my mind to move to the other end of the corridor, but before I took a step, I heard the door open. She beckoned as I turned. After knocking, I entered. There he lay on the bed. If he had not turned his head towards me, I would have presumed he was dead.

She beckoned to me not to move to the bed. My presence was announced by Elsie. She mentioned my name and told him that I was from another country. I had been recommended by a friend whose name she did not mention. I had an international driving licence without blemishes and was a member of the Red Cross Society.

In less than ten minutes, it was all over. She directed me to the kitchen. I left the room and she joined me in the corridor some minutes later.

"You'll have to be very careful. I mean, extra careful. The kind of expression on your face; I did not like it. Our relationship must not come before your work. When it comes to work, I am the boss, but when we are alone, having fun, you'll be in command. Without it, we'll give ourselves away."

"I know I have to be careful, but you should also do the same. When I am forced to do things at the wrong time, restrain me."

"The other driver who left before you came was not serious. Always in a hurry to go to the boys' quarters. He had so many visitors that he could not concentrate on his work. The visitors were mainly of the opposite sex, he drank a lot and, worst of all, some of his girlfriends came here to quarrel. If you behave like him, then you'll have to call it quits."

"I know why I am here," I said. "I do not need anybody to teach me my work. 'Cautious' will be my watchword."

"Let it be. Don't let me down."

"I am hungry and tired, so please let me go for my food."

"Okay, you can go. I will also go and have something little to eat, but before you go, let me tell you who you will be working with. Follow me to the hall."

In the hall, she put on the television and went to sit on the arm of the sofa close to where I stood.

"Rebecca, the woman who opened the door for you. She takes care of the cooking. You should know how to behave and do things when she is around. She is a close relative of his late wife and came to the shop I worked in before I resigned. She never agrees with me, and I know she prays for the day when I would be thrown out of this house. She will be watching every step you take. You'll never know. Ajegunle is where she resides. Every evening at eight, she leaves for home."

"Any other person who works in the main building?" I asked anxiously.

"Yes, Kate, a nursing sister with a private hospital. A niece to my husband. She also dislikes me. Behaves as if she is the wife, the mistress of the house, which she is not. I overheard her telling someone that she is surely going to get some of his property. The room next to his is for Kate. She is on permanent day shift. Always in her room. Every Friday, she goes to see her children. Her husband divorced her on the grounds that she cannot bear male children who can continue his name. Kate did not want the husband to take a second wife. Every Sunday night, she does not miss her evening prayers at the chapel which they call 'Confession Night'." She sneezes. "You'll have your day off on Sunday, she'll have hers on Friday, whilst Rebecca takes Saturdays. When Kate is off, I have to take her place. I hate being by his bed all day. Since I have no love for him, I don't see the reason why I should be by him."

"Elsie, so I have to be careful about everyone, don't I? Even about myself."

"Yes, if you really love me."

"What about the gardener? Does he come indoors?"

"No, don't call him the gardener; we call him 'Papa'."

"Is he also in the team?"

"No, you saw him outside, old and tattered. He cares about nothing, only his work - the lawn and the flowers. There is a housekeeper who comes only in the mornings. The gardener has no wife and kids; the lawns and flowers are his family. He has never married before. Dr Parkings is his personal physician and an old friend. He knows all about our business here and abroad. He never gave his blessing to my husband marrying me. He was out of the country on our wedding day. On Tuesdays, Thursdays and Saturdays, he comes here. He even comes anytime he drives to this area. When he hears my husband is ill, he will leave whatever he is doing and rush down."

"Even when on top of…"

"Jerry, be very careful," she said, cutting off my sentence. "He says it was because my fiancé died, that was why I succumbed to his request to marry me. I don't love him; it was because of his wealth. Always try to stay out of his way and, when answering questions from him, be very careful."

I took out a cigarette.

"Put it away; you can't smoke here. Don't let any of them see you smoking."

"This place is like a prison. Even inmates are allowed to smoke and talk freely."

"When you go to Rome, you do what they do there, so you have to abide by what I tell you to do and not to do."

"The moment I came to this hall, I knew it was not my type of place. I would not fit in. But because of you and because I have no work or security, I will try my best."

"It has not been easy for me," she said. "They like to criticise everything I do in this house. That's how I have lived all the years in this house. Just try and be careful, for my sake. Do not get annoyed easily. A devil may say something, but you have to control yourself. As I have already told you, when it comes to work, you are under me, but in times of fun, I am under you. Never make an attempt to hold me or behave foolishly towards me or anybody. The smallest mistake we make will let the cat out of the bag. It is very difficult, but please, for my sake, do not try anything. You can now go for your food. Till tomorrow - I can't see you today."

Chapter Fifteen

All that she had said did not come as a surprise to me. I knew it had to be that way. The rules of her type were what I was expecting. She also had to be careful. For me, I would play it cool. If that would keep us together, then it was fair enough. I knew how to play the game. She took me for a kid, but to me, I was an expert in this field.

If she kept her side safe, I would play mine free from any suspicion; I could guarantee that. She would never regret bringing me to this house. Next time I was with her, I would give her my word.

I knew I couldn't do without her; she had the beauty, the type of body I wanted to touch and feel. The money I needed for my project. If you have been in a love scandal before, you'll know what I am talking about. Oh, God, help me. I asked for it, but it is too much - the dos and don'ts - I have to be very careful. Oh, Lord, see me through.

The whole house was quiet, so I made up my mind to meet her in the dining room before I went for my food. Someone might just walk in. I entered the dining hall and she was sitting behind her food with a glass of orange juice in her hand, staring at the ceiling. She did not notice or feel my presence till I got to the edge of the table where she sat. I took her by surprise, and she spilt the drink on her dress.

"What do you want here?" she asked as she cleaned the drink from her dress with a napkin. "I was thinking of you and me being together and then someone walks in without being noticed. Go back; this could give us away. Go back; someone is coming, I heard the door..."

She had not closed her mouth when the woman came in. I moved back and stood at ease with my hand behind me, taking orders from the mistress. With Rebecca in the room with her, I left the two and went for my food in the kitchen. It was warm because it was kept in the oven.

The boys' quarters consisted of two bedrooms and a kitchen, a bathroom and toilet combined, and a large hall. There was also a garage by the bedrooms. The boys' quarters had two entrances, one entering from the veranda, and the other from the side of the toilet. I loved the veranda because when I sat there, I could see the water and everything going on. One of the doors was locked so I did not waste time going for the keys; I just moved into the unlocked one. Moreover, it was in the corner of the corridor and had a window facing the water.

The walls of the room were dirty; cobwebs hung on the ceiling and in every corner. Old cigarettes littered the grey and black tiled floor. There was a double bed with a mattress as dirty as the room with stains that made big designs. Three or four old nude pictures of a white girl were pasted on the wall. I noticed that someone had tried to peel off two of them, but it wasn't possible to get it off without the paint coming off too. From the main building came a cream sofa with part of its upholstery torn, a white sideboard with one side of its glass broken, and an armchair.

I placed my small bag on the sideboard, removed my shirt, went out for a broom, and swept the whole place, dusting everything after I had cleared the cobwebs. After showering, I fought a battle with my food, which I won. With only my trousers on, I smoked two cigarettes and then went to bed.

The following day, I went to work early, dressed in my well-ironed uniform. Uniforms were not part of me, but I had to put them on. After cleaning the cars, I was about to go into the main building when one of the morning shift security men asked me to come to the gate. I hurried to the gate and was told a policeman wanted to see me. I put my eyes through the hole and there he was in his uniform. In fact, my heart jumped, and a cold shiver went down my spine.

"Good morning, young man," the policeman greeted me.

"Good morning," I replied with an unsteady tone.

"Are you Jerry?"

"Yes, anything wrong?"

"Cool down," he said, noticing my unsteady voice.

"Do you know Benroe?"

I was confused.

"Don't you know Benroe? Do not be scared."

I paused for a while. He then described him, how he was arrested and where he had been living – in an uncompleted building. When he mentioned that Benroe lived on a building site, I knew who it was.

"What did he do?" I asked. "Please open the gate and let me outside. He was my classmate," I told the security man.

He unlocked the two padlocks and I went out.

"You know something? I know of two Benroes. One, I do not know of his whereabouts and haven't seen him for about two years, and the other, who lives in an uncompleted building, was my classmate. It was only yesterday I started work here. I told him I would come to work here. I am sure you might have gone to my former place."

"Yes, I did go."

"You must be a very good man."

"I am just trying to help." This was the policeman speaking. "He was arrested last week, on Friday evening."

"Oh, poor boy," I said, scratching the back of my hand. "Could you please tell me why he was arrested and detained for so long?"

From where he stood, the policeman moved two steps back and stood in the flowers at the frontage.

"Please try not to stand on the flowers."

"A video recorder," he began, "was stolen two weeks ago. The guy who did it escaped when the policemen went to arrest him. Benroe, being innocent, did not run. He was arrested with two other boys who also claimed they knew nothing about it."

"So, they are being treated as scapegoats? Aren't they? But they were very foolish for not running."

"In Lagos, most of the occupants of uncompleted buildings are criminals. He asked me to let you know so that you can arrange for his bail. Do try and come into the station."

"Which one, Sir?"

"Bode Thomas."

"Thank you, Sir. I am very grateful."

We shook hands and he left. I called one of the security men to open the gate. As I was still waiting for the gate to be opened, I saw Rebecca coming out just two buildings from ours. I gave her a smile, but she did not return it. Till she reached the gate, I kept on smiling as if I had seen my love. At the gate, she forced a smile, but then withdrew it.

She just stood in front of me like a piece of log, then put her bag down to adjust her headgear. The bag she carried in her right hand had nothing much in it, but when she was going out in the evening, it had a lot of things stuffed in it.

"Are you her latest catch?" she asked.

"What do you mean by that?" I asked, holding the gate. I was surprised by the question. "I am here to work, to replace the driver who left." I bent to pick up the black leather bag.

"Don't bother, I will carry it," Rebecca said as she bent to carry her bag.

She said nothing again. Rebecca stretched her hand to open the gate, but I did it for her and allowed her to pass before I followed.

"By the way, who was that policeman and what or who does he want?" she asked after entering.

"A friend sent him."

"Mmm! It was only yesterday you came here, and you have started having visitors."

I stood looking at her whilst she walked away.

"Don't mind her," one of the security men said after Rebecca had gone far enough and would not hear.

When she got to the porch, she opened the small gate and put one foot on the terrazzo floor and one on the steps, turned and looked at me. Hurriedly, I went to her, and she asked me to wait in the kitchen. I followed her through the hall into the corridor where she disappeared into the master's bedroom.

Left alone in the corridor in front of the kitchen, I tried to search my mind about her behaviour and what had made her behave rudely towards me this morning. It seemed she thought there was something fishy about my being in that house. After some time, she came out and asked me to follow her to the kitchen. In the kitchen, she showed me where she would keep my food, and told me the things I was allowed to do in the kitchen and those not to do.

I should always be in my uniform; I should be around always not just when I am wanted so that people don't have to go everywhere searching for me. I must be neat from head to toe, fingernails well-trimmed, and abstain from cigarettes and alcohol when on duty.

"That guy who just left," she said, putting a bottle of milk into the fridge, "he was of no use. Only God knows what would have happened if he was still around."

She closed the fridge.

"Always drunk and smelling of cigarettes."

The way she spoke and looked at me was embarrassing. I got the message that she was trying to put across. I knew she would talk all that morning if I did not find an excuse to leave her.

"Excuse me, I have started to clean the engine of the Peugeot 505, so let me go and finish it."

"Anybody coming to stay with you?"

"No," I replied.

"No wife or girlfriend? The other driver changed them like a baby's nappies."

"I have a girl but she stays on her own with a brother and sister; I don't mix my work with pleasure."

"Young man, beware of them," she advised me whilst she bent down to open the fridge. She brought out an orange and started to peel it with a small knife. "They are very dangerous. I know you are handsome but don't let them pollute your mind. One day…"

"Don't worry, mum," I interrupted. "I will be very careful. Thank you for the advice."

I turned to leave the kitchen.

"You better be." I heard her say as I walked out of the door into the corridor.

I smiled and she did the same. Surprised, she would have told me more about the driver who had left and even madam. I was reluctant to leave but I had to because of my work. After finishing the work on the engine, I went out to the main building through the back door. Elsie was not in the dining hall or the sitting room. I saw her on the porch, reading a magazine, with her favourite drink, orange juice with ice cubes in it, on the table.

After greeting her, I stood by her side with my hands behind me.

"Have you finished with the cars?"

"Yes, ma'am."

She looked up at me with seriousness.

I smiled.

She did not reply.

"What are you smiling for?"

"Is there anything else I can do?" I asked childishly.

"No, just go away."

I turned to go.

"I will see you tonight. The doctor can come in at any time, so be very careful of what you do. I heard you talking to Rebecca; don't let her influence your thoughts."

I remembered what she told me earlier on.

As I opened the door, without turning her head, she asked me to stop.

"I forgot; the doctor might come for one of the cars today."

"Has he got no car of his own?" I asked, turning the handle of the door.

"He has a black Mercedes, a 1979 model, and a white BMW; I don't remember the year it was made."

She had finished drinking the orange juice. I took the tray containing the glass and the glass jar and left.

"You'll see a packet of cigarettes with a silver lighter; bring them with an ashtray."

After I had taken the tray to the kitchen, I went for the cigarettes and the rest. She lit one and crossed her legs.

"That night we were at the restaurant having a nice time, he was having a bad time," she started and put the cigarette into the ashtray. "He was involved in an accident; a ghastly one."

This time I did not stand with my hands behind me, but by my sides.

"He drove into a stationary long vehicle on a highway; it was travelling without a parking light or any sign to warn him. It was so late that you can imagine the speed that he would be driving at. It was too late when he noticed the lorry. He said he wanted to dodge it, but there was no way and that night he was a little bit tipsy. He tried to swerve but the passenger's side crashed into it."

"Who was the passenger?" I asked.

"His twenty-year-old girlfriend."

"I thought as much."

"He said the girlfriend died instantly with her tongue cut. They were there till the wee hours of the next day when the fire service came to remove them. The doctor said as soon as he saw the girl had died, he collapsed in his seat. He suffered some minor bruises and a fractured knee. I think what saved him was the seat belt. He had some amount of alcohol in his blood. The quantity showed that he was heavily drunk." She coughed. "The Mercedes is an odd number and the BMW was even but it is no more."

"Can't it be repaired?" I asked.

"As a matter of fact, I have not seen the car with my own eyes, so I can't say much about it. He arrives here in either a friend's car or a taxi, but most of the time in an ambulance."

"Has he no wife?" I asked, inquisitively.

"He has divorced one; even the present one is threatening to sue for divorce on the grounds that he neglects her. The first one, he had two girls from the marriage. They are both in Germany. The second wife is a banker. She has had two boys and a girl - one is at school in London, one in France, and the third is here with them."

"What was the reaction of the present wife when she got the sad news?"

"She went to see her attorney to sue for divorce for neglect. On that rainy night, he had left the house with the excuse of seeing a patient. Then he went to pick up his girlfriend and wine and dine her. So, on returning, karma caught up with him."

'Sad story,' I whispered to myself.

"Better hurry; go and make sure the cars are all ready. The 505. I don't want him to complain. He is always finding faults. There is nothing much for you to do, so ask Rebecca if she needs anything. I'll see you tonight."

"Yes, ma'am," I said.

She looked at me as if I were a fool.

"You know we are in an open place; I don't like the way you behave," she complained, a little annoyed.

Elsie could pretend. I did not blame her. Someone might have been listening or watching us.

"Do you pity him?" she asked me.

"No, but…"

"But what?" she cut in. She moved her chair back and lifted her body from the seat. One side of the morning gown covering her left thigh fell apart and my eyes took a sharp look as I knew she had done it intentionally. But why would she do something like that when she knew very well that people were watching? She was behaving like a pastor when they go to the pulpit to preach about what they don't do.

"He had many friends who came to eat and drink but after the accident, many of them don't visit this house anymore. They even drive past this gate. They have forgotten that we live here; such is life. You have to reason with me and understand my actions; if not, it would be too bad for us."

"You also have to understand me; everyone who comes across him for the first time would react in the same way. I feel sorry for him. Why should a human being suffer like that? He is really feeling the pinch, poor soul."

"I see. Get out of here!" she shouted.

Without saying a word or looking back, I hurried into the hall.

Chapter Sixteen

When I got to the boys' quarters, I kicked the door of the store with my canvas shoe and went in. I used my leg to close it and leaned my back against it. I collected some of the cleaning materials and took the toolbox. I changed my mind and put the toolbox down. I opened the door, slammed it, put the things on the wall of the veranda and went to my room to take a shot of dry gin. I felt fine.

Rebecca, in a blue dress with a white apron and white scarf, came out of the back door of the main building as I left the veranda pretending as if I had not seen her. I went to where the 505 was parked.

Happily, I started working on the car. I noticed her coming towards me, but when she saw Elsie on the porch, she changed her mind and went back. Singing and whistling, I carried on with my work. She came into my mind, and I stopped to look in her direction. She was not there. Elsie had been sitting there one minute, and the next minute she was nowhere to be seen.

All who worked in the house had some kind of sympathy for the boss. The breadwinner of the house; what would happen to everyone when he died? What would the wife do to them? What steps would she take? These were some of the questions the workers in the house had asked themselves.

Before the accident and what followed, he had been a lovely man most of the time. How can a wife live with a husband who is deaf and dumb, could not function as a man, had eyes but could not see?

I went to him after I had finished washing the car. He was alone. The room would have been silent as a graveyard if not for the low, soft music coming from the music machine by the window. As I was coming out of his room, I bumped into madam. She asked me to help her to put the boss into his wheelchair and push him to the dining hall to have some lunch. He always looked tired, sitting all day, but he had no choice but to remain like that. Only God or a miracle could save him. Who knew? He might live like that forever.

When he had started eating, I left for the garage to return the cleaning materials and turned the 505 so that it faced the gate. On my return, he had finished the food. I do not mean that he had finished all the food put before him. With great care, I pushed him slowly so as not to jolt him, through the corridor into the hall and onto the porch. I pushed the round table aside and placed the wheelchair with him facing the gate. As I pushed the wheelchair to a stop, he ran his slim, weak fingers into his hair.

Elsie was already on the porch when we got there, but she did not give me a hand or even turn her head. Instead, she went on sipping the brandy on the rocks in a crystal glass, and puffed her cigarette, releasing the smoke through her nostrils and mouth, up into the air.

On my way to the back of the main building through the hall, I changed my mind at the door entering the corridor. Since there was no one in the hall, I hid behind the curtain and began to watch them to see how she behaved when the two were together. I didn't think she had any sympathy for him, but I did, and she knew it.

Still behind the window blinds, I heard someone slam the door. Since I had not seen Kate, I waited in the hall to see whether it was her or Rebecca. It had to be one of them because the cleaner had already left. I moved to the door, pretending to be coming from the porch.

It was Rebecca; we came face to face once more. She stared at me, and I winked at her, then she turned her face and I smiled. Sluggishly, I walked to the swimming pool.

Not knowing Rebecca was in the kitchen, I opened the door and pushed it with such force that it banged on the refrigerator. Rebecca, who was eating off the cupboard by the sink, jumped in fright. I opened my mouth in surprise when I saw her.

"Sorry," I pleaded. "I did not intend to frighten you. Just don't know what came over me."

"Why are you opening doors like that, and with such a push?"

I forced a smile, but it did not work.

I looked at her with a friendly interest whilst she ate hurriedly. Rebecca was not paying attention to me, but I kept on talking, telling her about the work I had done in the morning and what I intended to do for the rest of the day.

She stretched out her hand and took a glass of cold water with ice cubes from the other side of the sink from where I stood. She nearly pushed her food down in a rush to get the water before I did.

I tried to tell her how I had cleaned the inner and outer parts of the car and checked the oil and water, not forgetting the brake fluid. The brake fluid had almost finished, the water was down, and the oil level was half of what it should be. I went on to tell her how I took the trouble to clean the engines of all the cars. The mud beneath the cars was so thick that each of them took a fair bit of my time.

She finished the whole plate of jollof rice with spaghetti, topped with red stew and roasted pork. No wonder her heart sank when I opened the door. Elsie cannot eat that amount of food and she would never give that to me, not to mention the boss.

She placed the tumbler on the plate then put them in the sink. Our eyes met and she asked if I wanted to eat. Rebecca got a positive reply from me.

From the oven, she brought out a blue plate with white rings on it, dished out some rice, a bit of spaghetti, shredded lettuce, sliced onion, and fresh, hard tomatoes topped with curried chicken in sauce. It was rather a mouth-watering meal.

"Whoa," I exclaimed as she handed over the food to me.

The aroma of the sauce was nice, and it made me grab it like someone who had not eaten for days. The problem with me was that I liked good food, but to taste good food, you have to put down a lot of money.

On my way out, she told me I could use the kitchen if I wanted to. I pulled a small, white stool with my leg from the side of the gas cooker. I settled on it and began to spoon the food into my mouth.

"Can you cook?" she asked, looking at me and, at the same time, putting a saucepan on the shelf. It missed and fell, making such a noise that I placed my fingers in my ears.

"Yes, I can cook. One of these days, I will come and do the cooking. You'll be surprised."

"When will that day come? I don't think it will ever come," she asked and answered herself, teasingly.

"Do not worry; very soon. First, let me settle, Auntie Rebecca. That day, everyone will be my guest in this house. A meal you've never tasted or seen before. You'll love it. Just for a change."

She stared at me without voicing a word, just nodding like a lizard. Rebecca told me she'd love to taste the food. What food it was would remain a secret until the day.

On her way out, she asked if I could bake, but I could not answer since I had more rice than my mouth could take at a time. I tried, but the rice came rushing down and I covered my mouth with my left palm.

Chapter Seventeen

He was alone on the porch when I got outside through the back door. As I opened the small door to the porch, I heard the sound of the padlock. It was one of the security men unlocking it. Two middle-aged men walked in after the gate had been opened. At the same time, Kate came to the porch from the hall. Since she was around, she asked me to take my leave.

Before opening my door, I lit a cigarette, removed my jacket and went inside. I hung it on the nail on the window frame, then removed my trousers and hung them over the jacket, but they fell. I picked them up and folded them neatly, putting them on the table. I sat at the edge of the bed with only my pants on and continued smoking.

Since it was sunny, I opened the louvres facing the water for some fresh air. If it had been a Saturday or Sunday, there would have been many speedboats passing on the water. From my room, I could see the nice buildings on the other side of the water.

On Saturdays, Sundays and holidays, the water becomes colourful with different decorations on the boats and the many mixed colours of the sails. Sometimes the colours clashed. It looked like a regatta or a carnival on the water. Some of them speed, to the extent that when you are in my room, you could hear the girls and kids screaming, whilst others drive leisurely.

As I sat on the edge of the bed smoking, I heard the engine of a boat approaching from a distance. Hurriedly, I put something on and ran to the swimming pool. It was a white couple who I presumed to be in their early thirties. The lady was behind the wheel with the man sitting at the prow of the boat, drinking from a can. He was clad in a blue and white striped cotton shirt with white slacks, a white sunshade topped with a blue cap. She wore a white cotton sleeveless shirt with blue bands at the edges, white fisherman's shorts with turnups and covering her eyes was a round, blue sunshade. Her hair was tied up in a red and blue scarf and she was laughing and joking. She had no lipstick on but had rosy cheeks.

When they got to where I stood, they waved after the man whispered something to the woman, and I waved back. Gracefully and peacefully, they drove past and disappeared under the bridge. I picked up small stones and threw them into the water and watched the circles they made and listened to the sound.

Sitting on the wall of the swimming pool, swinging my legs, I began to think about him. It made me feel uneasy. I had to think of myself before anybody else. This was my chance. If it slipped through my fingers, I was doomed. If she had not chosen me, someone else would have got it. Although I needed the money badly, it had to be found in the proper way.

'Oh God, help me and deliver me from this terrible plot,' I prayed. If I say I am leaving today, somebody would be happy whilst another would be sad. Here, I have three square meals a day and a roof over my head. I can drive or walk confidently into the compound, not dodging and sneaking in and out. I just don't know what to do. She is beautiful and tempting, and good in bed. I just can't let her go. Tonight, I will be on her, riding her; I will be the boss of the well-shaped Elsie.

'I am being stupid,' I said to myself. I should not allow myself to get carried away. No way. These daughters of Eve; they can pretend. Who knew what would be my fate after executing the plan? She might get rid of me - maybe she had planned that already.

With her money, status, and beauty, she could have brought someone else to work in here. I began to ponder over it for a long time. Men with property, flashy cars; she wants money but not love. We shall see.

I tried to figure out how, overnight, we became intimate friends at the restaurant. It seemed incredible but true that a lady of her type would fall for a waiter without a permanent residence. Maybe she knew something about me and wanted to find out more or use me? But I didn't think she had any sinister motives for employing me other than what I already knew. Far from that, tonight was going to be special.

Maybe she was one of those ladies who go in for the younger ones or those who cannot stay long without a man touching them - any man at all who comes their way.

"But why me? Would anybody tell me?" I shouted with clenched fists and burning anger. I hit my thighs.

Why did John have to go? No one knew; she was the only one who knew. After she had finished using him, she sent him away. I didn't believe what I was being told to believe. I knew many had left before John did. What did I know about her? Nothing. Maybe she had been telling me lies all along? That's a better reason why she does not want me to be friendly with anyone in the house. I had to get things straight.

I began to shake. She was beautiful, I couldn't deny that, but she was hiding something from me. Elsie wanted me to do a job for a certain amount, of which I wasn't sure. Always hidden behind those sunglasses, she might even be staring at me when I think she is looking somewhere else. I just didn't know what was in her mind. She knew best.

Elsie was on my mind for a long time. I couldn't come to a conclusion on what was going on. I tried to forget about her, but no way. I tried singing and got up to throw stones into the water again, but it did not help. Swinging my hands, I went to my room to sleep. It was not easy for me to doze off. I had to smoke one cigarette after another.

It was dark when I woke up, with the light in the boys' quarters out. No one had been there. After putting on the light, I sat on the floor, leaning on one of the pillars of the entrance with my back to the main building.

As soon as I settled down, I felt a finger touch my shoulder. On turning my head to see who it was, another finger went into my left cheek.

"I did not hear you come. You frightened me. Why do you behave like a ghost at times?" I said as I stood up.

She was leaning against the pillar from under the roof. With my arms folded, I sat on the wall guarding against any intruders.

Her hair was divided into two, one part to the left and the other to the right, tied with a white ribbon on the left and a shiny red ribbon on the right. She wore a light red, short-sleeved shirt with white shorts. She looked cute and smart in it and looked younger than her age. There was something I did not understand. Elsie and her husband always overpowered my feelings. For the husband, it was sympathy, and for her, it was love and affection. She held onto the pillar like a kid, moved towards me and sat in front of me.

I pulled her up and held her in my arms. The scent of Chanel No. 5 overpowered the scent of the river when she raised her hands to put them on my shoulders.

"Happy to see you," she said in a low voice.

She put a kiss on my forehead, both cheeks and a long one on my lips. She got a good response from me. She withdrew and leaned on the wall. I opened my mouth to say something but I paused.

She wiped the lipstick off my lips with a pink tissue she brought out from the patch pocket of her shorts.

"Let's go in; the mosquitos are disturbing me," she complained.

"Okay, let's go in," I said whilst I moved towards the door. "You are sure no one saw you coming here?"

She did not answer.

I had pushed the window blinds aside and opened the louvres for some fresh air and sunlight, but now I had to close everything for security reasons. The moonlight still lit the room together with the light from the bulb.

My wristwatch read eleven. I moved to the sideboard and poured myself a drink of brandy and water. I sat on the arm of the sofa sipping from my glass.

She had removed her clothes and lay on the bed with only her panties on. I was admiring a figure, even though the room was not clear. She reached for a cigarette, lit it, and placed it between her lips. She puffed the smoke through her nostrils and lips steadily in my direction. Whilst she lay there, I began to imagine her husband trying to mount her, which I knew he couldn't do. After she had finished smoking, I joined her. We did not talk to each other; we were like strangers.

She groaned from the time I entered her till she reached orgasm. After I had released into her, and lay on my back, staring at the ceiling, I heard her snoring. My eyes were wide open, pondering over my affair with her. I climbed over her and reached for a cigarette. One, two, and three cigarettes and the room was filled with smoke. I just had to smoke to relax and clear some of the thoughts from my mind.

Elsie started to chew in her sleep, then started talking, paused, and lay on her back with her hands covering her pubic area. I went over to the wall and put on the light, then came to sit beside her to listen to what she was chattering about, but I got nothing clear.

It was getting louder and it might have got to the sharp ears of a passer-by, so I stopped her.

She opened her eyes and stretched her body.

"Dear, it is not over yet," I told her as I patted her. "Relax your mind and sleep."

She was in the middle of a dream. Dreaming about the good times we would have some time to come, she told me. She smiled at me and I sat on the bed, smiling back.

"You had a nice dream."

"Yes, it will come true," she said, confidently. "A reality."

She rolled to my side and put her head on my lap.

"The expression on your face made me feel you were having a good dream," I said, whilst I made a sketch on her face with the middle finger of my right hand.

"What is happening now is like a farmer getting his land ready before the planting season. We have just begun."

"So, I was dreaming," she said as she got to her feet. She looked around and came closer to me. "Not here," she continued, "a different place."

Elsie knelt down by the bed and began sobbing. When I got up and went to where she knelt, like a spring, she jumped to her feet and began to hit me on the chest.

"Jerry, can't you do something? Are we going to live like this forever?"

"Take it easy."

As if she had forgotten something, or heard a noise, she rushed to the table by the door and checked the time.

"Ten minutes before two," she said, facing me. "It's early in the morning, still young."

"Do you want to leave?"

"No," she retorted. "If you want me to, let me know."

"Why? If you want and if it is good for both of us, stay."

"I don't want to go," she said as she smiled and moved gorgeously towards me. She put her hands around me and drew me closer, kissed me and began to stare at me with her eye wide open.

"What is it?"

"I want to have a word with you," she said, releasing me. "Would you do anything I want?"

"What is it that you have to ask before talking about it? Let's be serious."

She went and poured herself a drink, moved to where the packet of cigarettes was, drew out two, lit one for herself and brought the other to me. With mine between my lips, I lit it from hers between her lips.

With my back to her, I was counting how many cigarettes were left in the packet. She patted me in the hollow of my back. She moved slowly and came to stand before me. With her cigarette between her fingers and mine between my lips, she pushed me on my chest. The cigarette fell out of my mouth onto the bed sheet whilst I fell on my back.

"What's all this about?"

Smiling, she threw herself on me but I rolled to the other side and turned my face towards the pillow. With the almost finished cigarette between her lips, she tried to turn me with both hands. Elsie tried but it was fruitless. She gave up and pleaded with me to face her and listen to what she was going to say.

Reluctantly, I turned and lay flat on my back, staring at the ceiling. After drinking some of her drink, she put the cigarette butt into what was left of the brandy.

My cock, which had been silent for some time, I noticed, was in the mood of coming back to life once more. Both naked on our backs, staring at the ceiling, she broke the silence.

"Jerry, do you want us to be happy?"

"Yes, of course. Why not? When you are happy, I am also happy, and so it goes on."

"Sometimes, the way you behave does not go down well with me."

"Elsie, I want you to tell me about your dream."

"Why not? If I can remember everything vividly. But first, answer these few questions I would put before you in a second."

She sat on the bed.

"Why are you here? Because of me or my husband? Do you feel for me, or for him? Why do…" she paused when she realised she was putting too many questions to me at one time. "Okay, answer one first."

"Why all these questions? This is no time to ask these kinds of questions. If you feel like you are fed up with me, let me go. You can get the one who is well-behaved and more to your liking."

"Jerry, I am not saying I am fed up with you and that you should leave; far from that." She bent and came closer. "Just answer my questions."

"You brought me into this house, but I am working for both of you. You have the power to give me the boot anytime you so desire. As for your husband, the condition in which he is, anyone who would see him for the first time would do what I did. Sometimes, he tries to put on a face or, let me put it this way, he cheers up, but inside him, SADNESS is written. Don't you feel for him?"

"What about you, do you feel for me?"

"Elsie, be serious and let's forget all jokes. His condition is completely pathetic."

"Jerry, my dear, you have shocked me."

"Likewise, yourself," I retorted. "If I have, then you have more than I have."

"Let me put it to you; you are falling for him. His charm is overpowering. Do not let him cast a spell over you."

"Elsie, be sincere to yourself. Don't you have any feelings for him? Look at his condition."

"I am not pretending. It's the facts I am putting before you. That's the way he wants it. You don't have to force yourself upon someone. In flesh, I know he's dead, but he has a strong will to survive inside. His spirit is putting up a strong resistance to exist. He wants to punish me, but he can go too far. It must end; be cut short, but to do it, I need someone."

I said nothing, pretending that I was not interested, but I understood every word she said. She wanted me to say something; contribute to it. I tried to raise another topic but she overruled it.

"For how long is this going to go on?" she directed the questions to me after she became aware my eyes were staring somewhere else and I had not opened my mouth for some time to support or criticise her.

"Can't say and I don't want to guess. Don't worry, one of these days I will read his palm and tell you how long he wants to stay alive," I said jokingly.

"I have the feeling," she started, "that he'd like to hang on forever and make me suffer. To sue for a divorce, his people would tag…"

"Do not bring that up. Who knows, maybe by tomorrow in the morning, he will have breathed his last breath."

"I can no longer live in this fortress."

"Let's forget about this for now and talk of something else, like the dream you just had."

"The dream is part of it. It's what would happen later."

She got up and reached for her drink, forgetting that she had put a piece of cigarette in it. When she saw it, her face changed. With annoyance, she dropped the glass and the drink spilt on the floor.

"Poor soul; take it easy."

"It would be wonderful to be free from this bondage. Think about it; the fun and the good times we would have together. Do everything together of our own free will. Not live like cat and mouse. We can fly out if we like, get married and have children."

"Get married, you said?" I asked, and paused. Marrying someone like her would be a curse on my head. Her type doesn't make good wives.

"Are you thinking about the money that would be involved? Forget about that. Everything will have been worked out already. If everything goes well, money will be no problem."

"Of course, money is my problem. You know it yourself. If you have the money, no problem. Let me have some money. Let's talk about how we are going to make money rather than what you're talking about."

"For money, there is more than you want, but I will only let you have it if you can do something, you know that."

Chapter Eighteen

She got up and went to where the watch was.

"It's very easy; all it would take is just your brain and a little bit of strongheartedness. And I would give you more than you want."

"Say it, name it and I will be on my feet."

"Really? Are you sure you can do it? Do you have the heart to do it?"

She got up from the bed and went for her clothes. No one spoke. When she finished dressing, she came back. Caressing and fondling my nipples, she looked straight into my eyes the whole time.

"You say you can do anything for me? No matter the risks involved?"

I nodded.

"After you have finished it, we shall live happily. It's going to be a tough task, which you must not fail to do.

I know you to be a soft-hearted man, but for this task, you must become like the gladiator!"

I knew something fishy was in the air but I wanted her to speak to me. I knew the path on which I was treading was a dangerous one, but I wanted to see the end of it all.

"I have told you, anything, mention it and name the fee," I said, rubbing my forehead.

She rubbed her long, tiny fingers across my chest and down to my abdomen.

"Don't worry about the bread."

"How much?"

"About fifty thousand naira."

"Do you mean it?"

"You'll receive half now, and after you have done it, the rest will follow. If you fail, you will not live to enjoy what you would get before you do the jobs. No cheating and keep your mouth shut. If you like, I can give you the other part in dollars or pounds sterling."

"Are you sure of what you are saying or just blowing your own trumpet?"

"If you execute the job well, without any mistakes, and no traces left behind, I might even be compelled to give you more. Moreover, you can still have me if you so desire."

"Elsie, when and where? But are you sure?"

"You know my husband is wealthy, both here and abroad, with property in Africa and elsewhere. If you want to marry me, I can give you the dowry rather than you giving me. We can also go into joint business. If you want more money, I can lend it to you. Working together can bring us together as we are now, but with a difference."

"Are you sure you'll lay your hands on all his property in the future?"

"Why not? I am his legal wife, and I am entitled to most of his things. His money is not out of my reach. I have mine and, moreover, I have seen his will. The sad thing about it is that somebody wants the will altered and I won't accept it. I have a photocopy of the one he made before the accident. His daughter, the one who is at school abroad, is training to come and take charge, and the boy he has out of his marriage is getting something. We have to be fast."

"Hold on; I am coming. It seems there is an intruder," I said, lowering my voice.

Steadily and noiselessly, I put on trousers, opened the door and went out. There was no one there. I went as far as the gate. The security men were asleep. On my return, I stepped on some rotten fruit. It could have been dropped by one of those birds that carry fruit their beaks cannot support. The greedy ones.

"There was no one around; even the guards are asleep," I said when I got back.

I closed the door behind me softly and turned to lock it.

"As I was saying," Elsie said, "my husband's former wife went into labour. Both of them died. A baby boy. The daughter of our age is studying in London. After her education, she'll come down and be president of the empire."

"When is she returning?" I asked as I removed my trousers.

"I think this year or the next. Not sure about it. Let's act fast. There is no time to waste. You'll be rich, I will be rich. If you still want to stay on with me, no trouble. My dreams, all these have come true. Better days are ahead."

"How are you going to put all you have planned to work when he still has more years ahead of him? He has the heart of a horse."

I reached for a cigarette.

"It is very sad for him to lie there. I don't care how long he has. It must be cut short to relieve him of his suffering. No fun for him. One has to do everything for him. Don't you feel sorry for him? The earlier he dies, the better."

She turned and looked at me, expecting to hear a word from me.

"How and why are you going to force death on someone when he is not willing to give up? It would be murder!"

Her face changed and became cold when she heard that from me.

"He is fragile like the thread of a spider's web."

At this juncture, I became bored and concentrated on smoking. She continued.

"You can do it. Do it alone. One of these days, you can give him a ride to the seaside early in the morning for some cool sea breeze. When there is no traffic, you can either drive into a big pothole or brake suddenly.

I told you he is like a cobweb; he would not be able to stand it. The shock would kill him. You can even attempt something like an accident."

"What about me?" I cut in sharply. "Or do you want me dead too, eh?"

"No! Stop thinking about that. It's going to be done in a way that all anyone would say is that it was an accident."

"No, I can't. It can't happen without me being hurt. You must be joking. Stop these expensive jokes and be serious."

"Accidents do occur now and then."

She used her long, well-trimmed fingernails to scratch my chest towards my armpit.

"Man, we are talking in terms of thousands, and you are being soft. Are you a woman?"

"Elsie, do you really mean what you are saying? Get rid of him?"

"Don't you know he'll bless you if you help him travel to the beyond? He would be saved from suffering. He has to rest."

I just sat looking at her, then yawned. She was serious and wanted me to send her husband on his last trip to the beyond. It was no joke. She had meant every word that came out of her mouth; picked every word she used carefully, one after the other. Some women are wicked. Whenever you tell them they are wicked, they would say 'I am not like that' but when it comes to the day, you'll see how bad she could be. Very wicked.

After all that she had said, she sat undisturbed, smiling instead.

"Do you really mean what you've just said?"

"Yes, I mean every letter, every word, and every sentence. I have no regrets."

"Then you have made the biggest joke of the century. In my life, you are the one I have heard and seen making the most expensive joke."

"Jerry, don't be foolish. I never thought you were so useless. We are talking about money, and you are talking of sympathy. He is half-dead. You want the half-dead fellow instead of money. Do good and good shall follow you forever, wherever you go. You can do it; try it."

I became disturbed.

"This is the right time to do it, before she comes."

"And this is the right time to put it to you that you are being foolish and stupid."

She looked at me with her eyes glaring, courtesy of the moon.

"You want me to commit murder, don't you?" She did not reply, but slowly removed her hands from my body. "Why not do it yourself?" I asked, wiping my face with my left palm. "Since you are closer and have the heart of a devil and a lion, not a lioness. You are in a better position to do it. Then, you can keep all the money for yourself."

"Come on, kiss me," she said, bringing back her hands and starting to caress me again. I drew in a lot of smoke from the last of my cigarette and, when I got closer to her, almost touching her lip, I quickly drew my head back and blew out all the smoke in my mouth with force. She began to cough but she covered her mouth to stop herself.

If she coughed loudly, it might attract someone. In the first instance, she tried to say something, but it wasn't possible; then, she tried for the second time, but no way, and she gave up. Tears rolled down her cheeks whilst I sat there smiling. I wanted to laugh but it would be dangerous.

After a while, she returned to lying on her back five metres away from me. I also turned my back on her. She began to cough again and couldn't lie down with it, so she sat in the middle of the bed.

My intention was to make her shut her little mouth and kill the conversation. She lay back again after the coughing died down. Staring at the ceiling, rubbing her left palm against the other, there was absolute silence in the room.

"Jerry," she whispered and broke the silence.

I did not answer till she had said it three times.

"What is it? Can't you keep quiet? Even radios switch off. I want to sleep."

"What can one do with a man who cannot perform, I mean, can't screw? He has failed to honour his part of the marriage agreement. He can't fuck."

"Even a doctor has no right to kill someone who is struggling, suffering to die. You would be charged if investigations proved you killed him." I yawn once more, a long one, and I felt dryness in my throat. "Why not go to the court to file for a divorce? You would be paid some alimony."

"Look, don't bring that up; I have already talked to you about it. Divorce is out. I would not get what I want. We just have to play our cards right and we shall be the winners."

"So, you have still not forgotten about it?"

"Divorce; the reaction from the public won't go down well with me. You must be mad. The law my ass..."

"The law your ass," I cut in. "When it gets you there, you'll know that it is above everyone."

"With money, we can buy our way through. Don't care what happens, I want freedom. Freedom is what I need, not staying in this house like a servant with nothing happening. We are going to be rich and live together. On his part, we would give him peace and a long rest."

"What would be my fate if it is proved beyond doubt that it was a planned accident? When you are interrogated, all the strongheartedness would leave you at once. I know you'll turn your back on me."

"There is no way they would know we planned it unless you say it."

Without saying anything, I went and sat on the sofa. Elsie grinned at me and called me. All the heavy makeup she had on earlier had vanished. Reaching for the pillow under her head, she put it between her legs.

"Must you go and sit that far from me?" she questioned, as I moved reluctantly towards her.

"Look, baby, I don't care if you like it or not; forget about it. You can't use me for your selfish ends. The motives behind it would be investigated. I am convinced that when you are being interrogated and bombarded with questions, you'll let the cat out of the bag. So, baby, forget about it. People would gossip and rumours would spread like bush fires during the dry season. Already, eyes are on us. If we are found to be the perpetrators, we would be followed, and, if found guilty, we would end up at the gallows."

"Please lower your voice," she said when she noticed my voice rising and anger beginning to shadow me. "You know that if not for the owls and other night-crawlers, the world would be sleeping in silence. Calm down."

She removed the pillow and placed it on her face. I got up to where the drink stood, opened it, and poured as much as my mouth could hold. I put the bottle down and in one go, swallowed everything. I went for a cigarette, lit it, and smoked for some time. Back to the bed, I removed the pillow and passed it over to her; she took it with a flourish.

"Are you still aware of what you said and remember it all, or have you forgotten some of it? If I don't remember all, at least I have some stuck in my mind for the records."

"What do you mean by that? You are not so soft that you would forget about it! You are eligible to do it. I am serious and I mean every word I said, as I told you before."

"You want me to get rid of a father; what about if someone does the same to me? You'll be asked why, for a whole month, you didn't take him for a ride for some cool sea breeze till Jerry came." I got up to sketch our interrogation. "Everybody needs money, but why are you so eager to do it fast?"

"I am not what you think of me or take me for. I'm a woman who is ambitious, not cruel or heartless.

My freedom is what I want and to save him from his suffering. Put him to bed forever. I am hopeful to see that you do it without saying a word."

I picked up my towel, covered my body from below the abdomen and left for the bathroom to relieve myself.

"Will you do it or not?" she confronted me with the question as soon as I entered the room on my return from the bathroom. She was on the table by the door with her arms folded under her breasts.

I did not answer and passed on to the bed, throwing my towel somewhere near her. She just stood up and came to me with a broad smile on her face, then put her arms around my neck.

"Darling, I know what you think of me, but it's far from that. You are making a big mistake. Freedom and liberty are what I need; I want them at all costs. There is money, so let's do it now. Say something. Don't just stand there staring at me. Promise you'll do it. Nothing can stop us. Can't you see I am serious? Go on, open your mouth and say it. Convince me that you'll do it and let no one hear of it."

"Elsie, this is not the way to get freedom. How am I to convince you? Forget about it before it eats down into your brain like toothache. I don't think we can get away with it. There is this feeling that we won't succeed."

"Please don't say that. If I knew you would not cooperate, you would not have seen me naked, far less had sex with me."

"Do you know what you are talking about? Murder. Murder! M-U-R-D-E-R. His blood would stain us forever and me in particular. Let him live and get rid of this wicked stuff in your head. It is not time for him to die. When the time comes, no one will need to say 'pack your things and leave'. He'll do it willingly."

"No, I will get someone else to do it. And you better keep your mouth shut. Do not meddle in my business."

"Elsie, you can't go like that. Let's reach a compromise before you leave."

"Just forget about it and let me go."

"Elsie, you don't understand."

"Okay, if you say no, then let's live like this until he kicks the bucket."

"We better do that."

She walked over to the windows and stared across the lawn after she pushed the window blinds aside. For security reasons, I opened the door and went as far as the porch. With no sign of anyone, I returned to the room. Even the guards were still sleeping peacefully, like their master.

"You better go now and get some sleep before morning. I will do the same. The day is still young."

"Yes, I have to go. I am tired and feel sick."

She came over to me where I stood behind the door and kissed me passionately.

"Try and wake up, dear," she whispered to me.

The area under her eyes was a bit swollen and the traces of the makeup mixed with the tears left some smudges around her eyes. I think she left her face like this so I would feel sorry for her.

"It is better for you to leave now," I said as I unlocked the door, "but be careful no one sees you."

I smiled, she did the same, and I gave her two quick short kisses on both cheeks. I opened the door, looked around once more and gave her the green light.

"You believe in safety; I like it," she remarked on her way out.

"We will talk later."

I bade her goodbye, then she blew me a kiss.

"Hope you are not angry with me!"

"Why should I be? It's okay."

I shrugged.

"Hope you sweep it under the carpet."

"Bye and see you soon. Come back soon."

"See you, ciao."

She blew me one more kiss. I watched as she moved stealthily across the lawn toward the kitchen and opened the door. I really believe that if at the time of opening the door, she had met anybody, she would have collapsed. When she entered, I left the veranda for the bathroom to clean my teeth before going to bed.

Chapter Nineteen

Even though she had asked me to wake up early, I could not. I knew she would be going to do some shopping. Luckily for me, she woke up as late as I did.

"Thank God," I whispered when I went to the main building. The doors were not even open.

Since I first came to this house, I had my bath before going to the main building but since I had not wakened up early, I went straight to the building for the car key. I just went to wash the car without cleaning the inside.

The Volvo was the car I was washing when my brain picked up last night's scene from out of nowhere. I tried to erase it, but it wasn't possible. Was she serious or testing me by the way she behaved and spoke? I was sure that when she got the chance, she would do it. More so since she had told me that she would get someone to do it. I had to be very careful.

After she had gone, sleeping did not come easy for me at all. I had to think about it. It got to a point when I got worried. I needed some money for my ticket, a passport and, if possible, connections for the visa. I knew Elsie could give me the money I needed, but the job she wanted me to do was no joke. I had thought over it so often that it had turned into a boil in my brain. To get rid of it, I had to burst it. But how could I do it? Do her job, or quit the house?

Maybe she had knowingly picked me to do this heartless job for her. I just didn't understand why she fell for me so easily. She invited me, but she just wanted to use me. There are some women who would do anything to satisfy their desires.

Pondering over what happened the previous night, I became more worried, asking myself questions I could not answer. Was she drunk? Was she aware of what she said? Although she was sometimes disturbed, she soon overcame it.

Elsie was serious about everything she said. At times, one would talk, say something at night. In the morning, when you ask him or her about it, it would be denied.

The first time she talked about me doing something for her, my mind did not go as far as murder. I assured her I would do anything to get some funds to work on my personal project. As soon as I got the damn money, I would break loose from her. She might even have more dangerous plans; a dangerous woman, Elsie was a rattlesnake...

I should take my time otherwise she would give me hell by either reporting my presence as an illegal immigrant or getting someone to give me a deadly blow. She could make it look like an accident, just as she was planning for her husband.

If I did not leave this house, any time I set eyes on her, it would bring it all back to my mind. It would haunt me if I executed her deadly plan. She had left a piece of cotton in my brain like a surgeon forgets a piece of cotton in a patient's stomach. I would become a murderer. It would be on my mind haunting me for ages till I died.

"No, no, I can't do that," I said at the top of my voice. I stopped the cleaning, climbed onto the boot and sat on it. As soon as I sat down –

"Jerry, what are you doing?" she shouted at the top of her voice.

When I heard my name, I jumped to my feet. I could have ignored her, but someone might have been watching. Like a leaf, I jumped down.

She was clad in a white sports shirt with a round neck, over white shorts with tilted pockets on both sides, with blue striped socks in white Adidas canvas shoes and a white sweatband across her forehead. She had a blue towel on her left shoulder, a racquet in her left hand and a tin containing lawn tennis balls. It was telling on her face that she had not slept well. I forced an uneasy smile when she smiled.

"Forgive me, it is something I had to do so that they would not suspect us," she said when she came closer.

"I feel a little bit disturbed this morning so, in case I do anything stupid, try to overlook it."

She handed the keys of the Volvo to me and opened the door in front of her. She was going alone.

"I have a meeting in town today and need to collect some goods," she said as she got into the car, "I will need you."

"Alright, ma'am."

"By eleven o'clock, you have to be ready with the SO5 in a well-ironed uniform, not what I saw in your —" she realised her mistake and kept quiet. She stared at me and drove off.

I continued with my cleaning. After some time, I went for the rest of the keys. Before I returned, I popped in to see my boss. When the cleaning was over, I went to have my breakfast. I did not come across Kate or Rebecca.

At eleven o'clock on the dot and not a second past, I was sitting in the car, dressed in my all-white outfit, my ceremonial uniform. The long waiting began. Twenty-three minutes later, she was stepping out of the porch. Looking gorgeous, she stood waiting for me. I drove quickly to her. By the time she stretched her hand to touch the handle of the door, I was there. She was dressed in an all-pink attire: dress, bag, shoes, fake pearls, and earrings. It was nice; I just didn't know how to describe it. I spotted Rebecca behind the blinds, watching as usual. I released the brakes and set the car into motion.

"Drive carefully and don't go too fast," she told me as I passed through the gate to enter the street.

I pressed on the accelerator and changed the gear, bearing in mind what Elsie had said.

Five houses from ours, she told me the meeting would start at one, so we could go somewhere before going to the meeting. I neither said anything nor turned my head. Rather, I looked at her in the driving mirror and smiled.

As I was about to drive into the main street, she asked me to turn right instead of going left. It was a five- to seven-minute drive to the Island House where the meeting was supposed to take place. It would depend on how free the road was. At the end of the main street, she asked me to go over the bridge and drive along the lagoon and take the first turning on my right. That street led to the beach.

At the beach, she asked me to park the car at the side of an uncompleted building. As soon as the car came to a stop, I jumped out of my seat and ran to open the door. She had already opened it and had her foot out on the sand.

"We have to talk... this afternoon," she said when I reached her door. "I am very sorry for last night. Try to understand and reason with me. It should have been something else. I did not know what I was saying. It was like I had fallen into a trance. I don't know how that idea came into my mind."

"Never mind, if you say I should overlook what happened, that's up to you."

"Jerry, forgive me for what I said and how I behaved. Please, please," she stepped out of the car and held me close.

"Elsie, do not do that. Mind, you are in a public place," I told her.

Just last night and she had changed her mind. I knew what she was trying to do because I did not agree with her. Elsie was playing mind tricks on me.

"But Jerry, I want you to forget and forgive me for what happened. Bury it. Let me hear it from you." She closed the door and leaned on it.

"Elsie, you have to forget about it. There is no cause for alarm. I promise I won't tell anybody. Do you think parking this car here is safe from thieves and nosey parkers? It would have been better to park it at the car park and come here in a taxi. What do you say? Should I go and park it there or...?"

"Forget about it; we are here already," she said flatly.

She stared at me without saying a word. I did not open my mouth. When she noticed that I had refused to speak, she broke the silence.

"This morning, I noticed a change in you."

"Did you really? You are very observant. I just could not believe what I heard from you last night. It was like a dream to me."

"Jerry, I did not mean it; let's forget about it. It's all over. Your master will live as you want until he gives up the ghost by himself."

"Elsie, let me warn you, if you are a wolf in sheep's clothing, then you had better stop. I have a feeling that because I refused to do as you pleased, you want me to believe that it's all over. Then you will turn around and do it with somebody else. Don't make up your mind that you'll report me to the police or give me the sack. Anyone who tries it will leave without finishing the job."

Women are dangerous and can pretend. You can never tell what's on their mind. Pretty faces with wicked thoughts and devilish hearts.

"Jerry, let's bury everything in this uncountable sand, let the wind carry it away. Do not open your mind about it to anyone. If it gets out into the open, I will deny it."

"Elsie, let's forget about it; everything must be left behind. Yesterday is gone, today is a new day, and we don't know tomorrow."

"Some sayings bring trouble; others carry joy. Let's take it as a bad wind that blew by. I have never had a dream that could bring up trouble like that before."

She removed her shoes and put them in the car.

"One day, you'll put him in the car…"

I looked at her and she stopped. Without a word from me, I left for the driver's seat, removed my shoes and put them in with my white jacket. I closed the door and locked it. With my t-shirt and trousers, barefoot, I ran towards the sea. Elsie thought I would go to her, and she stood by the boot. Off I went in the opposite direction. She jogged after me.

After about fifteen metres, I stopped running and walked sluggishly, kicking the sand. All of a sudden, I felt someone holding my waist. When I turned, it was her.

"What are you doing?" I enquired. "Can't you see? Too many people around!"

"So what? Our affair is none of their business. We are at the seashore; let them paddle their own canoe," she said, still holding my waist.

"Don't give me that shit. I can no longer…"

"You can no longer what? Am I forcing you?"

"Yes, you are forcing me to do something I have not before."

"Jerry, lower your voice and mind your words. I think you are aware of who you are talking to. What has come over you lately?"

"I know, and I am very sorry. You made me do it. You pushed me into it." I left her.

"It's all your fault," she said, following me and pulling me by the trousers.

I pulled myself from her.

"It is over. Do not hold me. Let's walk apart."

"Jerry, I know you still have it in your mind. I have told you; it was a dream. I did not mean it. Please. You should have stopped me, woken me up. Instead of stopping me, you listened to every bit of it, now look at what you are doing. It's very bad of you. We were married and had two kids. I was heavily pregnant with another. It was a sunny afternoon at the beach. There were a lot of people, and we were having fun with our kids. Since it was only a dream, let's forget it. Let's change the topic. Jerry, don't spoil the fun. Let's go on well."

"We can only get on well provided you erase this dirty thought from your mind."

"When I left you, no sleep came to me till the morning, I was thinking about you and me. You said you'd call it quits."

"Forget it; I just wanted you to stop and that was all. I was fed up with that kind of trash."

"Are you convinced and trust that I would not harm him? I was even frightened when I left you. My hands would be soiled with his blood. I thought you'd be gone by morning. I knew you would not wake early, that was why I did not open the door in time. Trust me."

"No, I can never trust you. Elsie, you are very dangerous. Do you want me to believe what you are saying?"

She nodded.

"No way, Elsie, no way," I said and bent to fold my trousers.

"What more do you want me to say to make you believe me? Don't you feel for me? What I have been going through all these years? You do not know the ordeal I have been through after last night. If I was still interested, the first thing I would do was to send you away. Then, I would replace you with someone who would eat me and eat my words too. No, someone who would like my body. If you like my cunt, you have to do what I say as well as what I wish; what I desire. You have to do it. But I am telling you to forget about it. I love you and promise that nothing will happen to him. I am sorry."

"You'd better be," I said, smiling.

She hugged and kissed me.

Some people sitting under the sheds clapped and cheered.

"Thank you, Jerry."

"Thank you too for promising to forget about it. Don't dare mention it again; no more."

Chapter Twenty

Elsie jumped towards me with the hope that I would spread my hands and receive her into my arms, kiss, hug and embrace her. I moved aside and she landed flat on the sand. Those who had cheered earlier jeered. It was like a knockout. Without saying anything, I ran off thinking she would follow. After about fifty metres, I stopped and turned. She was not running after me or on the ground. Rather, I saw her in the water in her blue and white swimsuit with her hair covered with a black swimming cap. With a broad smile, she waved. I did not believe it – she had planned everything so well.

"Come on, Jerry, come on!" she shouted, forcing her way through the water towards me.

I removed my trousers and T-shirt, then went over and put them on a broken stool beside a white couple who were drying themselves in the sun. As she came closer, I was unaware that she had some wet sand in her hand behind her back. It was too late – before I even saw the sand, it landed on my chest. Without waiting for a second, she was on her way, running into the water and I chased her. On getting closer to her, she jumped and went under the water. Thus, she splashed cold water on me. I stood quietly in the water, then, when she emerged, I forced her back by pressing onto her head. She then emerged like a killer shark going to attack its prey. I helped her to recover.

"Jerry, I can't do anything without you."

She gave me her left hand. I pulled her towards me and kissed her as she came close, touching me. The coldness of the water disappeared at once.

"Elsie, aren't you going to the meeting anymore?"

"Which meeting? Forget about it," said Elsie. "There is no meeting going on anywhere. It was a plan. Are you not happy here? I just wanted to have some fun and talk to you."

"What? But this is ridiculous. What if someone comes here, let's say a family friend or someone like that?"

Without any more, I left her and cruised towards the shore.

She followed me but could not catch up with me till I got to where my clothing was.

"Jerry, listen to me," she said coaxingly as I bent to collect my clothing.

"Don't go. Why do you always try to spoil our fun? Jerry!"

"What is it?"

"Let's go to the uncompleted building. But first, bring my bag from the boot. Please, dear."

"Can you stand the stench in there?" I asked as I moved towards the car.

Whistling and nodding my head to a popular tune, I returned with the bag. She was not around. She had already gone to the building when I got there. Elsie had surveyed the place already. Nearby, a shed had been constructed. It was one with a difference. It was covered with woven palm branches. You paid a fee and you could go inside and get changed.

I asked her to go in while I went to the shed some metres away to pay the fee. On my return to the covered shed, I met her stark naked. What surprised me were the things in her bag. She put her arms around me and we kissed.

"Jerry?"

"Yes, darling?" I answered with surprise still showing on my face.

"I missed my..." she said, swallowing the rest.

"You missed what?" I retorted, moving back.

"I missed my period. I am pregnant."

"Then get rid of it."

"The doctor said it is dangerous for me. I don't want to go into details. Moreover, I am afraid."

How could I be sure it belonged to me? Only God and Elsie knew best.

She leaned forward and kissed me, putting her tongue in my mouth. She withdrew it and I sent in mine. I cleaned all the strawberry lip gloss from her mouth. My hand went to her back, then slowly to her waist and landed on her buttocks. I pressed on them and put my head on her bosom. Then I pushed her away. She almost fell on her back but she tried to control herself and stood firm.

"What is this about?" she enquired. "You always try to spoil the fun."

"I don't want to live on your compound anymore," I replied angrily. "Let me stay on my own, out of this place, then come in the morning."

"Someone must be watching. We have to be very careful. We can arrange and talk it over."

"Where?" I asked flatly.

"Anywhere that is safe for the two of us."

"I can still keep some of my belongings in the boys' quarters. Let's leave. What happened last night could have been recorded on tape by an intruder. Let's be careful."

"Jerry, I know you are afraid to let them go. Most of them do worse than we did."

"You are brave, Elsie. Never seen your type. I knew you were the type to go and live in those shanties; you like the life there."

"Yes, I like it. I don't belong to this place and I have lived there before. I would be free to do anything I like. You can even come there to my own room. Okay, do not..." She paused. "If you have made up your mind then it's okay and good luck. I can't stop you from going, but you have to satisfy my wants."

"Yes, ma'am, I will do anything," I said, saluting.

"It's okay for now. I have some shopping to do at the Eudo Supermarket. I like that place. The prices are reasonable and economical. Everything you want

NEVER TRUST A STRANGER

is there, from black soil to gold. Oh, I love to shop there. Even the atmosphere attracts you. They have a lot of things that most supermarkets have not dreamt of putting on their shelves. Their service is second to none."

"That's it – service. Good service is what brings customers, not those with sales girls who would shout and yell at their customers. You know, the customer is always right."

"It's alright, let's go."

As she turned around to walk out, I gave her a light tap on her buttocks. She turned and smiled. I bypassed her and opened the door.

Chapter Twenty-one

Back from town, I removed the things we had bought from the supermarket. As madam approached the porch, I heard Rebecca shout,

"Madam! Madam! Maria phoned."

Her face changed. Rebecca did not notice because she had turned her head away. When I passed, she was still standing on the spot where she had been when Rebecca gave her the message. Rebecca asked,

"Madam, anything wrong?"

There was no reply.

"Has something gone wrong?"

"No, my dear. It's just that I forgot something I bought. So, she is coming next month?"

"She will call again and let us know when she is coming; I mean, the date and time."

Rebecca was delighted but Elsie was unsteady. I wondered why.

"Her father will be glad. But how… why have you changed all of a sudden, madam?" I asked her after Rebecca had walked away.

"Leave me alone, you fool!" she shouted at the top of her voice.

"Are you not happy she is coming?"

"Jerry, do something for me and stop asking all these uncomfortable questions."

"What is it? Name it and I'll be on my way!"

"Maria is very inquisitive so I would like you to move out before she comes. I would appreciate it."

Is that what's bothering you? I told you I would like to get a room in the village but you didn't like the idea. I am going nowhere!"

"Is that what you are telling me?"

"No, no, I was just joking," I said, smiling.

"Why do you ridicule me? Let me ask Rebecca if she can get a room for you in the village. I will tell her your wife and two children are coming and I can't keep them in this house. Okay?"

"That's right, I trust you. Right, baby."

"You are mad, crazy fool."

Her loud voice brought Rebecca running.

"Rebecca, can you get a room for this good-for-nothing man? His family is coming and he plans to house them here!"

I overheard her say, "I will ask some friends if they can help."

"Okay; do try before the month runs out."

I passed them; Elsie followed and Rebecca went through the back door. She followed me closely without a word. At her husband's door, she paused then entered. After placing the box on the cupboard, I began to arrange the items in the cupboard one after the other.

As soon as Elsie stepped in, Rebecca also entered.

"Maria should have given us enough time to prepare. The room needs some painting. I didn't know she was coming now – August was what I had in mind."

"She is just coming for Easter and to see her father," Rebecca said.

After putting the groceries into the cupboard, I asked Rebecca to open the door of the fridge so that I could put some vegetables in. Before she did, Elsie asked her to give her the orange juice.

"When are you going to your friends?" She directed the question to Rebecca. "And you too; you have to do something about it before they come."

"Auntie Rebecca, I can see you are busy. You can send me to your friend."

The woman who spoke was called Auntie Matti. She was black in complexion with a small round face, a generous bosom and buttocks and was of average height.

"Okay, I think that would be quicker. Just after the first bus stop in the village, the one on your right, just behind is a white storeyed building. On the ground floor is a garage that has been turned into a store. The woman in it is the owner of the house. It would be faster and would cut a long distance shorter if you go by boat across the lagoon. When you disembark from the boat, all you need to do is cross the street. But take care when crossing."

Elsie walked out.

"Thank you," I said, bowing. "After lunch, I will go there."

"Provided madam does not need your service. Did you see the expression on her face when I told her Maria had phoned?"

With my food in one hand and a bottle of cold water in the other, I was on my way out when I heard Rebecca say,

"There is going to be a change in this house when she arrives."

Since morning, I had not had so much as a puff of a cigarette, so, at the boys' quarters, the first thing I did was to light one.

Elsie's behaviour when she heard that Maria was coming disturbed me a lot. There was more to it than what she told me. Was it in conjunction with the murder of my boss? Since I was around and the daughter too, it would be very difficult for her to go ahead with her plan. That was why she later endorsed my request to leave the house. She made me believe that what had happened the other night was just careless talk. But I didn't think so. She meant business. Elsie was a very dangerous woman. The amount she wanted… and the property too. She has a sugar-daddy husband who couldn't perform. She claims she is in love with me. I am young and can perform well. She would gradually push me into committing murder. I have heard of girlfriends murdering boyfriends or wives doing the same because of being jilted but not for money's sake. Already, I had one pinned on me, so I would try to walk away from this web of deceit.

I needed the money badly. If I went out of her life, where was I going to get the money? It would not be very easy for me. She was attractive; the charm was there. Time would tell; what I needed was patience and willpower to survive. To be put up with a friend did not appeal to me at all, but it would be better than staying with this murderer.

Very soon, Maria would be in this house. I had seen her photograph – she was not bad-looking. Or do I wait and make a pass at her? When I got out of this prison gate, I was going to ride these girls mad. After eating, I decided to go to the woman. I hoped she would not disappoint me.

I did not need to rush as she was not coming today or tomorrow. The month was drawing to an end so the time would come quickly for me to collect my salary. Then I could have some fun with her.

My passport was my headache now. William promised to help, but with the amount involved, it scared me. The price he mentioned was too high. Unless I cooperated with Elsie, I would not be able to get the amount. When I had been to the woman, I would pass on to his place. He could also help with the room problem. William, who knew everyone in town, might be able to tell me something about the bitch.

The guy who left before I came, I heard, lived in the village, and if you gave him money, he would do anything for you. No money, no work.

Getting out of this country was my first priority because I did not know what was going to happen from one day to the next.

There was this girl called Thawa who I moved with secretly, like Elsie. She found out and did not take it lightly. Since that day, I was not welcome in her presence. I had not been to her place, so, I might visit her after William's place.

Since I had made up my mind that I would not return until the following morning, I did not go after lunch as Rebecca had said. Instead, after eating, I went to rest.

Chapter Twenty-two

At seven, I left the house after I had greased the palms of the night-shift security guards as I would be coming in at dawn the following day. I didn't want madam to know that I had slept out, so when unlocking the gate, it had to be gentle. I strolled down to the main street and boarded a taxi. In it, there were two female passengers in the back seat. As I settled down in the seat by the driver, I turned and greeted them. Because of the light in the car, I was able to catch a glimpse of their faces, especially the one behind the driver. She was plump and fair with a round face, big bright eyes and a flat nose that looked as if it had been pressed down. Her mouth was small but the lower lip was thicker and longer than the upper. The taxi did not have a pleasant-smelling odour. Air entering the cab saved the situation but it did not help much. In a few metres, I turned my head to look at them, pretending to be looking at the car behind.

We went under the bridge and turned left onto Norman Street. Just before the Olympio Hotel, the two women spotted a nice-looking woman, probably about thirty, coming towards the taxi. The street lights were on so we all saw her beauty. The woman stopped the taxi but since we were going in a different direction, we left her.

"Mmm, she looks beautiful; look at that," the woman behind the driver said as soon as we drove off.

I turned and looked at her again.

"But you are also beautiful. Or is it because she is fairer than you?" I asked and turned my face.

"My husband has even warned me about the remarks I make about women I see on the road. He said I am also beautiful so I should stop it. My fairness is natural and the most beautiful on earth. I have to be sincere to nature. I know my beauty is natural, not fantasy."

We all laughed, but no one made any remark or spoke till I got out of the taxi.

It was not far from where we lived but because of the lagoon, one has to go a long distance. If I had gone in the afternoon, I would have crossed with the canoe

NEVER TRUST A STRANGER

or boat. I would even have walked along the lagoon to the bridge, but since there are no lights there, thieves carry out their nefarious activities there.

The description given to me by Rebecca helped me in finding the place easily. After telling her why I was there and saying who had directed me, she led me to a corridor with rooms on both sides and we entered the unoccupied ones. Later, she asked me to choose one. I chose the fifth room on my right since it was clean.

"Twenty naira is the rent. I collect two years' advance payment from my tenants, but since you are from my good friend, one year."

We went back to her store/bar. She brought out a white sheet of paper with 'Regulations For Tenant' as the heading.

There were no customers in the store/bar, only a small girl who helped her. As I was about to leave, she called me and offered me a bottle of beer. It was very cold and I was grateful for it.

"How is your madam?" she asked as she opened the beer.

"Fine."

"And your boss? Hope he's doing fine."

"He is in the hands of the Almighty," I replied prayerfully.

"What do you do in the house?" she asked whilst she drew a chair back to sit on.

"I am the driver," I said with confidence.

"So, Gola has left. I knew he would not last in that house. Anyway, he did not go there to work but for another thing."

"Why do you say that?"

"I am glad he left. Thank God he left."

"Why?"

"Why? That idiot, drunkard, lazy man, he almost killed us. Always going after girls like a he-goat does. Whenever he was sent there, he had to be held up. I wonder where Elsie brought him from. That madam of yours, she is another one."

"I hear he is living in this village."

"Yes, but he has packed up," she said and hissed. "He made a pass at his neighbour's wife. He fought with them and was given a sound beating. I don't think he will forget it till he dies. Before, he used to live in the boys' quarters. Thank God he left. He woke up one night and he was seen around the main building near the swimming pool. Later, Elsie, your madam, who is a real pig, was seen coming from the direction of the boys' quarters at that odd time." She got up, scratched her buttocks and sat down again.

"One morning, we were in the house when a girl came looking for him. When the security men told him about it, he told the security men to tell her he had gone out with madam. In the afternoon, the girl came back again. She waited outside till Gola came back with madam. As soon as the gate was opened, the girl hurried in. He then led her to the boys' quarters. He did not know we had gone to the kitchen. He tried to calm the girl down so she would lower her voice. She said, "I have come for my money. Don't make me yell. If you want me to disgrace you, I will. Bring the money and I will leave quietly. If not, I will give you hell. You think you can fuck me free of charge?" Her voice was going up, so he tried to take her into the boys' quarters but the girl refused to go in and stood on the veranda. She was shouting so we rushed to the veranda. Your madam did not come down. We met the girl holding Gola's trousers at the fly. She did not even care to leave him and give some respect."

Two men and three women entered so she excused herself to attend to them. After she had finished with them, she came back with a medium-sized bottle of Guinness in her hand. She did not sit opposite me but beside me. Those who came in sat at the corner of the bar/store. There was an old radio on top of the counter producing some old tunes. The sound was not very clear.

"Rebecca stood at the entrance, arms akimbo, whilst I stood on the lawn with my head on the wall. Rebecca moved forward and held the girl by her elbow.

"What is wrong?" she inquired.

There was no reply.

"Are you not the one I am speaking to?"

"Ask him!" she said as she shook herself free from Rebecca.

"He thinks he can just go away with my money. He does not know who he is messing with." She held him by the collar, pulled him towards the lawn and spat.

"He did not tell me he was having me free, neither did I tell him he could fuck me free of charge."

"So, you girls of nowadays, you don't have respect for your elders. You are not even ashamed of what you are saying?" This was Rebecca.

"It is my work. Why should I be ashamed of it? Don't make me angry. Just tell him to bring my money and stop what you are telling me."

Gola did not utter a word.

"Last Friday, I was standing at the bus stop," the girl continued. "I was waiting for a taxi when this idiot stopped and wound the window down.

"Which way? Where to?" he asked me. He was not going in my direction but he offered to drop me off first before going his way."

I finished my beer. She offered to give me another but I turned it down.

"It's alright, in case you say that I am a drunkard."

We all laughed.

She said that as soon as she entered, Gola introduced himself.

"I gave my name as Christie. We followed it with a conversation on the armed-robbery menace in town at night. That was why people now chose to stay indoors." She jerked Gola up and grinned.

"About two hundred metres away, he said we should drop into a guesthouse about fifty metres from where we were to have a drink, First of all, I refused, but he talked me into it and we drove there. After a drink, we went in. To tell you the truth, I gave him a nice time. He is a good fucker and I enjoyed it, but he did too. 'Look at the stupid girl,' I said. 'After the good time I gave him, releasing the tensions in his prick, he is now playing with me.' It did not dawn on me that I had let him climb over me without money. I thought he was a responsible person when I saw him, not a con artist. I don't mind – we can go to the police.

"This morning, I was here and one of the security men told me he was in. He left the gate to call him while I still stood outside with some hope that I would get my money. On returning, he told me it was not him. I did not challenge him or say anything. I told him I would return in the afternoon. Luckily for me and unfortunately for him, I got him as soon as the gate opened. He told me he would go out to buy some gas and drop me off. When we got to the bus stop, he asked me to get out. He gave me ten naira but I refused to take it. We started arguing. When he saw I would not give up the money, he left me in the car. Ten minutes later, he returned with a policeman. He threatened me and I got out of the car. Today, I am not leaving this house until he gives me my money. He did not tell me he wanted to fuck for free."

She pushed him towards her.

Rebecca looked at my face and I shrugged.

"Auntie, tell him if he wants trouble, I will give it to him. I don't care; it's my work and I am proud of it."

"I then left where I was standing and went to plead for him. The girl did not even listen to me. She dragged him from the veranda to the grass, shouting at the top of her voice;

"I want my money! Give me my money!"

She made such a noise that Kate, who had just returned from town and was changing, heard her. As Kate hurried to us, I heard the gate open. It was the doctor. Gola placed his hands on his head. The doctor had not even stopped his car when Kate ran to report to him. He came hurrying down the lawn. He was a nice-looking fellow, about fifty or over, with a childish face that made him look younger than his age. No wonder he went after the young girls and they also liked him.

He was clothed in a short-sleeved shirt, not buttoned correctly and partly rumpled, with trousers that had not been ironed neatly. He did not seem the type to dress shoddily. In fact, he looked bedraggled. It must have been the result of being in a hurry!

"He might have jumped into whatever his hand reached after he got the message. I heard that wherever he is and whatever he is doing, he gets a message from the house and he has to be on his way, even before the end of the message," I said.

"The expression on his face showed that he had made up his mind."

Kate led him to where we stood. Gola showed no remorse when he saw him.

"Gola, you are dismissed outright!" he said, fuming with anger as he reached the scene.

This did not stop the girl from holding him or disturbing him.

"Pack your things. I said, go and pack your things!"

The girl did not release him.

"You too; can't you behave yourself?"

"Don't say that, behave, when we are talking about my work."

"How much is it?"

"Thirty naira," she replied, still holding him.

The doctor put his hand in his pocket and brought out some notes. He went through them and then gave her a twenty note and a ten.

"I am surprised at your behaviour."

"Papa, don't be."

"Who are you calling Papa?" His voice overshadowed hers.

"This is money. Moreover, his thing is no joke." We all laughed.

"If you like, pack and come with me," she teased him as Gola stood, straightening his shirt.

"How did he get into the house at all?" he asked, refusing the cold water with ice that Rebecca offered him to cool down with.

"Can I have some?" the girl asked.

Rebecca hissed.

"It is not my problem whether you hiss or spit. All I know is I have got my money and I am going. Are you not a woman? Doesn't your thing pain you?"

She walked away sluggishly with steps that made her body move as if in time to the music.

"Are you sure of what you are saying? I heard he moved into one of your rooms."

"My rooms? Who said so?" she asked, scowling.

A customer entered and I took my leave.

Chapter Twenty-three

From her place, I made up my mind to catch a taxi to Thawa's place. As I entered the main street from the village and walked about twenty-five metres without getting a taxi, I heard the faint sound of a siren from afar. Gradually, it got closer and closer. Finally, it turned into a building, the fourth from where I stood. It was the police. Thinking there had been a robbery, I ran to the magnificent grey and white building. It belonged to a business tycoon but he had given it to one of his various wives.

Joana, in her early twenties, had been in the fashion business, shuttling from one fashion city to the other. Rome, Paris, London, New York; you name it. She lived with her auntie who owned a chain of stores dealing in clothing. She studied design and modelling. Fresh and cute, she was fair in complexion.

After graduating, Joana started as an emerging businesswoman going abroad to buy clothing. It was on one such trip that she met him. At the time they met, he was forty-four, tall and well-built. The father of four lived with his first wife in a comfortable mansion. They quarrelled the night before he had travelled abroad. Joana had slept with him three weeks ago.

When Joana married her husband, she became snobbish and had no respect for her elders, even the auntie who cared for her. Joana, the only child of theirs, had lost both mother and father when she was two. Her mother was in labour and being driven to the hospital by the father when they had an accident. They crashed with a petrol tanker and the two vehicles burst into flames.

The husband of many wives was her only hope with her household, who were confined to the boys' quarters when they finished their work, including the nanny.

He had important business to attend to and would be back in a week or less.

After seeing off some friends in the driveway, she returned to dismiss the cook, nanny and steward. Between the boys' quarters and the main building is a wall with a gate which she locks every night and opens in the mornings. As an early sleeper, she was preparing to go to bed standing behind the louvres with the curtain drawn to one side.

Before Joana went to bed, she got dressed and put makeup on as if she were going to a function. Because of her makeup and her jerry-curled hair, her bed was changed every two days.

A man in his early thirties, wearing a pair of black trousers, a black jacket with white lining, and a pair of black shoes stood at the gate asking when madam would be getting ready to go to bed. The security man lifted the receiver to announce the presence of the man at the gate. As he lifted the receiver, the stranger blew a white substance in his face. He was dazed and fell, collapsing into his chair. He tried to shout, but there was no way.

He removed his jacket, turned it and wore it with the white on the outside. He changed his mind and put the black on the outside. He moved a few steps to the right side of the U-shaped wall and climbed over. Bent, and crawling closer to the wall, he went to the main building. The lights at the gate were faint near the main building, so when there is light in the room, you would see everything inside. He went under the master's bedroom window and saw her reading on the bed.

Stealthily, he crawled to the main door of the sitting room. He put on the black gloves he brought from his patched back pocket and began to try about ten keys that he had in his side pocket. The fifth did it. He turned the handle, careful not to wake anyone and he pushed it halfway. He peeped in and gave himself the green light to enter.

It was expensively furnished. The carpet, which matched the wall paint, had a soft layer and a rug in the middle. Between two doors stood the chrome-plated room divider. A twenty-four-inch Philips colour television stood solidly in the middle, and guarding it was the Akai Video and spread on all the shelves were five pieces of music system from Panasonic. In all, there were four loudspeakers, with flowers standing on them in the four corners.

The swift shadow of a car outside made him tremble and move a bronze metal carving. The place was dead quiet. She came out to look when she heard the noise. The man lay flat on his back on the long sofa. Joana wore a transparent pink nightgown with only her pants on, no brassiere; even though she had just given birth, her breasts were still attractive and pointed. She never gave her baby breast milk. Her breasts were protesting against the material.

Thinking she had gone, he came out of hiding. When she saw him, Joana shivered and a chill ran down her spine. She began to sweat. She could not shout. Her breasts quivered as he came closer with a dagger in his right hand. She wanted to go into the bedroom where the newborn baby lay peacefully asleep. Her first into the world. She was confused and tears ran down her cheeks.

'Why me?' She asked herself.

She gathered her courage and came to meet him to prevent him from going to the bedroom. Her baby was what worried her, not herself.

'What would happen if he knew the kid was there?' Only the Almighty would answer her. He was the only one who could save them. She didn't want to make any noise. When he got to her, he pushed her backwards.

"To your bedroom."

"Oh no," she said as she knelt, pleading. "Don't do that to me, please. Please, I beg of you."

"Your room," he said, pointing to the door.

When he realised she did not want to move, he grabbed her nightgown just above her bosom, pulled her towards him and pointed the dagger under her chin.

"What is in there that would make you refuse to go in?"

"Nothing."

"Then you better move and be cooperative."

With Joana's back to the door, he pushed her towards the door. When he took in the sight of the baby in the cot, he smiled while Joana became sad. She pulled herself away and ran to the cot, kneeling beside it and pleading.

"Please, my baby, have mercy upon me. I will do anything, anything at all. Take whatever you need. Ask for anything, I will give it to you. Just mention it and it will be yours. Anything excluding him."

"So, he is a boy. Nice boy."

Joana had never thought of anything like that before. She would rather it be the end of her life than that of her baby. Tears ran down her cheeks.

"Stand up," he ordered.

She stood on her feet with an uneasiness.

"Carry your baby," he commanded.

"Please, please."

"Obey before you complain."

She carried him, cuddling him.

"Now put him down."

She opened her mouth wide in disbelief. Her eyes opened so widely that they might fall out.

"I said down," he began with a loud voice but ended with a low tone.

She had to obey orders, so she put the baby down on the carpet.

"Draw your nightie over," he ordered.

With trembling hands, she drew the nightie over her shoulders. The ordeal was too much for her; it was written all over her face. The expression on her face explained it. With her eyes shut and her face turned side up, she wouldn't see what he was up to.

"Look forward," he shouted, losing patience. As he looked at her, she dropped the nightie on the carpet.

The baby woke up crying.

"Can't you stop him from crying?"

She bent and picked him up. In her arms, she began to comfort him and sing a lullaby for him. With heavy eyes, the baby soon slept. The telephone rang. She moved towards the door, but he stood in her way. For the fourth time it rang; he marched her out of the bedroom.

"Pick the receiver up and drop it on the table."

She did as she had just been ordered to. She was at his mercy. Joana was marched back to the room. The stranger's thing was hard and protesting in his clothing.

"Now down. I mean bend and hold your toes. Easy and relax," he ordered in a friendly tone.

She did it with her eyes closed over the baby. When the baby woke, she would have to move so that he did not see what was happening to her. Joana had to obey. It looked like a day of reckoning. She prayed to God to send a saviour to lead her out of the way of the sadist torturing her mind.

He undid his belt and zip. He pulled down his trousers to his feet, pants down. All in haste.

"Now, turn around and spread your legs in the same position as you are," he ordered, sternly. With vigour and rigour, he entered from behind. For so many years, she had never had sex in that position with her husband. As he entered, cold ran down her spine and tears ran down her cheeks. Little drops of sweat assembled on her forehead and she closed her eyes in pain. She had given birth three weeks ago and her cunt had not healed.

"Oh Lord, have mercy upon me," she prayed. More tears ran down her cheeks than before. As he pushed in and out of her, the pain increased.

When he saw he was about to come, he withdrew his rod from her. She thought he had finished and was about to get up when she felt the glove of his hand pushing against her neck. He entered again, but this time it was too much for her. She wanted to shout but it would wake the baby. In no time, he rested on her back, fondling her breasts. He had finished.

"Lord, have mercy upon us for we do not know what we do," she pleaded with the Lord. He left her, took the nightie from the carpet, and used it to clean his friend. She did not move but bent still and remained silent. There was absolute silence.

"Get up, you bitch," he ordered as he tucked in his shirt.

She got up, trembling and sobbing. She held the baby's cot and bent over it.

He drew his white handkerchief from his pocket and, with the hankie in his right hand, went for a half-full bottle of whiskey. He opened it and drank almost a quarter of it.

She could hear the voices of her neighbours outside but they sounded far away. They were the voices of the neighbour's children who had returned from the club. She knew it was their voices, but there was nothing she could do. Joana had no bell to call her domestic. If she had, it would have saved her from all that agony. If she tried anything foolish, he could harm her, or the baby, which was more important. Joana needed a saviour to get her out of her predicament.

He hurried to the door, then returned, looked at her, and went to the built-in wardrobe. With a smile on his face, he opened it. Standing still, he turned his head in her direction in case she tried anything stupid. He went through the things in the wardrobe and found some money in a brown paper bag and her jewellery in a container. There was a briefcase locked with a code. He could not open it and asked Joana to unlock it. She told him it belonged to her husband so the code for opening it was not known to her. After pouring everything from the envelope into a green plastic bag, with a grin on his face, he went to kiss Joana on both cheeks.

From her handbag, he removed some notes and put them in his back pocket. She watched helplessly as he stepped into the living room, moved across the carpet and then towards the main door, unlocking it. Joana came to the door with the baby in her arms. As he was about to go out of the door, he stopped and blew her a kiss.

Shocked and frightened at what had just happened, she stood for a moment and began to cry. Joana heard him outside and so moved swiftly to the window and watched him go out as he had come in. She just couldn't believe it had happened.

Joana made up her mind to call the police but when she picked up the receiver, she dropped it again. Would they believe her or think it was another of those tricks that girls play? With the baby asleep in his cot, she buried her face in the soft cushion in the cane rocking chair by her dressing table and broke down. She wept; her ego had been humiliated. How would she tell her husband with many wives? If she called the police, the whole world would hear of it. She could carry the baby and leave the house and go into hiding. But where? There would be gossiping.

Then, there was a sudden pain in her vagina.

"Oh, God, save me from my enemies," she sobbed. Could this be a catastrophe? Was it the end of her marriage to her husband who was well-known?

She went to the cot. He lay there, calm and peacefully sleeping. She felt dirty. Joana went to sit on the bed and with her face buried in her palm, began to sob. It was like a dream, but it had really occurred. Some life came into her. She gathered herself and walked across the room to where the telephone stood. Sitting on the carpet, she changed her mind and lay down. She raised her hand and took the phone. She began to dial two, nine, eight, zero, two, nine.

Someone picked it up, answering for her husband. She was told he was on his way out and she asked them to call him back, as it was very urgent. After a few unbearable minutes, her husband was on the phone. She did not tell him what had happened but asked him to come and that it was very urgent. Then she went on to phone the police.

Chapter Twenty-four

The metallic grey two-eight super Mercedes arrived ten minutes after the police. It had not come to a halt when a middle-aged man with grey and black hair got out of the car, ignoring everybody, and hurried to the room. His driver, in a completely clean and well-ironed white uniform with a cap, followed the young man. The police who were already there had started their work. Everyone was directed not to touch anything.

Twenty minutes later, he came out with the victim clad in a housecoat, sobbing. He whispered in her right ear with his left hand on her shoulders. They walked through the small crowd of those who had come to sympathise with her, those who had heard the police sirens, and other policemen.

Everyone watched the sad couple as they moved towards the car behind the police car. The driver opened the door on the right for the master. He did not enter but allowed her to enter and he closed the door. Then he went over to the left door which the driver had already opened. When he settled on the seat, Joana put her head in his lap and began to cry. People came closer to take a look at her. The driver reversed, screeching, and disappeared into the dark street. There was a nodding of heads and, one after another, the crowd dispersed.

I made up my mind to go home. After the crowd had left, I hailed a taxi just outside the gate. Since it was speeding, it did not stop directly in front of me but screeched to a stop some metres away and reversed. He asked me to get in after I told him where I was going and agreed upon the fare. I sat, without a word from me to the driver, till I got home. All the lights in the rooms were out. When I peeped through the hole in the gate, the two security men were asleep. One was even snoring so loudly that I could hear it from behind the gate. I didn't blame them. When the master is asleep, why shouldn't they sleep?

Knock, knock, knock, and on the fourth knock they both sprang up as if they were having the same dream together. Noisily, one of the gates was flung open. I pitied them because the metal used for the gate was so heavy. As I moved towards the main building, the light in madam's bedroom came on.

"Jerry?" I heard her call as I paused under her window. "Where are you coming from?" She did not wait for a word from me to explain myself. "Do you think I brought you here to play, or what? You left here without my knowledge and look at the time you are returning."

"I am sorry."

"I won't take that nonsense."

"I am coming from the village."

"And so what? Is that where you spent the whole day? I have been waiting to send you out. If you feel you are too big for the work, let me know so that I can find someone else. Tell me. Would you answer me?" she shouted at the top of her voice.

Do you know why she did all the shouting? Because of jealousy.

"Wait for me, I am coming down."

I went to wait on the porch and a few minutes later, she was downstairs in her nightie and housecoat.

"My friend Agnes Wellis is travelling to London at midnight. I want you to deliver this parcel to her."

She gave me the brown envelope. I smiled.

"What are you smiling for?" she enquired, smiling. She snatched the envelope and hit me on the forehead. "It is very important. If you don't meet her at the house, go to the airport."

She gave me the key.

"Drive fast, but don't kill yourself."

"I have got the room," I said before I turned to go. "Sorry, madam," I bowed.

She nodded.

I left for my room.

Ten minutes later, I was speeding along Hill Point Street to Agnes' house. In another ten, I was at her gate, sounding the horn. The gate was opened and the mallam came out. I introduced myself and he asked me in. Mrs Agnes Wellis was in the hall with her kids and some friends. I delivered the letter and left.

I was stopped at two police checkpoints, else I would have made it in twenty minutes to William's place. He was sitting on the slab among the grass by the main entrance, his eyes on the lookout. I was sure he was watching out for someone.

"Hi, Jerry!" He jumped up, smiling and came to the car. "It's been a long time," he said, as he shook hands with me. "Why don't I see much of you these days? What's been happening? Hope something good, man."

"I am now working for the chairman of a chain of companies."

"No wonder you look healthy."

"I was at your place but the guy did not want to give me your address."

"In the meantime, I am very busy. Hope to see you at the end of the month. How are the business and your girls?"

"I am even waiting for one of them," he replies, smiling.

"Let's go out and have some drinks."

"I am very sorry to turn you down. I would have gone but it has been a hectic day for me. I need some rest. Sorry for turning down your offer. If not because of the baby I am waiting for, you would not have seen me outside. Every night, she has to call here. Just can't go to bed without her. My latest catch is a newlywed whose husband goes on a permanent night in one of the factories as a doctor in the industrial area very far from here. When the husband leaves for work, she also comes to her work here. She ain't bad, pretty intelligent and a bitch. Since you brought a car, I think we should go to her place."

"What about if we miss her?" I asked.

"If she gets here and I am not in, she'll wait till I come," he said, confidently.

"Okay, let's go."

"What's her name?" I asked him as he opened the door.

"She is Tamali, Mrs Sade Tamali. As I told you earlier on, the husband is a doctor in a factory clinic. In the morning, he runs his own. She is a teacher. I first met her when she brought the pupils to the National Theatre."

I was hoping to see the lady called Tamali who Williams was risking his life on.

"Very soon, I will fire her after I have tasted every part of her body. So, if you want to see her, drive fast to catch a glimpse of that lovely and intelligent bitch."

"Never mind," I said, changing the gear and pressing the accelerator to double the speed. He brought out a packet of Rothmans King Size. He gave me one and I pushed in the lighter of the car. We continued our conversation. It signalled that it was hot. He removed it, lit his own, and lit mine for me.

"What about the passport, any news?"

"Yes, there is," he replied.

"I hope it's good news."

"Why not? Don't you trust me?"

"I do; go on."

"My friend Lawrence who works at the passport office, I met him last Sunday at the Tarkwa Bay. He said things were a bit difficult now but they are coming back to normal. Everything is moving on gradually. Things will be okay."

"Let's hope so. Are you sure he can handle it? It's not everyone who works there that can do it."

"Why all these remarks? If you trust me, then trust him. He is the right guy for the connection, my anchor man there."

"Is that so? Do you mean it?"

Williams made a grin.

"How much?" I asked curiously. "Did he tell you the fee?"

"He told me but said as the time changes, so will the price change. There are other people in the group whose palms he has to grease. It could cost you as much as five hundred. For express, it will be extra."

"What? What does he mean? He must be mad. It is daylight robbery."

"Watch out!" he shouted.

I nearly ran into a broken-down bus.

"Do not make noise over it. You can go to the passport office personally. You might get it at a lower price, but don't say I did not warn you. The swindlers charge less and then zoom off with your cash."

"I don't believe all that you are saying; you are putting your own price on top."

"It's up to you to decide. I know many who have made theirs through him. I hate being a contact man for many of them. This is your chance to get it. It's a clean job."

"Williams, never trust a stranger. Since I don't know him, how do you expect me to trust him? As you know, by the way, I don't have enough money. He can take half, and, after the work, I will pay the remainder."

Williams shrugged and threw the end of his cigarette away.

"Can't you borrow from your master or madam?"

"Are you mad? What has it got to do with them?"

"Don't get me wrong, I am only trying to help. If you don't want me to contribute, okay. The next junction on your right."

"Williams, do you know something? I had a dream that I was in Europe. Before the year is out, I have to be there. I can't remain here much longer than summer."

"Do you really need the passport?"

"Yes, why do you ask?"

"Then you should double your efforts."

"There, I can further my studies and make a better living. Oh man, I have to be there. Please."

"Don't worry, I understand your plight, but it is the money. Next time I see him, I will talk to him about it. When he is in a good mood, he'll listen to me. He might even cut down the fee."

"How is Labala?"

"She is now a full-time call girl at night in one of the big hotels in town. During the day, she works with an advertising company. I don't want to talk to her. She does not move with good men, men of violence, bandits, they're bad."

"Look at you condemning some people."

"No, do not say that. Their ways of operating are rude. Try to understand me. There is a guy there who has been to prison four times, all with hard labour. The police are always on their heels."

"Where is Gola?" I asked.

"Anything wrong?" he asked me.

I knew he did not expect a question like that from me.

"Can you give me some information on him? I want the truth; no tricks."

"Okay, okay, I will let you have it. He is a bad man; notorious. I hear he fled the country, but some say he went into hiding after a murder case."

"A murder case?"

"Yes, the police are looking for him."

"Where did he work and did he ever live where he worked and later move to the village?"

"He worked for a beautiful lady with a bedridden husband. Before, he lived with them then later, he moved out into the village. Why, I don't know, so don't ask me."

"Where did he kill?"

"There was a daylight robbery in one of the big banks along the Airport Road. He led the gang. A huge amount, into the thousands, was stolen by them. It was said that he shot the policeman on guard himself when one of his men told him the policeman had recognised him, so in order not to implicate them, he shot him. The policeman was brave and survived. Two of them were arrested. Those arrested refused to mention his name or where he lived."

He exhaled a huge amount of smoke from his cigarette.

"The policeman, a good artist, drew him. It was given to most media houses to be published and posted at all major police stations. But no one had seen him."

I lit a cigarette and put the lighter into its hole.

I just didn't know why Elsie would employ someone like him. Maybe she was unaware of his character.

Maybe she went for a ruthless one who can make her dreams come true?

"Is he tall or short?"

"Big? He is not big. Because of his bad behaviour, one would think he looks big, but he is a smallish, tiny, skinny little man. He looks like someone sick. He looks like a monkey, with hair all over his body. Always elegantly dressed. Here, here," he shouted.

I could not stop instantly when I applied the brakes, because of the speed. We had arrived at a blue house with a big open compound. It was very quiet everywhere. There were no lights in the house.

"She must have gone," he said as he turned his head away.

"You very well know we would not meet her in the house at this time. What are you up to?"

He neither answered nor looked at me.

"Let's go," he burst out at the top of his voice.

From the girl's place to his house, there was only a little communication between us. There she sat, on the steps, with her face painted like a masquerade. She was really beautiful, no doubt about that. That was why Williams was risking his life.

"I am not getting out," I said as I pulled to a stop. "It is very late, so give my regards to her. Thanks for the information and hope to see you soon."

"Thank you," he said as he stepped out of the car. "It has been an enjoyable ride. Take care and come back soon."

He had only just closed the door when I set the car in motion. With my left hand, I waved, and in the driving mirror, I saw him wave back.

Chapter Twenty-five

I had almost finished bringing out my things from the portmanteau when it began to rain heavily without warning; no changing of clouds, lightning, or thunderstorms. It took me unaware. The room looked a bit disarrayed.

There was a loud knocking on the door. Since I wasn't expecting anybody, I walked sluggishly to the door without asking who it was. I opened it. She charged in, fulminating. She was partially wet.

"Where did you go last night?" She continued with a sort of thrash, anything that came to her mind.

I stood at ease with my hands folded, looking at her.

"Have you stopped working for me or what?" she asked as she pushed me aside and entered the room. "This is what you should have done earlier on, not now."

"Do you know something, Elsie? This is my room, so you should mind how you speak to me. Else, I would walk you out and I would not regret it or tender any apology later."

"Jerry, I think you are aware of whom you are speaking to."

"Yes, I am aware. When I come to your house, you can do whatever you like. For now, and here, I am the boss."

She put her racquet against the leg of the bed by the wall and sat on the bed, looking at me.

"Where did you go after you delivered the parcel?" There was no reply from me. "I said, where did you go? Didn't you deliver the parcel? You did."

"Then what's bothering you? Do not put words in my mouth."

She came back to her senses and apologised for the rude behaviour she had just displayed.

"I know why you are angry with me. We were to meet yesterday night but I failed to turn up, right? Only yesterday, and you are mad with me. What about you, who refuses to see me for a week? If you don't take care, I will give you one across the face."

"Try it and you will regret it."

"What can you do?" I laughed.

"Just touch me." She stood up and walked over to where I was resting on the coffee table.

"Elsie, you are tempting me. What brought you here this morning? Leave me alone in peace. A friend arrived from home yesterday. He is leaving today," I explained. "On my way to deliver the parcel, I saw him. The guy told me he had a letter for me so since I had a car, we should go for it. So, after I had dropped it off, we went out together. So, what you thought yesterday and are still thinking about, wipe it from your mind."

"I thought you'd had an accident or a mishap had occurred."

"Nothing can happen to me; I can take care of myself."

I went to sit on the floor behind the door. She brought out a packet of cigarettes from her grey tracksuit top. She lit one with a silver-coloured lighter, also from the same pocket. She offered me one by throwing the one she lit for me.

"What news did he bring from home?" she asked in a relaxed voice.

"Nothing new; always the same story. Things are going on well with me, I always tell him, but he says they are worried about me. They want me home alive, not my corpse."

She said nothing. Neither did I.

"Is that all?" she asked. "When are we going to implement the plan? You know, time is running out fast. The doctor says he will not recover from his broken spinal cord. Why should I sit and wait for him till he passes away? As for his eyes, he could see one day but it would depend on him. It was the glasses that did it. One operation after another and good care would make it clear. He has to make up his mind with zeal and will, plus modern science, then he'll be okay. And as for his speech and hearing, it is just the noise and sound effects. He might overcome that too. Haven't you realised that he is suffering? It would have been better if he had died. No fun."

"Elsie, stop it. Stop it. That's enough," I shouted at her.

"I feel guilty since I am the cause of it. Oh no, why didn't he die?"

"You have done it already. You can never turn him back to what he was before. Ask God. Pray to Him for forgiveness."

"The morning before the accident we had a bitter quarrel."

"About what?" I asked.

"I had this stupid maid. A bitch in her own right. She was lazy, and all over her were spots left from a skin disease. One day, I returned early from playing lawn tennis. I caught them with my own two eyes, having an affair. He was right on top of her in our bedroom. If you saw how he went in and out of the stupid girl… can you imagine that? Straight away, I asked her to pack her things and leave. He apologised, thinking it was all over. No, it had just started."

"Because of this, you tried to kill him."

"One day, Betty, a childhood friend whom I had not seen for years, emerged from nowhere. She told me she had seen my husband with this girl, my former maid. She told me she knew it would hurt me, but she had to gather up the courage and report it to me. Another friend also told me she had seen them in a club three times. Another even volunteered to take me there. She now rubs shoulders with men in town. I even saw the two of them at a club last week." She wiped her face with her hand. "What broke the camel's back was when I heard that she's been boasting about my husband including her name in his will. The same day I heard it, I confronted him about it. I did not give him the chance to explain, but I threatened to sue him. Later that night, I tampered with the screw of the brakes."

She walked to the window with her hand behind her. She opened the window, looked out and suddenly banged it. She went to the door, locked it, and put the keys in the left-side pocket of her trousers.

"Jerry, I want him dead, before it's too late." She pulled the zip of the jacket down and removed it. Then drew her trousers down to her feet and, with her left foot pressing against the right, she removed one leg and kicked into the air, but the clothing did not leave her. So, she stopped being childish and used her right hand to remove it.

Then, she came to me, her hand around my waist, and kissed my forehead.

"I can come to you but not as often and you know we can't do anything at home unless it's here. Dear, I love you but there is one thing separating us. Tell me you love me."

"What if I say it and I don't mean it?"

"You can't pretend?"

"Go and put on your things. It is late, I have to go," I told her.

I moved to the corner and picked up the trousers of her tracksuit. When I got to the bed, she pushed me and I fell on the bed. She followed.

"Darling, you are not giving me what I want."

"What do you want?"

"You mean you don't know?"

"Tell me."

"Jerry, I have always told you, you spoil our fun. What has gotten into you? I have noticed a change in you. Last night you stayed away from me and now you are refusing my passes. Please, I want you to go into me. Do it to me; let me feel your body."

She kissed me passionately and I replied. Then she lay on her back and I began to fondle her breasts. Not the entire thing, just the nipples.

"Hold it, hold it," she said, putting her finger to her lips. "There is someone at the door." She pointed. I kept quiet, staring at her.

It was her conscience disturbing her. There were children in the compound, so I saw no reason why she would say there was someone at the door. It could have been the window, but that's her own business anyway.

"Someone has been listening to us, Jerry. Why not go outside and see things for yourself?" she said with an undertone.

"Okay, hold on, I am coming."

Stealthily, I moved across the room to the door, turned the key without a sound and went out. I tiptoed to the end of the building to the back, and back to my door from the opposite direction.

When I returned to the room, she was lying sprawled out naked on her back on my bed in the small shabbily furnished room, looking towards the door.

"What is this, Elsie? Someone could have entered just like that."

"Has someone entered?" After all, it was my own room.

I locked the door and went through my bag. After removing something, I brought out two small pocket-sized bottles of gin. I threw one to her and kept one for myself. I put mine on the coffee table and removed the shorts I had on but kept my penis out of her sight by leaving my blue pants on. With the bottle in hand, I went to sit on the bed beside her. She had drunk half of hers and resealed the bottle and put it under the pillow. After taking two sips, I covered it and put it on the floor. I moved up and sat on the pillow, resting against the wall and looking down at her. She rolled to my side and stationed her head in my lap.

"Elsie, I want to tell you something."

"Go on, I am listening," she said as she pulled my pants off.

I looked at her and, with my hands supporting me, I raised my buttocks for her to draw them off easily, which she did.

"What is it?" she demanded after my pants came down over my feet.

"Do you know you have charm, poise and good looks? When I see you naked, I can't take my eyes off you. You are too seductive. As far as I am concerned, you have everything I want. You turn me on too often, Elsie. You are a luscious lady."

"Stop flattering me," she said, and rolled aside, back to her former place.

She started working on me, licking my thing with her long and slippery tongue. It made it very difficult to sit. Slowly, I lay flat on my back and threw my legs apart, wriggling my waist in excitement. She went on to lick my thighs while she used her fingers on my thing. Up, up her tongue went to my chest and to the nipple of my right breast. Whilst she was doing this to me, I had my finger going in and out of her cunt, my other hand caressing her back into her armpit, out and right across her breasts.

She put the thumb of her left hand into my mouth and I began to suck like a kid. Down to my prick with short intervals like a butterfly licking nectar from a hibiscus flower. I took over and started sucking her. She gave me a long kiss. Then, I am sure, if we entered a kissing competition, we would definitely win.

When my finger went back into her once more, I noticed she was wet all over. She began to wriggle, making little sounds and behaving like someone suffering from fits.

My penis had erected to its full length, strong like Hercules. She lay on her back and threw her legs apart. I did not enter her, rather, I placed my elbow under her knees and jerked her. Since it was already wet, I did not find it difficult to penetrate. It was like when you put your finger into butter not almost melted. Up and down my buttocks went, and in and out my penis. After some time, I capsized and she took over the ship from the pilot.

She did the kissing and fucking and fondling with my nipples whilst I did my own thing. With her eyes closed and mouth open, she began to call me "Jerry..." It was the climax, faster, stronger. She waxed and began to shudder when she reached her orgasm. Elsie discharged her cargo and, panting, rested on me. I began to push harder.

"Oh, my God, what are you doing?"

I started pouring out into her and held her and she clenched onto me. When it all ended, she rolled off me and lay on her back, still panting like a matchless horse who had just won a derby.

"Elsie, I told you a while ago that you are luscious."

"You are also sweet, and can perform well," she said, smiling.

Chapter Twenty-six

 That night, I did not return home early from work. Since I had not gone to work early, I had a lot to do in the afternoon. After leaving my place of work, I went to visit a chick. I asked her to go out with me, but she refused with the excuse that it was cold. I tried to persuade her but she stood her ground and refused to go. I could not carry her on my back, tie her, or force her to do it; it had to be of her own free will. So, I left her.

 A friend asked me to accompany him to a girlfriend's house. On our way to the girl's house, we met her with another guy, strolling with the guy's hand around her waist. I did not say anything, nor smiled even though she offered a dry smile. When I bypassed them, I saw the guy putting his hand on her shoulders, pulling her closer. My friend saw me off at the junction and I got a taxi home.

In the middle of a nightmare, I was awoken by a knock on my door. When I enquired who it was, they replied, "Dolly." Since I knew who it was, I rushed to open the door and ushered her in. I noticed the sadness on her face, a swollen lip and her right eye was black. As soon as I opened the door, she began to cry. I consoled her. Her boyfriend had beaten her as usual, but this time it was too much. It had not been like that before.

She told me she was cooking when the boyfriend came in with a friend, both drunk. She said as soon as he entered the room, he called her from where she was cooking and asked why the food wasn't ready.

"He did not wait for me to explain. Wham, wham. He slapped me on the face and when I turned to run, he punched me on the lips and the middle of my lower lip burst. Look at it," she said, showing me. "What have I done to deserve all this? I want to leave; it is all over. I can no longer stay with that brute, that monster. He'll kill me before I know. He can't even clothe or feed me well, but he beats me like a slave. If you like, go and ask him. He has not spent a kobo on me but likes to treat me like his property. If I leave him, no girl would waste her time on him."

After she had finished complaining and, on my part, advising and consoling her, I accompanied her to their room. The boyfriend was sound asleep on the only armchair in their room. He had poured out all the ingredients the girl would use to make the food.

After she had locked the door, I went back to my room to sleep. Some time ago, there had been rumours that there was an intimate relationship between us.

In the morning when I woke, the shadow of the rising sun had lit the room through the opening in the window. I felt weak and feverish. This did not stop me from smoking one of my favourite cigarettes. Lying on my back, I began to ponder what Elsie had said yesterday, about someone outside listening to us. How did she know there was someone outside? The smell of men's popular perfume? But why should someone come to listen to us? There was an expression showing that she was sad and disturbed over it. If I had told her about the perfume, I would have loved to see the reaction on her face.

'She was just disturbed by her conscience. It is haunting her,' I said to myself and brushed it off.

After she had left that morning, I put the finishing touches to my setting out of things before I went to work. I turned to go.

"Wait, I have not finished. What about the kidnap? Let's give it a try. Find someone good, let him mention his fee, a reasonable one, and let me know. No tricks."

"Okay."

She turned to look at me. I knew she was disturbed.

"We are going to give the ransom when everything is done. I will also let you go if you wish. I don't want you to feel that I am keeping you against your will."

"Thank you very much," I said, bowing. "I will do as you wish, but you can't keep me here against my will. Also, I know I am an illegal immigrant here, but don't even try to report me to the law enforcement agents. It wouldn't be good for either of us because if you give me away, I will do the same. Everyone suspects you but there is no evidence of what you are planning."

"It has never occurred to me before to report you," she said, sipping from her wine glass. "Forget about it. It is only that I am worried about how things are moving. If our plans fail to work out, you'll have to wait for a few days till I get someone to fill the vacancy you'll create."

"I don't think it would be important and all that necessary," I said without looking at her. "You can drive, and there are a lot of people to take care of your so-called husband. You can even bring in a relative."

"Don't be stupid and wicked. Do you expect anyone to come into our main bedroom?"

"You are trying to be ridiculous."

She was making a point but I wanted to leave since I had my own plan.

"Elsie, I am still working for you, so I will do as you wish."

"That's nice of you," she said, smiling.

She stood up and removed the sunshade, placing it on the table. Then she took another sip.

"Jerry, the very day you quit and walk out of the gate, leave everything here; bury whatever has gone on between us here. Don't carry with you anything that happened between us. I am even trying to forget that there is something between us."

"When I leave you now, I am going to the post office."

She moved towards the pool, throwing her hands up and down till she got to the wall, went down the ladder and disappeared into the water.

After I had collected the letters from the box at the post office, I drove to the car park of a multinational oil company. I told security that I had come with somebody, so he allowed me to park. Then, I went straight to the popular Ritz hotel to have some fun.

Elsie had turned me on, but there was nothing I could do with her at that time. Moreover, I had made up my mind not to do anything with her. I entered and headed for the counter. Lining the corridor were the bitches. Those with big busts, jumping and hopping, others with the correct statistics to win a beauty contest. It is not only good statistics that win a beauty contest; brains counted too. Some of them painted their faces like they would in masquerades in the villages.

As I walked past them, a fairer one smiled. It was a smile trying to win me. There were others too, towards the bar, many of them, as if to welcome an August visitor. One touched me. A plump lady, black in complexion, said hello. Another hissed, and a short, fair one said hello. A lady with a pair of neat, white, high-heeled shoes stretched her legs across. They did all this to woo me, but no way.

I bought a bottle of cold Fanta at the counter in the bar. Leaning on the counter, I began to sip it. After I had finished it in less than ten minutes, I decided to leave. As I was leaving, I got to the lady who stretched her legs; she repeated it but I did not say a word as I knew what she was up to.

When I turned into the tiny corridor leading to the main entrance, the lady who called when I entered took my hand. There was a touch on my left shoulder. They were hungry. No money. Who would use his hard-earned money to come and have sex with prostitutes? The touch on my shoulder was the one who had stretched her legs.

"Come, I want to ask you a question," she said, smiling and showing a set of clean, white teeth. There were nice, deep dimples on her cheeks. God must have done some extra work on her teeth because they were well-aligned.

She attracted me the most, so I followed her. The lady took the lead and I followed. Just by the reception was a door that she opened, leading to a corridor with six rooms on both sides.

"Where are you taking me to?" I asked as she passed the door to the first room.

"You come," she said and leaned on the wall between the first and second doors on my left. She put her arms on my shoulders.

"You see," she started, "you are a nice fat boy."

She moved closer. I did not say a word but forced a grin. The next thing she did was fondle my penis with her right hand and with her left hand, she stroked my nipples. I couldn't resist. This was free of charge but I stood my ground that I wouldn't succumb to her temptations.

"What do you want from me?" I asked, like a novice.

"Let's go in; I will make you fine. You'll never forget." She moved closer, hugging me.

"I don't have enough money."

"How much money do you have on you, nice boy?"

I did not answer.

"Why not answer me? Now. This place is special, twenty bread, and that one near the gate is thirteen."

"I don't even have thirteen," I said. My rod was very hot and was asking for something cool.

"Okay, bring ten."

The truth was I did not want to fall for her temptation.

She pushed me to the wall and put her finger in my ear and began to hum a tune and hugged me, forcing her pubic area to rub mine. I loved it, but it was just touching. She let me go when she realised I would not give in.

I hurried through the main entrance and quickened my steps to the car park. Without wasting time, I drove off. Time had gone but I had my usual excuse - there was a broken-down car or two cars had crashed and it caused a long hold-up.

When I had delivered the letters, I went to continue with the cleaning of the car. Whether it was on the road or not, it had to be clean both inside and out.

After I had finished with my work for the day, I went to the sitting room to find madam.

"I have finished and so I want to go home," I told her after I had greeted her.

"You can go, Jerry." She spoke like someone who was sick. She had her eyes glued to the television screen. I wasn't going out. I would watch telly till I fell asleep.

I don't know when she started watching telly; maybe of late, she had become a television addict. Only God knows what was on her mind that she allowed me to go so early, not even six.

"Thank you for allowing me to go so early," I said. Maybe it was the talk I had with her in the morning. "Since there is no one at home, do you think it is safe?"

"A relative might call. If there is anything at all, I will notify the security men. Don't worry, I can handle everything. Thanks for your concern."

"I am glad."

"I am also glad. By the way, come early; I am having a meeting with the bankers and insurance."

"See you."

"Bye, and take care."

Chapter Twenty-seven

As I got a taxi to take me home, I began to ponder over why she had allowed me to go home so early. Maybe she was expecting somebody or had a plan to execute tonight. If his daughter Aireen came and the kidnap failed, it would be very difficult for her to carry on with her faceless plan. Moreover, since the boss would soon be leaving for Europe for a check-up, she wanted to act fast.

Because of the water beside the house, no one thought it reasonable to put up a wall or put a guard there. The one whom she had planned with could come by water so as not to be seen by the security men.

Before I entered my room, I went to greet the lady and cooled down with a chilled beer.

"Madam, I want to rest for a while then go out. I am telling you in case you don't see me tomorrow because I could come in late."

"Please don't stay out at night too long. It is very dangerous."

"Thank you, madam. Can I have a bottle of beer?" I asked as I gave her the exact amount for the beer.

"Go for it. Feel free, and go for it."

"If you please, a lady might come here tonight. Please extend my apologies to her and tell her I will see her tomorrow night." I picked up the bottle and left for my room.

I woke up around ten pm. In under twenty minutes, I was in the vicinity of where I earn my daily bread. So that no one would see me, I went through the house before ours. Since we were good neighbours, there was a gate in the wall dividing the two houses. Pretending to see someone from that compound, I sneaked into ours. Stealthily, I moved into the flowers under the boss's window.

Seventeen minutes had gone past, seventeen precious minutes I had wasted. If I had stayed at home, I would have had my girl. Since I was not at home, she might not come again. As I was still thinking about the time being wasted by me, the light went out in the bedroom upstairs. Some minutes later, I heard Elsie's voice in the master's room. Then, the door closed, and the back door opened.

Stealthily, I crawled and stationed myself in the corner of the building where it was possible for me to view the surroundings of the pool, right down to the edges. It was very dark on the water.

Elsie came out and closed the door. Moving swiftly, she headed for the boys' quarters. She disappeared into the tall flowers by the side of the boys' quarters.

Now I understood why she had asked me to go. From where I had stationed myself, it was possible to see Elsie and anyone coming from any direction. There was no light from where I was. I noticed a shadow moving behind the hedges and went straight to where Elsie had positioned herself. Now, the shadow had become two, then I heard a male voice.

"It is very cold here and the mosquitos... I have donated enough blood. I am even scared."

Everywhere was very quiet, so I heard every word Elsie said

"Didn't you know before you arranged for us to meet here?" the male voice asked.

"What time did we agree on? And you have just arrived? Do you think I live in the water? You know I come from far away. Moreover, I have to come undercover."

"Okay, let's get straight to business. I don't want any mistakes. Everything will go according to plan. It's just that I have brought in the kidnapping of Aireen. I have asked Jerry to deal with the arrangements. After Aireen is kidnapped, it might shock my husband, and this could kill him. You know she is his hope. He is training her to take over from where he left."

"What about Jerry?"

"You'll get rid of him."

I nearly revealed myself to let them know I knew their secret.

"Jerry no longer lives here. He has a room in the village. He moved in with a harlot in a hotel in the area. So, you can track him at night and club him or knife him. Whatever you want to do to keep him out of my way. Before the week is out, I have to get out of the country. I don't want any delay tactics.

"We have to be very careful. Extra care has to be taken. I don't want mistakes and I mean it, no mistakes.

From this very moment, I don't want to see you till we execute the plan. If the kidnap goes through, you'll definitely hear about it on the telly and radio. You might even read it in all the dailies. I will make a big advert and posters everywhere. So, watch out."

"I need some cash," he growled. "You talk too much."

"Don't you have any?" she asked. "What about the five grand I gave you last week? I hear your new girl is very demanding."

"You forced me into it," he said angrily.

"Take this," she said. "This is another ten."

No word from either of them, but they made noises which meant they were still around. They made noises like cats when they are having an intimate session. The bitch was being fucked.

I pressed the button for the light on my watch. I had been there for almost two hours. A shadow moved behind the hedges towards the pool and disappeared. Then, Elsie moved across the lawn to the back door.

Before the shadow moved, Elsie had told him that if everything went well, he would get the fifty grand he asked for and she would offer him her body once more.

You can't refuse her body.

"No tricks," she had warned, "else you'll have only yourself to blame."

"Don't you trust me?"

"This is not a matter of trust. I want a clean job. I am not joking."

I hurriedly moved to the back of the house, right to the back of the dining hall and to the back of the sitting room. The lights were on. I saw her pouring herself a drink and heard her humming happily. From there, she moved to the couch and lay on it with her glass held on her chest, staring at the ceiling.

She stood up and walked to the curtain, drew it to one side and looked out. Only God knows what she was looking for. Elsie looked tired and drunk. Of late, she had taken to drinking. With a hand raised, she stretched herself and yawned. She went to put out the light and walked over to the door leading to the corridor.

Then, like a cat, I moved to the back and down to the back of his room. She was already talking to him. I saw her kiss him on both cheeks, then his forehead, and a long one on his lips. He would smell the alcohol but he couldn't complain. He couldn't see the look on his wife's face. The bitch that she looked like.

Elsie ran her tiny fingers through his hair and kissed him again. She moved to the window and with her elbow supporting her, leaned on the window. Then she put both hands in the two front pockets just above the waistline of her housecoat, removed a packet of cigarettes and lit one.

"Dear," she began. He turned his head towards her voice.

"You set spies on me. But now you can't. Whatever I do is out of your reach. If I tell you what I did twenty minutes ago, you'd pity yourself."

She placed the cigarette on the table by the bed and folded her arms.

"I have come to talk to you," she said as she moved toward the bed, scratching the back of her neck. "This is a day I have been waiting for a long time... for years. It has finally arrived."

On my knees in the flowers, I watched and listened attentively to catch every action she made and every word that came out of her mouth. She continued in a high-pitched voice.

"I wouldn't have bothered, but when you found out, you could not cope with my friends calling you by your first name. Especially when your daughter was around. You knew I was the same age as your daughter, but you kept on coming to me, bringing me all sorts of presents that came to your mind and your hand and that money could reach. When it became apparent to you that I was not the type that you wanted, you relegated me to the background of everything you did. Formerly, I went on business trips with you. Pleasure trips and functions. Then, you left me behind."

She went for a cigarette, lit it, and drew some smoke into her mouth. With her eyes set on him, you could see from the expression on her face that her mind was not on him.

"We had no children, so you thought you could toy with my love life. I could not stand it. So, I made up my mind about you."

She laughed gorgeously.

"We used to watch this program on the telly - Do It Yourself. I learnt how to do minor jobs on the car like changing the tyres, topping up brake fluid and about batteries. You set spies on me and I had to do the same.

It got to the extent that we did not trust each other. I got to know that you always went out with that bitch of yours in the evenings. Instead of the driver taking you, no way, you would go by yourself. Don't you think it is risky to drive at night by yourself? A man of your status. I had the lite phone bugged. When the telephone rang, you knew the time was at hand and so did the caller. You were at the table eating and you rushed for it upstairs. Every word you spoke is on tape.

"I hurried to where the meter is and since there was no one to start up the generator, I tampered with the fuse and the lights went off. With a torch in hand, I hurried to the garage and tampered with the brakes. Before the generator lit the house, I had done the deed and returned to the dining hall. I wanted you dead. It would have been better, safer and more peaceful if you had died than to be in this miserable and pathetic position."

She paused for some seconds, staring at him. I raised my body up with my knees and bent forward to see what was going on. Suddenly, she burst out angrily towards the bed.

"The best thing you could have done was to sit and settle things without a third party and if things did not go well, then a divorce whereby you paid me some alimony, but you weren't wise enough for that. I was not interested in you anymore, and you were not interested in me, even after the wedding with all its ostentatious pomp and ceremony."

She took a long sip and licked her lips.

"You only thought of yourself, not me. Even your daughter came before me in everything. Why did you not go over there and lick, suck, and fuck her cunt? I am sure that bitch came before me in everything. Gossip and rumours were what you relied on most of all, in a country where rumours are as old as the sea. You told that bitch that you would delete my name from everything of yours. I have friends very close to her, so, whatever you say or tell her gets to me in no more than a day. I put it to you that she is now your mistress and you are paying her rent and footing her bills. You bought all the furniture and everything is in her name. What has she got that I don't have? Those fallen breasts and watery cunt as big as the sea. Is that what you want? I am very sorry for you. You should have kept quiet about the affair I was having outside of my matrimonial home since you did the same."

She bit her lips and wiped her face, then, with the heels of her palms, rubbed her sleepy eyes. I was tired and my eyes were begging for some sleep.

I stood up to see what his reaction would be but there was no sign. Her voice was loud and anyone passing by would have heard her.

"You were very much aware that I was married and was four months pregnant. You used your money and influence to set spies on me. My movements and everything I did were brought to your notice. You had lost your wife and so you wanted me by any means. Who knows, you might have even planned it that way. From the beginning, I told you I don't go out with married men. I made you understand that I did not have even a small amount of love for you. You showered presents on me then went on to arrange to get rid of my man. With the way your thugs killed him, the shock made me miscarry. Yes, the same shock could kill you one day."

She turned and moved towards the built-in wardrobe, then, as if possessed, she turned towards him.

"Yes, it will surely kill you," she said as she walked slowly in his direction with her hands behind her back.

She paused for a time then continued to the bed and sat beside his legs.

"After the death of my man, I wanted someone rich to marry. Since you were rich and wanted me, I gave in, not knowing you had planned it all. When I found out you would not spend money like I had dreamt of, I realised I had made a grave mistake in marrying you. You found out from that friend of yours – the doctor – a friend indeed. Did you know he made some passes at me? You didn't know! He thinks I have told you, that's why he dislikes everything I do or say. He told you I cannot bear children. It is true. When you heard it, you began to mistreat me. You treated me like a maid. You began to hate me.

"Whenever you went out to meet business associates and whatnot, every night, they were all lies. Let me tell you, it was that bitch you went to meet. She is a real *bitch*," said Elsie, stressing the word 'bitch'.

"Your manager at the supermarket is having an affair with her. Likewise, your cousin, the engineer. That's not all. Three close friends working for you had an affair with her some time ago. They had what we call a sex orgy. Why do you have to associate yourself with such a loose girl?"

"I am very sorry for causing all this for you. Please forgive me."

"I know how much you are insured for, both accident and life insurance, and I have all the names of the beneficiaries and the percentage for each and every one of them, including the little you left for me."

She sat on the arm of the armchair with the glass of brandy in her right hand.

"Me! Your wife! Why didn't you give me the biggest amount? Instead, you are leaving it to your daughter whom you are training to take over from you. Most of your properties you have left to your children. Your son is getting the same amount of money as me. Your son is too young to bother me. Aireen is coming home soon. We shall see," she threatened and moved over to the window where I stood. Stealthily, I got down on my knees. It was a cold and quiet night – I would have said 'quiet as the grave' if it had not been for Elsie's hysterical speech.

Chapter Twenty-eight

As I waved to a lady at the first turning on my right in Kobi Street before entering Kudu Avenue, Elsie was once more on my mind.

I could leave without informing her or maybe just tell her I would be back and that's all. She knew more than I thought. I would have to be cautious in everything I did or said. The drought in some parts of Africa and the worldwide economic crisis with the small and poor countries owing the big and wealthy countries have always appeared in the newspapers and on television, but nothing about me. Maybe I had not seen it. Sometimes, I felt like going back to my country but the damage had been done already. They had tagged me as ungrateful and, worst of all, a murderer. I would have gone home earlier but now it was too late. They wouldn't believe me.

If I were in my own country, by now, I would have climbed up the ladder and been given the respect due to someone of my age. I have not made enough money. Who would listen to me when I go home to defend myself?

I drove to the pavement and came to a halt. I unlocked the door on my side, stepped out onto the sand and locked all the doors again. As I moved towards the sea, not ten metres from the car, sand began to enter my shoes. I returned to the car, removed them and put them in the boot.

My buttocks had hardly touched the bench in one of the coconut-palm sheds when a man, almost naked, came in demanding the fee for using the place. I dropped a note in his palm and he left. In all the years I had been in this country, I had never been so frightened. I gazed at the waves, pondering what to do next. Why did she employ me when she knew the type of person I was?

Perhaps she wanted me to satisfy her longing for sex and help make her dreams a reality. After sitting for some minutes, I decided that as soon as I got home, I would call it quits and go back to my country to face my people. Then, I changed my mind since leaving the job would not bring an end to my various problems both here and at home. The overall conclusion was that I should stay and see out the course of her plan.

Since she is a well-known person in social circles and very influential, Elsie could go to the security agents, offer them some money and, with falsified information, they would be on my back.

After all, she had known about me for a long time. However, she did nothing about it. Perhaps she wanted to use me for her faceless and wicked plan. Since I did not agree with her, she would get rid of me. It would be safer for me to work in this house than to work outside. I decided to wait and see.

The following morning, she asked me to distribute some letters and invitations, knowing very well that I would not return early, but later in the afternoon since it was Monday, the first day of the week. When I left the compound, I drove straight to my house and stuffed my pockets with money. Early in the morning, the hold-ups are not as bad in some areas as in others.

Kate would be having her day off. She was leaving this morning and would not return until tomorrow. Since Elsie had decided to send me out, she would have to do everything by herself. After all, she was the wife.

From my place, I went to the restaurant that Fibe owned. It was set up for her by my master, or so the rumour-mongers have it. Since my master's accident, it had not been functioning well. It was a chance to have a closer look at that bitch, and, if possible, have a go.

As soon as I sat down at a table, a girl walked towards me in a blue skirt topped with a white blouse. She was pale with smudges under her red eyes. I smiled but she did not return it – instead, she yawned. She must have had a sleepless night. One could tell from her appearance that she was suffering from a fever, even though she had painted her face with make-up. What did my master see in her that Elsie had not? Maybe she worked as a call girl at night and came to the restaurant during the day.

"Morning," she said.

"Hello."

"Can I help you?" she asked, holding the chair facing me.

"Yes. Can I have a plate of rice? I mean, the white one?" I continued before she could open her mouth and ask, "White or jollof?"

"Fried plantain, two pieces of meat, an egg and a bottle of cold Fanta. A bottle of iced water too," I concluded before she turned and walked away at a snail's pace.

I did not understand why my master should leave Elsie and go after the likes of her. Maybe she had a taste inside of her that Elsie had not.

I did not expect the food to be on its way so soon. It was hot, with the Fanta and water served on the same metallic tray. She was about to leave the table after she had placed the tray before me.

"Hello, Miss," I said. "Could I have a word with you? I am Jerry – pleased to meet you. When are you closing?"

"I am Fibelia," she answered, smiling for the first time. "We close at five. Can you come back at that time because I would like to go home early?"

"Sure. I'll be here."

"I will be expecting you."

She turned and walked away as before and went to the back of the counter.

Since we were meeting at five o'clock, I thought I'd better hurry up. I even thought of leaving the food behind, but I was damn hungry. Then I thought of making love to her for the first time. She said she would like to go home early which meant I could not do anything today.

Maybe it would be better to forget her since I was not really in love with her; I just wanted a round with her to taste her, see how good her cunt was and how she performed. I wanted to know what makes my master mad about her.

In less than ten minutes, I had finished and was on my way to the car. From the restaurant, I went to Ikeja, did most of the distribution and then went to Surulere. At Surulere, I discovered that I had two letters for Ikorodu which I had to deliver before the hold-ups started.

I returned home at about five and reported back to Elsie, then went to the kitchen to have my meal. After eating, I washed and cleaned all the cars in the yard.

At 8.30 pm, Elsie was making her way to the lawn, noticed me and walked over to me. I knew she had just returned from playing tennis as she was clad in a white T-shirt over a white skirt with grey stripes at the sides.

"Hi, Jerry."

"Good evening, madam."

"You are still around. Can I have a word with you?" she asked, smiling.

"Why not?"

"Here?"

"Wherever you wish."

"Jerry, there is nothing secret between us anymore so let's stop pretending."

"That would be better, but it all depends on you."

When I had finished washing and cleaning the cars, I went to sleep on the table on the veranda of the boys' quarters. I had just woken when Elsie saw me.

The boys' quarters were only partially covered by the main building so, from where I sat, anyone entering the main building would see me.

"Elsie, I have already donated much of my blood to the mosquitos so let's go indoors."

I took the lead and she followed at a distance. I turned the knob and kicked the door to open it, put on the light and switched on the ceiling fan. She bypassed me and headed straight to the window facing the main gate. Elsie looked tired but not exhausted.

Her presence in that room made me feel unsteady. I wished there was a bottle of brandy as I could have done with a couple of drinks to steady my nerves. There was none, so I erased it from my mind and waited for her to begin but no words came from her. I took the lead and set the ball rolling.

"You know I don't sleep here anymore."

"Yes, it's been a long time since we were together here, hasn't it?"

"It seems so," I replied.

"To be frank, I miss your company, Jerry," she complained.

There was no word from me, but rather, I got up and went to switch off the fan.

"Why?"

"I don't like it."

"By now, I am sure we know each other really well, so let's stop beating about the bush."

"I don't understand you. Who is pretending? You are rather doing that so what's all this about? What has happened?"

"Don't you know? Stop pretending!"

She moved to the window, peeped out and then placed her right ear next to it. I was sure she did that because of an intruder. Then she walked back to me.

"Have you locked the door?" she asked, caressing me.

I shook my head.

"Please go and lock it."

I went to lock it and, on my return, she had removed her top and brassiere.

"Come and play with me," she said as she threw her hands wide to receive me. I walked straight into her open arms. As soon as she closed her arms around me, Elsie began to kiss me and fondle my rod as if she was sex-starved.

"If you want to play with someone, why not go to him? I mean Chris!" I said as I prised myself from her arms. "Do not pretend."

I noticed her face change.

Sometimes, mentioning names brings happiness, and at others, sadness.

"What about that name?" she asked.

"What about that name? It is written all over your face. You cannot keep me here and use me for your shameless and faceless activities."

"How did you come by that name?"

"You know I have friends."

"Friends indeed."

"Yes, your friends told you about Fibe's affair with your husband. My friends also told me about yours. Gossiping and spreading rumours, that is as old as the hills up-country."

She stood up from the bed and moved quickly to the door. Elsie remembered her racquet and returned for it with the same speed. She looked very angry and I even thought she would walk out on me. It was what I needed, but as she turned the knob, Elsie controlled herself and pulled herself together. She turned and looked at me then leant against the door with her eyes closed and fists clenched, breathing heavily. After some time, she walked to the bed like someone exhausted.

The name Chris had dug deep into her flesh. Elsie thought I would now need to know about it.

"Let's settle everything...everything on this name tonight and bury it right here."

"Whatever you say."

"If your friend told you this, it means that many know of it."

"Rumours spread like wild bushfires. I knew it would cause a lot of harm to your name. Anyway, they are my close friends. There is no cause for alarm," I said.

"Jerry, you've been spying on me!"

"I hate cheating, but that is what you've been doing. I don't even know how many more you have had. I can't trust you since you are not dealing with me alone, so it is useless going on with you. You are not satisfied with me, that's why you have others, so let's forget it. I'm calling it quits."

"But...t...t..." She prolonged the word like a stammer.

"But what? How could you associate yourself with such a deadly person? Out of all the handsome men in the world... I know you are very much aware of his character, so is it just because he is handsome or does he fuck you better? Let me warn you, he is more dangerous than you know. Better watch out!"

She bowed her head in shame but I knew, deep inside her, she had no regrets and was rather proud of him.

"Your hubby set spies on you, then you did the same on him and me. I am doing the same to you."

"You think I have not done my homework on you? At least he is trustworthy. He would not abscond when he is needed to serve the company that helped him. You murderer!"

"He is the murderer, and, very soon, you will be Mr and Mrs Murderer. I know you know a lot about me, but since it is all false, I am not worried."

"Stand here and say it is not true when the police come after you. Don't run away!"

"Some time ago, I heard a rumour about you asking a friend questions about my background. This is the hour I have been looking forward to. I did this and that, but one day, posterity will be the judge," I said and got to my feet, burning with anger.

"Look, my dear, you don't have to be angry and frightened. We know ourselves – let's continue our relationship. And if I have said something to cause this anger, then please forgive me, but you started it all."

"Whoever told you all this is a crazy liar!" I said flatly. "The murder of that prostitute was done by him, not me. Do I have the money to go in for that kind of high-class bitch? I was framed."

"But by whom, poor soul? You know I have travelled a lot and I make friends on almost every trip I make."

"Say boyfriends, not mere friends," I cut in.

"Call it what you like. Two months or so before I met you, I was alone on a business trip to Europe. My seatmate was your Managing Director. We were watching a video of a murder just like the one you performed. He gave me a vivid description of you and said that you had performed one at home and then fled to Nigeria.

"When I saw you at the restaurant, I phoned him but did not tell him I had found you. Since I needed someone to do a job like that for me, I became interested in you instantly."

"Oh, that was why you gave yourself to me – not for my love but for your selfish ends. You have made a big mistake. It is the wrong man you have come to lure into murdering your hubby. I am very sorry but my heart cannot face it."

"You are right. If it wasn't for the murdering of my husband, a lady like me would not have given herself to you."

"But why did you not try any of your various other boyfriends before coming to me?"

She smiled and walked to the window with her right fist hitting her left palm.

"If you did not kill the lady, why did you abscond?"

"I told you; I was framed. It was a setup. I am losing my temper. Don't let me do anything stupid. It was my boss who did it as he has a bad temper."

"You should not have run. What you should have done was to go to the police. Instead, you wanted to run from your obligations at home, you being a man with two wives and many mouths to feed."

"You know more about me than I thought you did. No one would believe me. You believed I did it and that's what everyone else would believe."

"At least the court would hear your case."

"Why did you not get someone else to do the job for you?"

She threw forward her right hand as if playing lawn tennis, then got to her feet and looked down at the floor.

"I picked on you because of your brain. You are very smart. Before you, there was a guy whom I thought would do the job, but he was so stupid even though he had the heart to do it. I tried him out the day before, but I noticed he was clumsy and would make mistakes. He was in a hurry. I wanted him to do it but he was bound to fail, so I got rid of him because he knew too much."

I listened attentively.

"So, you really meant all that you said?"

"Why wouldn't I when there is a huge amount of money involved? I am waiting for the one who can do it neatly and at the right time. I would surely get him out of this mess. It has been started already so it has to end. He thought he could maltreat me because we have no kids. And the money – the money he showers on his girlfriends. He killed my fiancé."

"You would never get away with it. It would be the biggest joke of the century, murderess!"

She laughed.

"He did not feel for me, so why should I feel for him? It's been a long time. I have waited for too long. The earlier the better. It is rather sad and a pity that I have to take a step like this."

"I cannot do it so please find someone else more suitable and callous like you to do it."

"Do not make me force you. If you refuse to, I will call the police."

"Go and bring them! Police my ass!" I said as I turned and showed her my ass.

Elsie stretched out her hand and reached for her racquet, got up and headed for the door. She held the knob with her left hand and turned the key with her right. Before she turned the key to unlock the door, Elsie turned and looked at me.

"Hope you'll have the guts to tell them that. It's already late, so let's wait until tomorrow. Sweet dreams. You can sleep here tonight if you want to."

"Are you threatening me or what? You can't scare me."

She opened the door and stepped out.

"I am stopping working for you tomorrow," I said, not looking in her direction.

"You better not – wait till I give you the green light."

"Why not give it to me now?"

"Do not rush. Take your time."

She moved forward and closed the door. I waited for some seconds and then rushed out to call her.

She came back, burning with anger.

"What is it? Haven't we finished?" she burst out as she kicked the door to open it.

"Cool down, baby, or should I say, lady. Let's try to kidnap…"

I did not finish my sentence but began to laugh as I noticed the happy expression on her face.

"Kidnap who?"

"The daughter. After all, you don't have a kid for him. The daughter is all he hopes for. You know he is training her to take over the business? When he hears about that, it would give him a shock. He might collapse or something of that sort. I can arrange it. The ransom to be demanded would have to be great. Give part to the men who would do the job and share the rest."

"That means many people would be involved. I don't want that."

"There are professionals who can do it. Clean, without a trail to implicate us. So, think it over. If you decide to go ahead, let me know first thing in the morning so that I can make the arrangements."

Chapter Twenty-nine

I woke up early in the morning. Since I had cleaned all the cars the night before, I did not have much to do, just wipe off the dew that made the cars wet. Stirring my tea in the kitchen, I heard Elsie and Kate exchange greetings. Elsie entered the kitchen while I was sipping my hot tea. I paid no attention to her until she greeted me and I responded.

"I am still thinking about it," she said as she looked away.

I munched my bread with groundnut paste.

"When I make my final decision, I will let you know."

We did not talk to each other until I finished, cleaned my cup and made my way out. She had bent over, removing a plate with sausage. I touched her lightly on the buttocks and she jumped. I ran off to the boys' quarters.

I woke up before noon when the sun was high. Feeling thirsty, I hurried to the kitchen for some cold water. I noticed Elsie relaxing on a garden chair by the swimming pool, clad in a blue striped swimsuit and sipping some wine. On my return, she beckoned and I hurried down to where she was sitting.

"Aireen is coming tomorrow at night," she said, looking down at the water." I would like you to go to the airport to pick her up."

"Okay, madam," I said and turned to go.

"Where are you hurrying to? I have not finished. I want us to try the kidnap. Get someone competent to do it and let me know his fee," she said, still looking down at the water.

"Okay," I replied.

She turned to look at me and seemed disturbed.

"We are paying the ransom if everything goes well. You'll also get your freedom from me. You think I am keeping you against your wishes and I don't like that."

"Thank you very much," I said, bowing. "I will do as you wish, but don't even think about reporting me to the law enforcement authorities. If you do, I will also give you away. Most people believe you have a suspicious character; I have evidence."

"Do not spoil things. Erase that from your mind," she said and sipped from the wine glass. "Forget what I said last night. The way things are going, I am very worried. In case our plan does not go through, you may have to stay for a while, or maybe until I get someone to take your place."

"Can't the security men help? What about all the drivers?"

"Don't be so stupid and wicked. How do you expect anybody at all to enter our bedroom... sorry, the master's room? It is ridiculous."

Elsie was making her point, but let me put it this way – I had my own plans.

"As long as I remain under you, I will do as you say, but do not push me too far against the wall, for, if you do, I will push back,"

"That's nice of you," she said, smiling.

After she got to her feet, she removed the sunshade and placed it on the table by the glass, took a long sip then turned to me.

"The day you quit this job and walk out on me, leave everything you have come across behind and let sleeping dogs lie. Do not take a single word or memory away with you. Bury everything in the sand or throw it all into the water."

"Already, I am trying to forget but I just can't."

"You have to."

"Madam, I am going to the post office."

"Okay."

She turned and moved towards the pool. After she had entered the water by going down the ladder in the corner to my side, I left.

After I had finished with my work for the day, I went to the sitting room to meet Elsie. I knocked and she asked me to enter. I greeted her as soon as I stepped onto the carpet and she responded.

"I have finished for the day. Can I go?"

"You can go home, Jerry," she said, paying attention to the television.

"I don't think I will need you again till tomorrow. I have some video cassettes that I want to watch then return them to their owners."

I don't know when she started watching videos like this. Only God knows what she was up to. It was very unusual for her to allow me to leave so early.

Go early and make the arrangements for the job."

"If you think you'll need me, let me stay."

"Don't worry. I will be okay. That's nice of you. Try to come early tomorrow."

I noticed she wanted me to go so she could carry on with the viewing.

"Tomorrow, I have an appointment with the bankers and insurers. Good night."

"Night, Elsie. Take care."

I closed the door behind me and ran towards the main gate. Before I got to the gate, one of the security men had opened it, so I did not stop; I continued with my running.

It was very lucky for me to get a taxi before the main street. As I entered the taxi, I began to ponder over why she had allowed me to go home so early. Maybe she was expecting someone. If her kidnap plan failed, it would be very difficult for her to carry on with another plan with Aireen in the house. Moreover, my master would soon be travelling abroad for a check-up.

NEVER TRUST A STRANGER

I did not return home early even though I left my
working place before dark. By the time I got home,
everyone had gone to bed. On my way home, I changed
my mind and got out of the taxi. Then, I picked up
another and headed westwards from this direction. I
was going to my friend's house to discuss the plan after
we agreed we had about a carton of beer. This made it
impossible for me to wake up early. It was when I was
coming to the end of a nightmare that I heard some
knocking on my door. When I asked who it was, a voice
said "Dolly", so I managed to open the door and usher
her in.

We talked for about thirty minutes, but I don't
remember what happened afterwards. It was around
noon when I woke up feeling thirsty, hungry, and, to
top it all, tired. My drawer was not fully closed. I tried
to recall what had happened earlier. I reached for a
cigarette and lighter. I lit it and lay on my back with
the cigarette between the fingers of my right hand and
an old newspaper in my left.

I had not gone through all the pages of the
newspaper when Elsie came to my mind. As if
possessed, I dropped the newspaper and flicked the

quarter-inch ash onto the carpet. I began to stare up at the ceiling, pondering over the sentence Elsie had said about someone at the window the last and only time she had been here. Why and how did she feel that there was someone at the window? Of all the rooms in the compound, why only mine? I had noticed she looked disturbed when she was leaving.

"Wait a minute," I said and jumped to my feet. The perfume – it was the same scent when she said someone was at the window and when she had met him at the boys' quarters.

I managed to bathe before cleaning the room and left for work, bearing in mind what the consequences would be for being late.

Chapter Thirty

The time for the arrival of the plane was 9 pm but I was in the arrivals hall thirty minutes earlier in case the plane arrived earlier than scheduled. At ten minutes to nine, a female announcer's voice was heard from the public address system announcing the delay of the Nigeria Airways flight from London. It would arrive at 9.45 pm. After the voice had died down, I did not wait a second. Angrily, I hurried to one of the bars in the hall, climbed onto a stool and ordered two bottles of beer. I asked for any brand at all – I just wanted a beer and that was all. The delay of the flight would not tamper with the kidnapping plan at all as they knew the number, colour and make of the car.

At exactly 9.45 pm, the arrival of the flight was announced. I rushed, leaving the rest of the beer on the counter. Everything had been paid for already. From the bar to the entrance, after going through Immigration and Customs and the health checkpoints, was about fifty metres. Before I got there, law enforcement agents were trying to control the rowdy crowd, including relatives, touts and drivers.

With her photograph in my hand and a vivid description of her and the clothes she was wearing, there was no way I would miss her. Forcing my way through, I got to the aluminium barrier the authorities had built about twenty-five metres from the door. Every minute, I studied the photograph but paid close attention to the entrance until the passengers started pouring out.

I would have missed her if not for the description of me sent to her by someone she refused to name. Before the passengers started to emerge, two more flights were announced belonging to Nigerian Airlines and that made the place even rowdier than before. The touts and the airport taxi drivers made a lot of noise, some hurling abuse at others for snatching their customers. Some even went to the extent of throwing punches. The police intervened and at once brought sanity into the hall. My eyes were averted and my mind was set on two drivers having a heated argument over a passenger when someone touched me on my left shoulder. Instantly, I turned and looked at her then glanced once more at the photograph. It was her.

"Aireen?"

"Yes," she replied. "You Jerry?"

"Yes; welcome."

"Thank you."

She was a buxom lady in her late twenties, like Elsie, clad in a pink and white silk two-piece suit, a pair of white shoes and matching handbag. Her thick eyelashes were coated in mascara and she had rosy cheeks. She was very attractive; almost irresistible. As soon as I set eyes on her, I needed no one to tell me more about her.

"How are Dad and Elsie, not forgetting the household staff?"

"Dad's doing fine," I replied, forcing a grin. "Everyone else is also fine. Dad is looking forward to seeing you."

We moved to the main entrance of the hall that leads to the street with the porters following closely. She stopped by an empty public enquiry counter.

"You were telling me about Dad," she said anxiously.

"It is rather unfortunate that your father will not be able to see you, not even to touch you as it would be very difficult for him."

By the time I said my last word, her face had changed.

"What do you mean by that?"

I realised the grave mistake I had made by telling her. It had been kept away from her. But I kept looking at her face.

"Why are you looking at me like that?"

"Nothing. I'm sorry. Let me get your luggage."

"We can't carry everything. Let them carry it." The two porters standing nearby pushed the two trolleys before us.

"I have some things that will arrive at a later date."

Outside, I hurried and opened the boot for the porters to put in the luggage. Then, I hurried and opened the back door, the one on the right, for her, but she refused and entered the one on my side. Without closing the door after her, I went to supervise the porters. After they had finished, I dipped my hand in my back pocket and dished out a twenty note, at which they protested. I refused to give them more and they left frowning.

We did not say a word to each other until we had passed the first police checkpoint on the airport road. It was only the kidnap plan that was ringing in my mind because, as I closed the boot of the car, I noticed my friend, whom I had talked to about the kidnapping, dashing across the street towards the parking space.

"What is wrong?" she enquired as we approached the first filling station on the road.

"Nothing," I replied without turning my head. I then forced a yawn.

"I see you are feeling sleepy," she said as I yawned.

From the left driving mirror on my side, I noticed a car tailing us with two occupants in it. As we went up the bridge at speed, they overtook us and blocked our car. I pressed the brakes and screeched to a halt. I nearly hit the rear of their car. As soon as I came to a halt, two men came out, one with a pistol and the other with a knife. The young man from the driver's seat went straight for the tyres whilst the passenger went for Aireen. All four tyres went down one after the other. Aireen and the man who came for her occupied the back seat while the driver sat alone. They reversed and fled under the bridge.

I shouted at the top of my voice but no one came to my aid. Since life was more important than the car with the luggage, I began to lock up. When I opened the door at the rear, a Volvo car came by. I waved but they did not stop. A solo taxi approached but it was full and the windows were all wound up. After locking up, I ran down towards the filling station as fast as my legs could carry me. Before I got to the bridge, I met a mobile police unit in a Land Rover. I waved and they stopped.

After making my complaint, the officer radioed to the police station. Since all four of the tyres had been deflated, two of the policemen helped me to move the luggage into their vehicle and they drove me to the station. At the station, I made my statement and I was allowed to phone home. It was picked up by Elsie.

"Hello, this is Jerry," I said with an unsteady voice.

"What is it?" she shouted. "Where are you speaking from?"

"Airport police station. Aireen…"

"What about Aireen?"

"She has been kidnapped."

As I finished saying the last word, she dropped the receiver and screamed.

I called three consecutive times but she did not answer, so I replaced the receiver.

After giving a description of the two men, I was taken home in a police Land Rover.

Chapter Thirty-one

At 7 am the following day, the national radio station announced the kidnapping of Aireen Oglow, the heiress to the chairman of the Highends Group of Companies. After the announcement, telephone calls start pouring in from near and far. Relations, friends and business associates started trooping in to sympathise with the family.

On the second day, nothing was heard, just announcements on the radio and television. All the newspapers carried her photograph. On the third day, it was the same.

I was sent on an errand on the fourth day in the morning but was soon back in the house. On almost every street I drove along, I saw her photograph on buildings, walls, trees and billboards.

As I reached for the handle of the door, it opened and Elsie was standing there, hands on hips and burning with anger. She was dressed in a red kaftan with matching headband. She wore no makeup and was barefoot.

"Good day, madam."

There was no reply from her.

She flung out her right hand to slap me but I moved backwards to dodge it. She nearly fell but was able to remain standing on her feet.

"So, you have been transporting girls with my cars, eh? Haven't you?" she wanted to know from me.

I didn't say a word. I just stood with my hands by my side and at a distance away from her reach.

"You even gave out your master's complimentary card with the excuse that you had run out of yours. The Head of the Accounts Section of Highends (WA) Ltd. Head of Accounts Section indeed!

"Whilst you were out, she called to find out if you really live here and if you are what you claim to be in the company. She comes from your place so do not pretend as if you do not know what I am talking about."

Because of the sympathisers in the hall, I just bowed my head in shame without saying a word.

"Don't bow your head," she said as she tried to reach for my head. "Be proud of your head and stop telling people you are this and that which you are not. This is your first and final warning!"

She turned, hissing, and closed the door on me.

It had been three weeks since Aireen's abduction and there had been no call from the kidnappers or the law enforcement agents. However, day in and day out, telephone calls and people came and went. The telephone calls became so unbearable that she sometimes refused to answer them. She even refused to open the mail and gave it to the secretary. She kept a record of those who had telephoned, those who called in person and those who had sent mail.

Elsie complained of having nightmares and went to see the doctor. Some people accused her of having masterminded the whole incident. She was accused of being lazy and wicked for not going to the airport herself.

Another time, she complained of having sleepless nights, refused to eat and cried when she saw her friends. I knew she was only pretending.

Aireen's photograph continued to appear in newspapers, on televisions, walls and trees. The Friends' Committee was set up. They produced car stickers and established little groups throughout the country to search for her.

On the Sunday of the second week, there was a phone call just as the sun was going down. The caller said he had seen the mutilated nude body of a lady at the beach bar. It had no head. Elsie broke down and cried like a baby when she heard the news. We rushed to the beach bar. Elsie cried the whole way. It was not difficult to locate the body because many people had already gathered there. The body was not fat and did not look healthy. Even if Aireen had been on hunger strike to protest her abduction, her body would not look like the one on the shore.

After the scene at the beach, we did not see Dr Parkings for the second day. In the evening, it was raining heavily and most of the well-wishers who came had left. Elsie was in the guest room cum master's bedroom when the phone rang. She rushed out to pick up the phone, spilling some coffee on the rug.

"Hello? Hello?!"

"This is Dr Parkings' secretary. My boss received a call this morning. When he picked up the receiver, his face changed. I saw him write 100,000 on a message slip, and after the call, he tore it out and put it in his pocket, went for his briefcase and left. Later in the afternoon, around four, he returned with a huge amount of money which I helped him count. It amounted to the same number that he wrote on the slip. After I had packed the whole amount into a milk carton, he asked me to put it in the boot of his car, which I did. I was locking the boot when he came out, got the key and said he would be back at 6 pm. But up till now, he has not returned. If he goes out and stays out beyond the time he gave for his return, Dr phones the house. Hold on; the other phone is ringing."

Five minutes later, she was back on the phone.

"The police have just phoned. Dr has been found unconscious and with a battered head. His left eye is almost swollen shut. His right leg is bruised at the knee and he has a swollen lip, but worst of all is a big cut under his right ear. The message said he must have lost a lot of blood."

Maybe he had received a call from the kidnappers to come and pay the ransom. He had refused to mention it to anybody, went for the money and took it to them. If he had told the police or anybody, it would have helped. Who knows, they might have warned him not to call the police or bring anybody with him. After he gave them the money, they produced Aireen and this sparked off a brawl. He wanted names but all he got was pain. Some crooks might have done it. Maybe they had seen the doctor's telephone number accompanying Aireen's photographs everywhere. We went to see Dr Parkings at the hospital where he was being given drips and blood transfusions. I doubted if he would recover.

The following night, at midnight, the telephone rang. Elsie told us it was Aireen's voice. I did not believe her, but when I picked it up, it was her.

"Please, please…" she began to sob.

My eyes were filled with tears as I had arranged it all. I wondered at the expression on Elsie's face. She was now Dr Jekyll and Mr Hyde. A sonorous voice came on the phone. I knew who it was but I did not say a word. Our telephones had been tapped by the police.

The agony people were going through because of me! Of late, I had added more pains to those of my master.

"We are for the trodden masses," the voice said. "We have been cheated for far too long. This is our chance. Our homework has been done well and very carefully. We have been pushed for far too long and we hate it. We are now pushing back. By the way, our ransom is ☐ 500,000 and we want it in cash."

"Do you mean half a million?!" Elsie exclaimed.

"Yes; don't you have it? Or do you mean it's just chicken feed to you? It is to be delivered to the old cemetery at King Close. There is a thick bush around a tall black terrazzo cross just by the gate. No police, but only you. It must be there before 6 am."

"Where do you want me to get the money from at this time?" Elsie asked.

"If you value her life, you will get it."

Aireen screamed.

"Okay, make it 6 pm the following day," the voice said. "No tricks, no police and it must be 6 pm. If by six you are not here, collect her body at seven. She will be lifeless."

He banged the receiver down and we did likewise. I rushed downstairs to see what her face looked like. When I got there, she was holding a discussion with two plain-clothes police officers by the main door. After the discussion, the taped version of the telephone call was played back for everyone to hear.

Chapter Thirty-two

Early in the morning, on the way to the gate to see off my master's cousin Eric, Elsie's friend, they met Arch. Williams. Neither said a word or smiled. Elsie's friend, who knew the archbishop, said hello and then they passed each other.

Elsie had been to the hospital only once to see Dr Parkings since the incident. That did not disturb her; only the money disturbed her. She even thought I knew something about it but I warned her if she wanted everything to come out of the bag, she should do whatever she liked. By all means, Arch. Williams would ask about the husband and Dr Parkings because he had been out of the country when Doctor Parkings' case took place. Most of her husband's friends had not given their blessing to the marriage.

On her return, Arch. Williams was having a word with me. As soon as I saw her, I left.

"What is wrong with him?" he asked as she drew nearer, his small cat-like eyes staring at her.

"Nothing. He is just sick about Aireen. He wants her and has a feeling that something has gone wrong."

"He looks very pale. When is he going abroad? I think this time you are accompanying him?"

"Next week, but if things get worse, it has to be earlier than next week."

"I am going. There is something more to this than meets the eye."

He hurried out of the hall. I took the cigar that he had left behind on the sideboard. Doubling my steps, I reached the car before he released the brakes to move. I tapped on the boot. He looked in the driving mirror, saw me and wound the window down. When I put the cigar in his hand, I was about to go when he asked me to wait.

"You have been in this house for some years?"

"That's right."

"Tell me something – I want the truth. Do you have any complaints about her behaviour?"

"Yes," I replied, scratching the back of my head. "I am happy with the way she comports herself, but most of the time, her attitude leaves much to be desired. Some days, she'll go out, leaving him in the hands of relatives, friends, the cook or anybody at all, especially at night. I feel very sorry for his predicament."

Elsie was standing at the door watching us. After he had left, I went to Elsie to obtain permission to go out. She granted it without any hesitation.

I was waiting at the junction near the bus stop by the shopping centre at a quarter past eleven when I saw Sussie, one of my old birds. She went on a transfer upcountry. We exchanged a few letters and that was all I had ever heard or seen of her until that moment.

"Hi, Jerry," she said, smiling.

I took a step back.

"Whoa! Is that you still around in town?"

"No, I am back on an official assignment."

Her outfit was superb; a white jacket and pink V-neck top over white trousers with bow pockets.

"Where to?" she asked.

"Home; would you mind coming along?"

"Why not, if you invite me?"

"Okay, I wouldn't mind but you won't leave until tomorrow."

"Jerry, you've not changed!"

"It was only a joke!"

"I missed you. Let's pick a taxi and go, dear. That settles it; if you did miss me, I also missed you, so let's go and have some fun. We'll go to the beach bar and then later to the amusement park."

"Alright. I like that."

I hailed a taxi. It stopped just in front of us. After renewing our friendship, we had a happy reunion and had some real fun when talking became unbearable.

Afterwards, as we lay silently, wrapped in each other's arms, Sussie told me how she had missed me, how she had been willing to meet me but did not know where to find me.

We left for the amusement park after we had some fun at the beach. Sussie and I behaved like kids watching the tourists then went on to the arts and crafts site.

At the beach, she asked me about the wave of crime in town and told me about some of the robberies I had heard about or come across. The kidnapping of Aireen shocked her most of all. Sussie agreed with me that our lives were not safe in the city.

The conversation between us was more casual and friendly than on the first day we met. She had changed entirely. Was it because we had been by ourselves for a long time? As we sat under one of the sheds we had paid to use, time took us unaware. It had gone faster than we had expected. Without wasting any more time, we hurried down the street and got a taxi to the amusement park. After we had paid at the gate to get in, our first port of call was the ghost train. The building which held the railway was very dark, and, as you rode on the train, all of a sudden, a ghost would spring up from nowhere, scaring the life out of you. I vowed never to set foot in the ghost train building again. People call it fun but it can kill you!

From there, we rode on the artificial horses and the Ferris wheel, which let you see over five hundred metres when you are up high. This one, though, was no joke!

Our next port of call was the casino and the shooting range with targets that hardly anyone could hit. In between these, we had some snacks and cooled off with some cold drinks. To me, it was a day of stepping out of boring times and having a reunion. I have had a lot of fun days, but this one at the amusement park was one with a difference. It was just the two of us, talking and cracking jokes.

I nearly spoilt the fun when I missed my step when climbing onto the carousel. Sussie screamed at the top of her voice and everybody turned to look at us.

At around six, we went to a restaurant forty metres from the fun park after it had closed for the day. The atmosphere was exquisite and we talked a lot over the food and wine. The food, which was mouth-watering, comprised potato salad as a starter and the main dish was fried rice with roasted chicken with curried sauce. Jam tart was the dessert served with strawberry ice cream and topped with cashew nuts, all washed down with white Concorde. Mind you, not all the bill was paid by me. She shouldered part; after all, we had both enjoyed it.

She tried to recall the exact date and where we had met for the first time. I am not good with figures so I could not help, but I remembered meeting her at the National Theatre in the company of some girls and a male friend. The theatre's hall was jam-packed. She stood on my right-hand side, stretching her neck like a giraffe, so I offered her part of my chair. She refused but her friends persuaded her to go and have a seat and not to reject the kind offer from the handsome guy. She was dressed simply but was rich in beauty and smiled all the time. When I set eyes on her, it was like a dream come true.

Sussie was not aware that I was in love with her. From that day, we started seeing each other. It was one evening when I went to her place. While sitting on the wall of their terrace, we found out what we meant to each other. It had rained the previous day and the weather still brokered a chill. We sat on the wall a metre away from each other. A cold chill ran down my spine and I grabbed her. She looked into my eyes and I did the same. Without a word, we found ourselves kissing and caressing.

I was in love with her the first time my flesh touched her but I just didn't know how she would react. We stared at each other in silence.

She got down from the wall and I did the same. My mind was set – if she refused my approach, it would mean an end to seeing each other. Moving towards her,

I reached for her waist and pulled her from behind. When I kissed her lips for the second time, Sussie responded.

"Will you be mine?" I asked her.

"Yes; why not?" Sussie replied and she put her hands on my shoulders. "I have been waiting for you to say you love me. Jerry, I would have asked you to be mine but you would have thought of me as a spoilt and cheap girl."

We raised our glasses and drank from each other's glasses.

"Jerry, why...?" She paused

"I am listening," I said, looking into the food.

"I just don't understand why you are doing this kind of job; a driver's job. Can't you get a more decent and respectable job? One with more pay? Formerly, you were a waiter, now a driver. God knows what you will be next. I love you, but you know that with this kind of job it would be difficult seeing each other, so think about it. If you decide to change it, let me know. I will see if I can do anything about it."

"What you are saying is true, but you don't understand me," I said then took my glass to drink some water.

"Continue; I am listening," said Sussie.

"Do you care about me?"

"Yes. Why do you ask?"

"You say you cared about me for all the time that you've been away. Today, you are sitting before me and saying you love me and care for me. I don't think you are serious." I laughed

"I have a roof over my head and a job; at least I am satisfied with what I earn. With the little I earn, I can take care of myself."

"I know you can but it is your future I am thinking about. It is not a decent job you are doing. No one has respect for you when doing that kind of work. Everyone pushes you around. Are you not qualified to work in the offices of an oil company, multi-national firm, insurance company or in a financial institution?"

"Sussie, you know I am a foreigner residing here illegally, without a passport or resident's permit. I would also like to stop the work."

"That's good; let's drink to it."

"Don't misunderstand me. I am not resigning to find another job to stay here. After I resign, I will be leaving for home."

"Why? Don't go!"

"Because I don't belong in this place. I have to plan my future. Here, I don't have a future. My people want me at home. I don't fit in here."

She sat for some minutes, staring at me with her hands folded. I also said nothing but she finally broke the silence.

"Oh, Jerry, you are spoiling the fun. I have missed you and I knew very well for all the time we were apart that one day, we would meet and come together as before. It wasn't my fault – my work took me away from you, so forgive me. Now that I have found you, Jerry, you say that you are leaving. Erase that from your mind!"

"I did not say a word."

"Man proposes but God disposes. If it is the will of God, we will be together as one. Everything will be alright. Promise you won't go."

I smiled and looked at her.

"No, Sussie, I must go. I have already made up my mind."

"So, you won't change it? Jerry, you have not changed a bit. Still hard and strong-hearted."

"You said a few minutes ago that I had to do something decent; I should plan my future. That's what I am going home to do. Baby, allow me to go in peace."

"Jerry, don't go. I can get you a job right here."

"What work could I qualify for when my certificates are not here? Moreover, I am a squatter."

"Before I met you, I was working with a lady whose uncle is a director in a big multinational company. He can fix you up. I am sure he will be able to connect you. I have the right connections so do not fear."

"Okay. Give me time to think it over. I would not be able to see you very often as you are aware of the trouble in the house. So please, bear with me. Never try to come near my workplace."

"Don't worry, I will try not to do anything that stupid."

"I have been longing to work in one of the places you mentioned but I am handicapped."

"Jerry, it's going to be alright. Leave everything to me. I will take care of it."

"Don't you think you are being selfish? You have your family here; mine is far away and they want to see me, but you don't want me to go. Try to understand. As soon as everything is over, I will resign and leave."

Angrily, she got to her feet and took her bag.

"If that's the way you want it, fair enough. It did not occur to me that this is the way it would end. You can go to hell. Who do you think you are?"

"Sussie, mind your language," I warned her as I noticed many of the customers looking at us. Her voice had risen with every word.

She stopped and we stared at each other. I looked around. The eyes of others were still looking at us. I cautioned myself not to say a word. We left the restaurant without talking to each other. This had never happened to us. I did not blame her but for the first time, we behaved like strangers as we sat in the back of the taxi heading back to my place.

After having my bath, I changed into white cotton trousers, a blue shirt and a white jacket of the same material, and a pair of white shoes. I sprayed my armpits and the back of my ears with the perfume called Men Only.

After standing by the roadside for about twenty minutes, we got a battered Datsun taxi.

Our behaving like strangers had ceased on my bed. We talked about politics, music and the drought problem in some parts of Africa. The driver and his friend beside him contributed to topics they were interested in. At their house, I waited on the terrace whilst she went in to change. Sussie's younger sister brought me a bottle of chilled Coke. She spent about thirty minutes inside before coming out. She was dressed gorgeously and was very colourful. With bare shoulders, she wore a well-fitted strapless multicoloured bodice and a white skirt, with a white shawl draped over her right shoulder. Her makeup was excellent; it was like the work of an expert. However, I did not like the retouching of her hair. The perfume was strong – Christian Dior, she told me.

We went to Lords' nightclub to celebrate our reunion. We danced and drank till the early hours of the morning.

The next day, I saw her off early so that I could report for work early although I looked tired and my eyes were heavy with sleep.

Chapter Thirty-three

Since the first day I had been to see Dr
Parkings at the hospital, I had not been back. It was not
my fault – the doctor in charge only allowed a select
few in to see him and I was excluded. He had made no
progress and I was worried, more so when I knew I had
a hand in him being in the hospital.

My master liked fresh vegetables so, every week,
we took delivery of some in the morning. I was helping
the supplier to take some of them to the kitchen when
Elsie emerged from the back of the main building.
Pretending as if I had not seen her, she passed on
without a greeting or asking me any questions. She
went straight to my master's room, then checked in
the other room and went to the hall. For over thirty
minutes, she was in the hall talking with some people.
One of the visitors asked me to prepare a black coffee
with no sugar for him. I had rinsed the teacup, put
in a heaped teaspoonful of coffee and was stretching

out my hand to reach for the electric kettle when she came in. She crept in like a cat so my heart jumped and I missed the handle of the kettle and my fingers touched its body. Ignoring her presence, I turned on the tap and ran water over my fingers. After the pain had died down, I mopped my hand with the multicoloured napkin I took from my shoulder.

While I did all this, she stood in the doorway, her hands pressed to either side of the frame.

"So, you can't greet me because you are now older than me and the boss of this house. I want to talk to you as there are only a few visitors around. The other members of the household are not yet in. Also, I want you to do some work outside for me. The gardener is not coming for a week and I want the work done today. I want you to cut the hedges close to the swimming pool so that sunlight will shine directly onto the pool and give me a good aerial view of the water."

I took the coffee to the owner, then, straight from the hall, I went to the garage to pick up the hedge-trimmer, then went to meet her in the kitchen. She took the lead and I followed. When we got to the place, she pointed at the spot and I began to do the work.

"Hold on, why did you refuse to report here last night?" she asked.

I did not answer but she stood there frowning and my head turned towards the water.

"The seamstress phoned complaining that she had finished my dress last week. Last week, I sent you there. You came back late and told me the apprentice said she had not finished it; moreover, she was not in."

"That was what I was told."

"Shut up, you liar. I will give you one across the face if you don't behave yourself. You left without telling me you would not return, or you just decided to stay out when you met that Sussie."

I paid no attention to her.

"Do not shout at me. If you like, you can pay me off. You had better stop spying on me. We are lovers no more and I am aware of all your plans so you better watch out before they turn against you. Your beauty is nothing to me anymore. You think I would fall for you because of your beauty once more? Your tricks are nothing new to me. Whether I come back or not is none of your business. Did I not obtain permission from you? Don't ever think you can push me around."

I turned and continued with the work.

She stood there burning with anger but she had to control herself otherwise we would have washed our dirty linen in public with Rebecca in the house. It would have been disastrous and she knew it.

"Do not double-cross me or else you will regret it!"

"How much were you given when you refused to return?"

"Given for what?" I forced a grimace. "You are kidding."

"How did those guys come about that information?"

"Who are these guys you are talking about? Be serious and stop beating about the bush. I know you have something in mind."

I am talking about Dr Parkings' case. He was swerved and you know something about it."

"What has it got to do with me? Please, take this trouble away from me."

"What has it got to do with you? That's what you are asking me? Where did you get the money to go to the beach, the amusement park, eat at the restaurant and then conclude it with dancing at that expensive club?"

"Elsie, I put it to you that you were spying on me," I shouted angrily. "Is it your business? What I do outside of your working hours is my private affair so leave me alone."

"As soon as I heard of it, I knew you had a hand in it."

"You are a liar. The spies you set on me; do you trust them when you don't trust yourself? They would ditch you, crazy fool!"

She did not say a word.

"Since he is not making any progress…. I think she has a feeling that something has happened. You know he is very sensitive to things. If he continues like this, we'll have to travel earlier than expected. I have ordered the travel agent to book some seats for us. On the day that we leave, you will take your master and Rebecca in the Mercedes. I will drive the SO4 estate with the luggage."

I did not say anything or react because I knew of her plans. Afterwards, I began to sweat. This was in the SO4 estate.

We were the three people she wanted out of her way.

Last night, the kidnappers dropped off a note and a dress soaked with blood to warn us that they were aware of us informing the police and to let us know that they were serious. When the police traced the telephone number, it led to a brothel outside the city.

Before morning, one of the security men picked up a note warning us that if we cared about Aireen, we should do as they say otherwise there would be more bloodshed. We were not sure where these notes came from. The police were following every member of the household now, so I could not go there. They might dupe us.

"Are you sure they are the right people?" she asked me, shivering from the morning dive she took in the pool. She used her fingers to wipe the water from her forehead to her chin.

"We have to be very careful."

"This morning the money will be brought in. I am taking it, alone, later in the evening."

She turned and hurried to the back door.

Chapter Thirty-four

It did not take me long to cut the hedges, gather the clippings and dump them at the black spot where the gardener burns his debris.

After I had finished, my next job was to wash and clean all the cars in the compound. Soon, I had finished all the cars and I left for the post office.

The pressmen who had gathered at the gate tried to force some stuff out of me but I turned every question down. I utterly refused to talk to any of them so as not to commit myself. After all, they can ask the trickiest of questions.

While washing the cars, I noticed a blue Volkswagen pass three times but it did not occur to me that they were from Special Branch. As I was about to drive out of the gate, it passed once more. I then pulled over to the side of the street to see what was going on. The Beetle entered a close one hundred metres away. I was in the car for about thirty minutes, pretending that the car had refused to respect my orders to move. Then, I got out and went to the bonnet. Still watching them, for about an hour nothing happened, so I went to the car, fired it up and it did work. With my foot on the accelerator, I pressed it down for about three minutes so that anybody could hear it and then put the car in motion after they did not show up.

I was already on the main street when I saw them coming with two cars between us. They wanted to find out where I was heading. Not to give them the idea that I had seen them, I turned off somewhere else instead of the first turning on my right.

In less than thirty minutes, I was at the post office, after I had stopped off at a filling station to buy some fuel and engine oil. I did not even bother to look out for them anymore. As I drove out of the filling station, they were nowhere in sight. To my surprise, I caught a glimpse of their car at the post office. There were two male journalists in a green Mazda with the name of their newspaper inscribed on the two front doors. This time, I refused to speak to them.

Going back home, I pondered over what Sussie had talked to me about. Both in love with each other, she had promised to help me find a decent job with a fat salary. Sussie even wanted to marry me. If she finally did marry me, I would be a slave to her and her orders.

If things went in my favour and I left Elsie's house, she could harm me. I knew I needed money, but I could not kill for it. No way!

She had made up her mind to kill the three of us. I would have to kill her before she did anything foolish. To do it, I would have to get some slow-acting poison and she would have to take it before she left for the airport. By the time she got there, Elsie would be down and out.

What about if the post mortem showed that she died of food poisoning? Those of us in the house would be held as suspects.

No matter who she got to tamper with the brakes, I would be on hand to refix them. Later on, I would instruct the kidnappers to release the lady but I would have to be very careful so as to outwit the men from Special Branch.

At a quarter to six, Elsie left home alone with the large sum of money, leaving the orders that no one should follow her, which the men from Special Branch had protested against. She refused to listen to their warnings and advice. I knew the men working on the kidnapping case would follow and I was worried they would find out we were involved. The men behaved like amateurs and not like professionals. Every move they made was faulty and suspicious. Her reason for not allowing anyone to follow her was that they could kill the two of them or maim them when they found out that the police had got wind of it. It would fetch them long sentences, but they did not fear that. She made us understand that money was nothing but life was priceless and so she had to take the greatest precautions not to endanger Aireen's life.

Ten minutes after she left, the Special Branch men also left but before seven-thirty, they had returned complaining of the traffic hold-ups which had made them lose her.

We were all outside at eight keeping watch for their arrival. At 8.14, a blaring horn was heard outside the gate as if someone out of their mind was pressing it. Both security men rushed to open it. She drove in as if she was being chased by armed robbers.

When she brought the car to a stop, she put her head on the steering wheel. As soon as she did that, I knew there was trouble. We expected her to get out of the car but she did not. One by one, we began to move towards the car. Then, she opened the door and placed one foot on the ground keeping the other one in the car. She held the top of the door with both hands. I rushed towards her shouting,

"What went wrong, madam?"

The security men and the others, on hearing my voice, all rushed to the car. We all gathered to listen to the sad news.

She did not answer immediately but stood there staring at us like a fool, or someone who was hypnotised.

Madam, what is wrong?" the man from Special Branch enquired. "Why that look? Come on, tell us something, please, before it is too late," said one man.

Another said, "We are worried. Please tell us something."

Still no answer — then she took a deep breath and spoke.

"I am very sorry," she said in a husky voice.

"What for?" I asked.

"They took the money but did not release her. I did not even see or hear from her; they just chased me away."

"Why did they refuse to release her after they had taken the money?" I asked inquisitively. "No one dares touch her except yourself. I think you are aware of who you were talking to."

Instead of answering, she rushed over and grabbed my collar and pulled me towards her.

"Shut up!" she shouted when I opened my mouth to speak. She then pushed me back. I would have fallen on my back if it hadn't been for one of the visitors who held me.

"You better mind your language next time."

"Yes, madam," I answered as I pulled myself together and straightened my shirt.

"Forgive me; I am only trying to contribute."

I glance at my wristwatch and it read ten minutes past nine.

"By this time, I should be on my way home or already at home," I said, pointing to my wrist. "If you think I cannot contribute, let me go home and rest so that I can stop wasting my precious time here."

Everyone stared at me in disbelief.

She had lost the five hundred thousand to the kidnappers.

Chapter Thirty-five

From Elsie's house, I went to Sussie's place. I discovered she was not there but her parents asked me to wait if I could which I did without any hesitation. I settled in the cane armchair on the terrace for some cool fresh air.

She came onto the terrace without my being aware of her approaching. Sussie had been told of my presence in the house so she had removed her pink high-heeled shoes stealthily so that the noise would not give her away since my back was turned to the gate.

When she tapped me on my right shoulder, I jumped to my feet like a spring, not because I was scared of anyone in the house, but because my life was in danger. Somebody wanted me dead. I embraced her and kissed her on both cheeks. After all, it was not by sheer coincidence that we had come together once more, but God wanted it that way.

"Let's stroll down the street and talk," I said, holding her by the elbow.

She moved to follow my request.

"Hold on; I think it would be respectful to your parents to see you first."

"Okay. As you say. Your wish is my command."

She darted into the corridor. When she went in, I moved sluggishly, my hand behind me, towards the gate. About twenty metres from the gate, I heard the door of the building open and her footsteps running. I knew it was her but I kept going. Then she jumped on my back. We would have fallen down but since I was almost at the gate, I reached for it and it saved a situation that would have been painful. After going through the gate, she came down smiling.

"I went to your house but your landlady told me you had not returned. If I could wait, I would have been welcome. Please say thanks to her for her grand hospitality towards me."

She held my left hand, dragged me after her down the street and stopped at the junction, panting. She settled on a broken-down pillar.

"Sussie, I want us to correct some parts of the discussion we had yesterday."

She stood up.

"I thought it was all over and that chapter was closed."

"Sit down, my friend," I said as I pulled her down beside me. "I have not been able to erase what you told me yesterday. Did you really mean it?"

"Yes, I really meant every word I said."

"What about a passport?"

"That's chicken feed. Trust me."

"And the job?"

"You can rely on me."

"Now, everything is in your hands. I hate being disappointed. If you don't want to strain our relationship, stand by your words. I hate to trust women but you are special."

"Put your last kobo on me. I will do everything in time. Even this morning, I talked to my friend about it. She said it was no problem. After you've got the job and everything else, I will arrange for transport back to the city. It will be just the two of us."

She jumped up.

"I want to be with you, Sussie," I said. "Oh, Sussie, you are all I want in this world. Your charm and love have come over me once more."

She stared at me.

"What has come over you? Something must have happened. Why have you changed so from the other Jerry?"

"It's your charm. It is working. I have thought of it over and over again. I concluded that it would be good to give your proposal a chance."

"Yesterday, I thought it was all over. You were sure and determined to go home, but just today, you have changed."

"Yes, I have changed my mind. I don't want to hurt you. If you are happy, I am also happy. Be mine. You are mine."

"Jerry, you are also mine."

"Yesterday, Sussie, you put a proposal before me. You should have allowed me to think it over. Things done in a hurry are never successful," I said, staring downwards.

"No, Jerry, something has happened and it has made you change. Today, you are sober. Yesterday, you refused

412

to see reason and give constructive suggestions about my opinion."

"You are right, something has happened but it is not because of you. And it is not because of it that I have changed my mind."

"What happened?" she asked anxiously.

"That bitch, whore…my madam carried ₦500,000 to the so-called kidnapper just like that. She calls the money chicken feed. She did not bring Aireen back. It was because of her that you did not meet me at home. I am very sorry for that. When she returned, my madam called me names and I walked out of the house. When I asked her about the whereabouts of Aireen, what you said yesterday was true."

"Do not let any lady stand in our way. I am serious."

"I know you are."

"Tell me you love me."

"I do," I said as I reached for her lips.

"Today, you've made me so happy; the happiest moment in my life. You are about to change my life – let it be so. Stay with me and everything will be alright. Lean on me and I will do the same. Bring your troubles to me and I will solve them. There is nothing to worry about. I cannot afford to lose you. Promise you will never turn your back on me in the future."

"No, I would never do that. Never." I then kissed her on her forehead and stood up.

"Darling, it's late now and I have to go. I hate to leave but I must go."

"My parents are going out to a state function so I have to take care of the baby. You will never regret staying with me. So long as you don't turn your back on me, everything will be okay."

Arm in arm, we strolled back to their gate and I waved for a taxi.

As I sat in the taxi on the way home, I pondered over what had just happened between us. Had I made a mistake? I thought of my people at home. It was because of money and being a scapegoat that I had come here. At home by now, my woman would be under another man who would be digging her cunt. After all, we were not properly married either legally or customarily. She just moved in and that was all. If I left Elsie, it would mean that I would have to look for a new home so as not to face her wrath.

Chapter Thirty-Six

The next morning, I went to work late in my new stretch jeans and white sleeveless sweat top. From the gate, I went straight to the boys' quarters to change, which I did slowly. My coming to work late was intentional. I knew she had seen me from the hall or wherever she was. From the boys' quarters, I went to greet my master and then went to greet the people in the hall. When I got to her, she just nodded. I did not go to the garage to wash the cars but went to the lawn by the swimming pool and sat on a piece of a log by the hedge. I sat looking at the glistening water.

Thirty minutes later, I heard her voice calling from the backyard door. I turned when she called twice. There she stood in the doorway, clad in a blue dress with big red dots on it, a blue and white wide leather belt, white ribbons in her hair and a pair of blue shoes. She was carrying a blue bag with red and white dots.

"You will drop me at the lawyer's office and then go and meet my sister at her office. She'll give you a file; bring it to where you dropped me. It is very urgent so no delay." She had started giving her orders before I got to her.

"Do not take any detours. Go straight to where I am sending you."

Since not all the cars are kept in the garage, there are tarpaulins for the ones without shelter. The car we were using was one of those kept outside, so I just drew back the tarpaulin and I was ready for my madam. After checking the water, oil and brake fluid, I warmed it and put on the air conditioner. After some minutes, she came out and I drove to the front of the house. By the time I got round to open the door for her, she was already entering. Once she was in, I closed the door behind her. I settled in my seat behind the wheel, set the car in motion and off we went.

After dropping her off as she had ordered me, I left for her sister's place.

On my way, I branched off the route to the office to get to the key cutter's workshop. I had to make spare copies of both the key for the car she would be using and the garage. In the workshop, I asked the man in charge to make me copies of the two keys I gave him. He wanted to ask questions, so I told him that last night, I was so drunk that I lost both my car keys and the garage key. The next time I get that drunk, senseless, I would not have another spare so I needed another one cut. He asked me to pay for cutting the two keys and I accepted without bargaining. He then asked me to come back in the evening. That didn't go down well with me. If I wanted express, it was double the price. I frowned and grumbled till we finally settled on half the price.

Less than twenty minutes later, I was given the duplicate keys. Satisfied with the work, I left for the sister's place.

When I got there, she told me that Elsie had just phoned to see if I had arrived and was on my way back to her. Back with Elsie, I would give her the usual excuse. She would frown at it but there was nothing she could do about it.

As I was driving out of the car park, I noticed a white Golf GTi convertible flashing its lights and sounding the horn at me as I entered the street. I looked in the driving mirror and saw the lights flashing, then I looked in the side mirror. I pulled to a stop and a gentleman in a pink and white striped towelling top and matching jacket came over to me. He was clean-shaven with a well-shaped moustache like someone who worked for Special Branch, and he wore dark glasses to hide his small eyes. He removed the glasses when he got closer to me.

After greeting me, he said, "Sorry to disturb you". He spoke in an accent that was not Nigerian. "I missed the turning my friend told me about. I am going to the boat club and I was supposed to be there by three but it is three already," he said as he glanced at his watch.

"Drive in that direction." I raised my hand to point the way. "The club is about four hundred metres from here. When you get to the intersection where the police are standing, go straight on and take the next turning on the right. The next turning on your left leads to the bridge, so go over it then keep in the right lane by the rail. Just keep in that lane until you notice you are driving downhill. When you finally join a street, turn right and you will see the sign on your right."

"Thank you very much. You have been very helpful."

"You are welcome," I said as I placed my elbow on the door.

All of a sudden, he grabbed my wrist and my heart sank.

"You a Ghanaian?"

"Half Ghanaian and half Nigerian," I said. "You made my heart sink. I work with a firm near the boat club but I am not going there. I have been sent to the mainland."

He let go of me.

"The girl in the car is my fiancée. I don't work here; we are on a sightseeing trip. Where are those people on the boat off to?"

"Where is the boat?" I asked since from where I was standing, I could not see the creek.

"Oh, I see; that boat over there."

"Yes, yes."

"They are going to Sugar Island, a nice and beautiful island for swimming and picnics."

"Can we go there too?"

"Yes, of course, but you told me a while ago that you were meeting a friend at the boat club."

"I don't mean now."

"You can even hire a boat at the club as a guest with the assistance of your friend, but it would cost you a lot. But if your friend would foot the bill, no problem."

He laughed.

"Money is no problem. I am fucking loaded. Would you travel with your chick without preparing? Do you want me to disgrace myself? Moreover, I am here to please her. Someone's competing with me over her. I must win."

"Oh yeah?"

"We have a suite by the ocean and will dine in the floating restaurant on the lagoon. You are not bad, man, I know she'll love it. I have already won the race. Man, she gives me good digs in bed. Thanks for everything."

"It's a pleasure."

"Don't be offended, but have you worked for a company in Accra?" He kept on smiling as he asked the question.

"Not me; I have never worked there before. I was born and bred here and did all my schooling here."

"Do you have a brother in Accra?"

"Yes, a half-brother."

"Then you are almost identical."

"I hear my brother is abroad."

"It must be him if not you."

The expression on my face changed. If it had not been for the wife blaring the horn that made him turn his face away, he would have noticed it.

"The guy was trained under a scholarship scheme run by the company. After benefitting from the scheme, one had to serve for five years or pay back the money if one decided not to serve the company. He showed how ungrateful he was by absconding to Nigeria with the Managing Director's car when they were on a sight-seeing trip at home. Because of his company behaviour and intelligence, and because he was bilingual, he was chosen to accompany the new Managing Director, who did not know what he had in mind."

"Let me go. I am now late. We'll see you some other time."

He followed me till we got to the intersection where I turned left and he went straight ahead. They waved and I waved back.

From the moment he held my wrist until he left me scared out of my life, I was not myself. I was shocked and puzzled by the questions he had asked. Elsie might be behind all these since she knew a lot more about me than I knew about her. If she dared give me up, I would do the same.

Chapter Thirty-seven

She was sitting on one of the cosy sofas at the reception waiting for me. When I stretched out my hand to give her the file, Elsie frowned and snatched it from me without a word. She entered the lift, and fifteen minutes later we were on our way home, but before going home, we went to see the officer in charge at the Central Police Station. Till we got to the house, we didn't laugh or talk to each other like before.

I was surely going to frustrate her plans to get rid of her hubby if she was going to let her agents bother me.

After dropping her, I went to the boys' quarters, removed my jacket, climbed on the writing desk on the veranda and lay on my back. I felt tired and my eyes were itching to sleep, but I could not sleep because of the gentleman I had seen. It disturbed me.

'It has been seven years now that I have rubbed shoulders with the citizens of this country, been in love with them; none of them has disturbed me. Then, from nowhere, you want to disturb me. Too bad; I am going to fight it to the last bit.'

Despite my troubled mind, I managed to get some sleep but not without nightmares. As soon as I woke up, he was back in my mind. Would he ever think of me and come my way again? I couldn't even recall his voice or what he told me. To me, it seemed like it had been a long time. My home company was one of international repute, so we had all kinds of people working for the company. They came and went, especially in the Accounts and Technical Section. He might be an agent in disguise, hired by Elsie and working for the company or a company affiliated with it.

He could even tell those he had come to meet about me. I am sure he was working for the company. Elsie could not do that – if he was not working for the company, why should he ask questions on behalf of the company?

I pondered over staying in this house or leaving, which was safer. It would be better to travel to Europe. If I had to go, then as soon as I got my passport from Sussie, I would have to split without her knowledge, or else she would also give me trouble. When I get settled,

I will write and inform her of my whereabouts. She would be given a rousing welcome.

On a sight-seeing tour – he might have used that to stop me from detecting who he was or to remind me of some years back.

Around six, I went up to her room. I don't know what came over me but I just entered without knocking. There she stood, nude. Maybe she had seen me coming and left herself like that. I told her I was going home. She agreed but asked me to report on time in the morning as they would be travelling at night.

I hurried to the boys' quarters and changed into my latest outfit, then off to Sussie's place. As I opened the gate, she ran to meet me, smiling. When we met, we kissed and embraced. Arm in arm, we went to the main building. Her parents were there with her sister and her younger brother who had a camera on his lap. Her mother was reading and Daddy was listening to some classical music. He loved it. I greeted everyone in the hall, bowing to the parents. I walked out as Sussie whispered into her mother's ear.

Six minutes later, she joined me and suggested going to see a film. I did not say no as I had to make her happy. Also, I wanted to engage myself in any activity to keep me awake. She held my hand and we both went into the hall.

"Mama, please, we want to go to the films."

The mother looked up with a flash of her big eyes at me and her daughter without a word. I really didn't blame her. After all, her daughter was working in a big financial institution and befriending a common driver, as people say. She hated to see the two of us together. Sussie kissed her mother on both cheeks and we left.

"Sussie, I will bring you back after the film and go back to work," I told her as we got nearer to the gate. She was not happy about it but I had to be there.

As we walked side by side, I began to ponder over what would happen after Elsie had travelled. I would let the world know what she had planned. Even when arrested, I would be given the chance to defend myself. There, I would let the cat out of the bag.

"On our return, please kindly give me your cassette recorder. I need to do some recording tomorrow and since I will not see you until the evening, I think it would be wise for me to take it with me tonight."

"Do you have an empty cassette?"

"No, I don't."

"Okay, I will let you have both when we return. Let's hurry to the junction; it will be easier to get a cab."

As we walked out of the gate, I asked,

"Sussie, did you see the way your mother looked at us? I am worried about our relationship."

"Are you after me or my mother? Whether she likes it or not, she cannot stop me. I don't think she would have been able to marry my father if her mother had done the same thing to her. She had better mind her own affairs."

"Don't say that. You are still under their roof so they have every right to stick their noses into your affairs. They have to control or criticise you when they feel you are going in the wrong direction or moving with the wrong people. What you have to do is convince them about our relationship to gain their blessing."

On our return from the film, she gave me the empty cassette tape and the cassette recorder. It was getting closer to the time when the meeting of the callous planners would take place. As soon as she gave them to me, I kissed her on the forehead then ran off. I was very lucky to get a taxi just outside the gate.

Instead of alighting at the gate of Elsie's house, I got out four houses away from hers. Then, I walked to the house before Elsie's compound. The security men of that house let me in when I told them that the security men on my side were asleep and calling them would waken my madam. Also, since I did not want her to know that I was only now returning, I had chosen to pass through this house. There was a communal wall at the back of the building and I could use that.

When I got to the small gate, I opened it gently so as not to make any noise and wake anybody. I tiptoed under the cover of darkness to the hedges by the boys' quarters. At exactly one o'clock, I went to fix up the machine with a twenty-minute blank cassette in it. Stealthily, I bent and hurried to my secret hideout.

I had not long settled down when I saw a shadow coming from behind the hedges. The part I cut had made it easier for them to come in. When the person came closer, it turned out to be a man in a mechanic's black overalls with black gloves and shoes with soft soles which made his movements noiseless. In his left hand, he had something wrapped in a duster. In the other was a flashlight. I thought he had been given instructions already. He went straight to the garage through the backyard door.

I went around the building to the window, which I had cleaned that afternoon. Since the window was a little above me, I had to stand on my tiptoes which was very painful. The bonnet of the car was open and he was using the tools he had concealed in the duster to screw up some parts of the car. Later, he went under the engine. I knew he would be working on the brakes. It did not frighten me as I knew what to do until I got to a mechanic's workshop, but I would have to report to Rebecca, or whoever might be in the car, that the brakes were faulty.

It did not take long before he came out from under the car, wiping beads of sweat from his forehead with the duster. He wrapped the tools back up in it and closed the bonnet. Then I hurried to my hideout. As he was closing the door, I saw the light go on in her room. Minutes later, I saw her moving towards the boys' quarters. At the door, she tapped and the door opened, then she went in and the door closed behind her. Hurriedly, I moved to the window.

"Why has it taken you such a long time to finish the job?" she asked from inside.

"Why didn't you come and do it yourself like you did the first one?"

"Don't be stupid. We are not talking about the past. It is the present. Make sure you have done it correctly. No signs or anything. You still have some money?"

He did not answer.

"Don't tell me you have finished every kobo I gave you? How is she?"

"Fine, but insists on seeing her father."

"Don't touch her. Still on the hunger strike?"

"No."

From this little conversation, I knew that Elsie had played with my mind.

"As soon as we travel, put her to sleep for good and dump her somewhere in a park. I think you understand me?"

"Yes, but when are you coming back?"

"You can fly and meet me there if you like. I could let you have the address."

"What about the promise you made?" he said as he moved towards her.

"Don't be stupid and stop where you are. That is why I said you can come over if you really want my cunt."

"Okay, let me have a look at it once."

She undid the belt of the morning coat she had on and threw both parts aside – no pants and no brassiere. The guy stood there like a fool and she covered her body.

"Try and meet me there and you'll never forget it," she said as she fastened the belt. Elsie opened the door and went out.

I hurried to the back of the building.

Elsie moved stealthily out onto the lawn towards the door at the back of the main building by the kitchen. The guy also moved out of the compound the way he had come in, disappearing behind the hedges.

I was glued to the spot where I stood, my heart pounding like a pestle in a mortar while little beads of sweat covered my forehead. Then I began to shiver.

After all, it had been worthwhile being there. I hurried to the veranda and stopped the cassette recording. I turned it off and watched for any movements. The light in the guest room went on and then off a few minutes later. I hid the cassette recorder between the hedges.

With the duplicate keys, I was able to enter the garage and unlock the car to open the bonnet. Stupid and unwise for them and fortunately for me, they had left the brake fluid they removed in the container beside some old ones. Before I poured it back, I sealed the hole he had left under the container. With the screwdriver and spanner that I found in the boot, I tightened every screw and nut I found loosened. When I had put everything in order, I locked the car and the door. Then, I went to the side of the passing water and zoom, off went the keys! No one would ever find them now or in the near future.

When it was dawn, I woke and went out through the place I had come in, this time greasing their palms. I went straight to my little abode and played the little drama I had recorded some time ago.

And the truth was shining right in my face. The tape recorder was still on but the drama had ended.

'Yes! The day has finally arrived,' I said to myself and yawned. Where would I be by this time tomorrow? With my wrapper on my pillow, I sat on it with my pants on. The children on the compound were already up, some playing and others crying, calling for the attention of their mothers.

Tomorrow, would I be at the police station, dead, or in the arms of Sussie? Only God had the answer. As soon as everything was over, I would go to her place.

May God help and guide me and most of all, guard me in all I am doing. Forgive me for all the sins I have committed and those I am about to commit.

Chapter Thirty-eight

$\mathbf{A}$lthough I had a table fan, the room was becoming hot and unbearable so I had to open the window for some fresh air from the sea.

Still sitting on the bed, I listened to a kid crying, then I went into placid thought about how everything would end. The slow poisoning that Elsie would die from disturbed me. It was a pity, a sin I was about to commit. It was not my fault for she was also planning to eliminate a number of us, some of whom I didn't know.

I went to the kitchen taking extra care not to be seen by anyone, and not to leave any fingerprints.

On my way to work, I stopped at the shopping centre and purchased a big white hankie. I knew she had been monitoring my movements but it did not deter me from performing the execution of my plan. I just had to use my priceless gift from God to play on their minds. I had a friend who worked at a private veterinary clinic and he gave me a small amount of slow-acting poison after I had explained that I wanted to get rid of a mad dog that was terrorising lives in our area, especially at night. He refused to give me the name of the poison.

That morning, when I came to work, on the porch in front of Elsie was a tall glass of orange juice and a cigarette in a square glass ashtray.

"Good morning."

"Hello!" she said, looking cheerful. She had taken her bath and looked smart in her white outfit.

"You are always late. Even when I tell you to come to work early, you choose to be late."

"That is not true," I protested whilst I opened the door of the hall. The guest room door was closed and there was no one in the hall. Whenever the guest room was open, it meant that my master was being washed or relieving himself.

From there, I went to the kitchen and opened the fridge. Keeping the handkerchief around my hand, I brought out the bottle containing the orange juice and poured the poison into it, closed it and shook the bottle to mix the contents. Then I put it back into the fridge. Hurriedly, I went to throw the poison container into the water then passed outside to where Elsie was sitting.

She was retouching her fingernails when I got there.

"Jerry, what is this all-black outfit for? Is your mother or anybody dead? Or are you planning a funeral for us?"

We laughed about it as I was dressed in black trousers, a black short-sleeved shirt and black shoes.

"This afternoon, you will take Rebecca out to purchase some goods we will need abroad."

"Okay, madam."

'Today is your last day on Earth, so give me every order you wish to, because slowly, you will die,' I thought. Since Elsie liked swimming, she might even decide to have a deep dive before she left for abroad. By that time, the poison would have taken effect on her. All her dreams of the life and accident insurance, the landed property and the cash would be shattered; they would all elude her. She could send me to every corner of the world now, but tonight, she would finally go down.

"Are you alright?"

"Yes, ma'am," I replied.

"Are you sure?" she asked.

"Why do you ask? Or did I not hear you well?"

I moved towards the small gate and then to the boys' quarters to change into my uniform. I was sitting on the grass with my back to the house throwing stones into the river. Twenty minutes later, I heard the back door being opened. I thought it was Rebecca, but no, Elsie appeared in a blue and red backless swimsuit and a round blue sunshade. She had a bottle of white wine in one hand and a wine glass in the other. On top of the glass was a packet of cigarettes and a lighter. I hurried to help her carry everything.

"Thank you."

I placed the things on the round white table with its yellow and white striped umbrella. She settled on the sun lounger. She asked me to open the wine, which I did, and I was about to fill her glass but she turned me down. She did it herself and I left to sit on the wall of the veranda. Ten minutes later, she went over to the hammock. By this time, I was leaning against the pillar supporting the roofing.

"Jerry! Jerry!" I heard Rebecca calling.

"I am coming!" I replied as I ran over to meet her.

"Are you ready?"

"Yes, I am."

"I am also ready," she told me.

Rebecca hurried down to the pool to talk to Elsie in the hammock. As she was coming towards me, I heard the splashing of water. I did not turn my head but I knew that Elsie had dived into the pool. Rebecca turned and shook her head.

I drove Rebecca to the shopping centre. She left me in the car park whilst she went in to purchase some things. Twenty minutes later, I saw her approaching the car park, struggling with two large and, I presumed, heavy brown bags with the name of the store emblazoned on them. I reversed the car and went to meet her. It was a sunny afternoon. The air was hot and not to my liking, but it was to her liking. She disliked air conditioning. From the shopping centre, we drove to the Federal Palace Hotel where she purchased some crafts and animal skins. These she bought in large quantities.

Since we had left the house, I had not glanced at my watch. On our way to the market, I did just that and saw that some time had passed. We got to the market when the sun was rather high. After she had climbed out and made me understand that she would be back in an hour or so, I knew that it would be more than an hour.

As soon as she disappeared out of sight, I set the car in motion and went to Sussie's house. I had the chance of putting on the air conditioning.

From the car behind the gate, I watched as Sussie jumped down from the wall of the veranda and ran to open the gate for me, her beloved.

She gave me a kiss before I stepped out of the car. We went to greet her mother together.

The gate opened ten minutes later and in walked a man dressed in white and blue-black trousers and grey shoes and a lady, dark in complexion, dressed in an all-red outfit with matching shoes and a white bag. Sussie jumped up shouting, "Brother! Brother!" and ran to meet them. The mother and the rest of the household also ran to meet them., embracing and hugging one another. The lady accompanying the brother wore high-heeled shoes and while she was being embraced by the kids, she missed her step and fell on her back. This did not stop the kids. The two kids climbed on top of her before their mother came to the lady's rescue by pulling them away. They walked in with the lady limping.

I was kept waiting after they had gone indoors. Sussie ran back and apologised and asked me to come back later.

I kept myself busy by counting the number of people on the street in front of the gate. Since the gate was not fully covered but in a trellis form, I found it easy to see outside from where I sat. I did this in order not to think about what would happen tonight. Then I began to form a picture of Sussie and me and what the outcome of our friendship would be, and whether a blessing or a curse would come from the parents, especially the mother who had shown a negative attitude towards me.

Just as I counted the two-hundredth man, the door opened.

"I am sorry to have kept you waiting."

"So, you do receive people nicely like that in your house? I loved that piece of drama you people just acted out."

"Ah, ah, Jerry, patience is what we need. Forget about it, my dear."

"The clouds are changing; likewise, the air. Let's hurry up before it starts raining. I dropped Rebecca, the housekeeper, at the market and I have to go back for her."

"Has your madam travelled out already?"

"No. The flight is coming in tonight. She had to buy some things that they would need abroad, like local foodstuffs, crafts and other things. As soon as she went into the market, I rushed over here."

"What if she came out and you were not there?"

"What could I do? I had to come and see you."

"Okay. Hurry and go. I will see you tonight."

"I think so. Take the key and go to my place."

I gave the keys to her.

"Let me see you off."

"What about your visitors? I mean, your brother?"

"Don't worry. I think you were here before them."

"I know, but..."

"But what? Don't start!" she retorted.

"Okay, okay."

We went into the car and I put on the air conditioning since I was soaked.

"Oh, I forgot to tell you."

"What about? The passport or the job?"

"The job first. We went to see my friend's uncle and he says he will get you a job with an oil firm but it will be in two months' time."

"Did he ask you about my nationality?"

"Yes, so I lied. It's no problem. He has the right connections so don't be disturbed. As for the passport, I will start work on a Nigerian one next week, then later, you'll get your own country's one. Before I leave next Friday, I will have good news to tell you."

"Sussie, you are a rare bird. I just wouldn't have believed all this could happen."

"You just wait and see. For your information, I have already drafted a letter requesting my boss to send me back to Lagos. I will soon be joining you but, before that, I will see you every weekend. Why aren't you saying anything?"

"I just don't know what to say, baby. I really need to go."

"It has even come to my mind already. I did not like the atmosphere where you live. It is dangerous. But never mind, I will find you a house in the city, a more decent room and at a decent price."

"I have to go."

She gave me a kiss – a short one.

We both went to the hall, arm in arm, and I bade the family goodbye. In the corridor, I pulled her over and gave her a long kiss.

Chapter Thirty-nine

I arrived at the market ten minutes before she came out with two other men following her with baskets on their heads and carrying a leather bag between them. She was carrying a black animal-skin bag.

Madam Elsie was digging up weeds from the flower bed with a hand fork when we arrived. As soon as Rebecca got out of the car, she went directly to meet her. Some relations in the house were helping to carry the things when it began to drizzle. Bit by bit, it turned into heavy rain.

I went to the kitchen, washed my hands and took my food at my usual place. After eating, I went to the boys' quarters to rest on the table on the veranda. Rebecca woke me up after the rain had stopped. She stood at the back door shouting my name at the top of her voice as if I were her slave. It was already six-thirty, my watch displayed.

"Madam is having her supper. You have to get the two cars ready as she told you. Kate is dressing. Don't forget your white uniform."

I jumped to my feet after I replied, "Yes, ma'am!"

"We have a lot of luggage so you have to call in the security men to help you. Hurry and come for the keys."

She placed the keys on a box by the door and went in.

After taking the keys, I went to the kitchen to have some iced water.

"Jerry, this cold weather… with iced water?" said Elsie.

"Is it any of your business or am I drinking it into your stomach?"

The orange juice was in there. When she set her eyes on the bottle, she pushed me aside and grabbed the bottle, took a glass and ran out.

Oh, thank God, otherwise, my plan would have failed!

Off I ran to the boys' quarters for the duster, then set up the hose and began to wash the car, which was among the ones in the garage.

In forty-five minutes, I had finished washing and cleaning the cars and had checked the engine oil, water and brake fluid. I even topped up the brake fluid in the car she wanted me to drive.

With the help of some of the visitors and the security men, I put most of the luggage in her car, especially those belonging to her, and put those of my master and Kate in mine. Knowing what she had planned, she had directed me to do that. Since my master's doctor was not coming, he was given another doctor to accompany him abroad.

The atmosphere in the house was a sad one. My master's relatives, friends and business associates had all put on sad faces. The cold weather worsened the case.

The telephone rang and Elsie asked Rebecca to answer it. She picked up the receiver and placed it by her left ear. As soon as she did that, Elsie asked who it was but she did not get a reply from Rebecca.

"Yes, yes," Rebecca replied. Then she put on a sad face. "Oh, no! May his soul rest in perfect peace." She then hung up.

"Dr Parkings died twenty minutes ago," she told Elsie.

"Jerry, bring me the brandy with a glass," she ordered me as she fiddled with her nails. Her hands were unsteady. After I had given the glass and brandy to her, she poured herself a large quantity and drank most of it, then sat down for a while without saying a word to anybody. I sneaked out to change into my ceremonial uniform; white jacket over white trousers.

At exactly eight o'clock, after I had parked the one I would drive in front of the porch, I drove her car out from the garage. Then, I went to announce that I was ready. As I was about to enter the corridor, I met Elsie who stared at me. I had not realised that tonight, she had set in motion a plan to murder three human beings. I knew she was gradually dying. With the help of some others, we put my master in a wheelchair and I pushed him gently, taking great care not to jolt him as it would have finished him off if that happened. And in the car, too, I had to drive with extra care if I wanted him alive.

Elsie was in the hall sorting things out with her lawyer, some men from Special Branch, some relations and some officials from his companies who had come to bid him farewell but found it more appropriate at the last hour to hold an emergency meeting on hearing of the death of Dr Parkings. The moon was now full and the compound lit, with the shadows of the trees and plants on the well-trimmed lawn.

Since I was not feeling fine, I got out of the car with my legs and arms a bit unsteady. I tried to control myself but I became restless. I kept reminding myself not to speed, slow down or else I would kill him. Since I didn't want him dead, I would have to take care.

Elsie was the greatest pretender I had ever come across and she knew it very well. Moving towards the SO4 from the rear, I saw shadows coming from the veranda. Elsie wore a red two-piece suit, black skin shoes and a black skin handbag with a black hat. Around her neck was a red silk scarf. She walked straight to her car and stationed herself behind the steering wheel.

As I drove out of the compound, the weather began to change; the clouds became dark and a strong wind began to blow. As well as this, there was lightning and a loud thunderstorm. About two hundred metres from our house, it began to rain heavily. It was very difficult to see.

On the main street, I noticed the unsteady movement of her car. My legs and hands were still unsteady but I drove slowly with care. Since I had noticed it, I kept some metres away from her car. I was sure the rest in the car would think it was because of the slippery surface caused by the rain. Going over the bridge, it became serious. She applied the brakes, and, all of a sudden, her car swerved and went through the railing and plunged into the lagoon.

I was out with the doctor and Kate, shouting. Other cars had stopped and drivers had come out. When I went back to the car, my master had bent his head forward. I touched him and he was cold. I raised his head but it fell back to its position. I yelled and people came running to the car.

Because she knew what was in her mind, Elsie had turned down the doctor's advice to drive her husband in an ambulance. The police and the doctor had offered to get one but she turned it down.

Elsie was bent on destroying others, but now, she was nowhere near claiming the accident and life insurance. All the landed property and cash she had been dreaming of had eluded her. When next she came to the world, she would have to be satisfied with the little she had.

The men from Special Branch had been following us from the house in order to prevent another occurrence of any attempt to kidnap anyone.

Chapter Forty

Soon, the blaring of sirens was heard far away. A police ambulance arrived before a police towing vehicle. Many cars and lorries had stopped and those occupying them had rushed out to the railing to see the car but it had gone under the water. In no time, a helicopter was hovering over the scene. A Mercedes Benz 911 specially built towing vehicle with special gadgets arrived. With the helicopter lighting the area, a frogman was lowered into the water on a big iron hook. The firemen also came with their own vehicle. Three more frogmen climbed over the railing and were also lowered into the water. They all had powerful torches in their hands, so they were well-equipped for the search and had all the things they would need to retrieve the body and the car from under the water.

I stood on the bridge, far from the others, looking at everybody and feeling satisfied with what had happened to her. After all, I had reciprocated what she had planned for me and others. I bowed my head and closed my eyes to pray for her soul and ask for forgiveness. When I had finished, I drew in a deep breath and went to the car to get a cigarette from the glove compartment. As I lit the cigarette, I noticed that my hands were unsteady once more but I pulled myself together.

When I got over to the rail, someone pointed at me and they came rushing.

"How did it happen? How many people were in the car? What type of car? Was it the brakes?" These were just some of the questions they asked. I just stood there with my arms folded, staring at them.

"She was alone in the car," I started saying when I had decided to answer their questions. "When she was driving over the bridge, I noticed the unsteadiness of the vehicle, but since she had drunk a lot this evening and with the slippery surface of the road, I was not surprised. Then it became more serious than before. In the wink of an eye, zoom! The car went flying and plunged into the water after she had applied the brakes.

"Please, I don't want to talk about it, so kindly leave me alone. Please!" I pleaded as they opened their mouths to ask some more questions.

The streetlights were not working but the spotlight from the helicopter and the cars that had parked with their headlights on lit the area. In a few minutes or so, they would come up with the car. I knew she would be dead. I would get away with it, but in my mind, it would keep on lingering.

If I had given her away, it would have saved lives. I flipped the butt of my second cigarette into the water and it was washed away. Then, I strolled to the car and placed my troubled head on the steering wheel.

It was in the hospital that I recovered the following day with a nurse and Sussie by my bedside.

"Has the car been retrieved from the depths of the waters?" was the first question I asked when I opened my mouth and eyes.

"Yes, but she was dead," the nurse replied.

"Why am I here?"

"After the accident, you started behaving strangely, then later you became unconscious."

A voice within me said, "You have done the right thing. You have killed another soul. Get ready for the reward. The flower vase – you can use it."

"Use it for what?" I asked, shouting.

The nurse and Sussie came to hold my hands down.

"You'll be alright," Sussie said.

I did not answer her but kept staring at the ceiling.

The nurse went out and Sussie sat, going through a magazine she had on her lap.

"You can do it," the voice said once more.

Then I sat on the bed looking at myself.

Sussie raised her head and smiled but I did not return it.

"Be careful not to fail," it said. "It's now or never!"

By the time she raised her head to see what I was doing, the vase was smashing onto her head which burst open with blood oozing out. With the broken part, I stabbed her several times and she fell. With blood on my hands and spilt all over my gown, I ran into the corridor, shouting, "I have killed her!" I pushed anyone out of my way, anyone who dared to stop me.

I heard voices and footsteps hammering on the terrazzo. The security men along with the other male workers had blocked the entrance I was trying to get through. A truncheon found its way onto my head. I stumbled as if to fall but I dived through a very large glass window in the corridor and fell into some garbage on the ground.

Today, I am in the Government Mental Hospital after I had been found to be insane.

Contents

9 781802 275810